PROJECT SUNDOWN

A VINCE CARVER THRILLER

MATT SLOANE

Copyright © 2023 by Matt Sloane. All rights reserved.

Published by Blood & Treasure, Los Angeles
First Edition

This is a work of fiction. Any resemblance to reality is coincidental.

No part of this work may be reproduced or distributed without prior written consent by the publisher. This book represents the hard work of the author; please read responsibly.

Cover by James T. Egan of Bookfly Design LLC.

Print ISBN: 978-1-946-00854-1

Matt-Sloane.com

Preface

I'm Matt Sloane, I like great stories, and I hope you do too.

The cool thing about stories is they come in all kinds. Everyone has their opinions and nobody's wrong. (Which must mean I'm right.)

So here's what I like in a story: Smart dialog between characters that feel real. Spurts of action, moments to breathe, and plenty to think about. Complex plots that aren't easy to predict, with realistic twists that don't make your eyes roll. And most of all, a satisfying ending, because you can't cheap out on those.

The Vince Carver books are high action, high intrigue spycraft on the world stage, and I hope they're your kind of story.

If you'd like to get in touch to say hi, offer a correction, talk shop, or otherwise gab, feel free to drop me a line:

matt@matt-sloane.com

Or you can get an email from me every time a book is released at: Matt-Sloane.com

Happy reading,

-Matt

Project Sundown by Matt Sloane is a powerhouse thriller stacked with gunplay and conspiracy. From rural electrical substations to the very heart of San Francisco, this book beats with the pulse of American adrenaline.

★★★★★ "**Sensational**. A taut thriller that has a great deal more to offer than bullets and brawn."

★★★★★ "The fight scenes are the **best you'll find** in crime fiction."

★★★★★ "Very real and **very very good**."

PROJECT SUNDOWN

"A great civilization is not conquered from without until
it has destroyed itself from within."

> •*The Story of Civilization,*
> Will Durant

1

Some days he moved in public like a ghost. Out there, in plain sight but out of mind. His early morning run was appropriately spectral, unimpeded by the community greeting the dawn around him. Aside from the aberrant nod of hello, his company was the crisp breeze and cloudless sky and steady rhythm of his breath.

His shooting afterward was similarly calm. Pistol and rifle ranges were rarely quiet, true, but they enveloped him in solitude and focus. Quiet of the mind. Row after row the shooters, the ghosts, absently minded their own haunted business.

At least, that's what they usually did.

Vince Carver was halfway between the rifle range and the parking lot when a man called out to him.

"Vince, wait up!"

Carver had a Lynx Defense rifle soft case over his shoulder and a pistol bag in one hand. His earmuffs were stowed in the range bag, unused today, but he still wore the noise-reducing earbuds. They were comfortable and featured voice amplification, though he preferred talking without them. Now far enough from the shooting, he pulled them from his ears as the acquaintance caught up to him.

"Good running into you again," said the man.

Carver had forgotten his first name but his last was Anderson.

"Nice tac bag," the man added with a point.

"American made," answered Carver congenially. "Like the gun."

"Was that a Golden Boy?"

"Sometimes you're in the mood for a lever gun."

Anderson nodded along with hands on hips, ticking off the small talk while eyeballing the padlock securing the soft case. California law had just saved Carver from having to trot out the steel-and-walnut showpiece.

"Yup," agreed Anderson, "sometimes you are."

He was about fifty, still in decent shape, not well-muscled or athletic but healthy. The two had run into each other lately, first at this same range, then with a visit to the Kinetic National Security office for a job offer. Anderson was interested in employing Carver, but Carver was interested in not being interested. Rather than the rejection spoiling a burgeoning friendship, Anderson had chased after the prospect even more.

"That was nice shooting," he continued, taking the long way to the point. "Prime technique. My boys already know how to shoot, I saw to that, but the offer's still on the table. Good money's waiting on you to come and train up my organization."

Carver smiled diplomatically. "I appreciate that, Anderson."

"Lester. Come on, we're not on duty."

A cordial chuckle. "Lester then. It's a generous offer, but my firm usually caters to corporate clients."

"Let the tech bastards pay through the nose," he chuckled, as if they were in on the joke together. "I'm aware. That's why I want you. You come highly recommended."

That bit got Carver's attention. No one should have been talking about him at all. "Recommended by who, exactly?"

Anderson waved the question off. "Listen, Vince, you were a green beret, right?"

"Operational Detachment-Delta."

His eyebrows went up. "Impressive. I served too but wasn't so much of a badass. 1st Marines. Saw a bit of Fallujah before being honorably discharged. And I'll skip the Army-Marine pissing match. The point is, you and me, we're cut from the same cloth. And we both know how it goes... The government doesn't always take care of us vets the way they should."

Carver's smile tightened. He had his share of gripes with Uncle Sam, no doubt, but he was too pragmatic a personality to aimlessly air his grievances. Complaining is like spinning a plate. You can keep it going as long as you want, but it only delays the inevitable. And when you're done, even if you manage not to break anything, nothing tangible is gained from the effort. You end up with the same damn plate you started with.

Effective outcomes are the result of actions, not words.

Carver had taken the active steps of going private, applying his discipline to civilian life, and starting his own company.

Of course, the government had sucked him right back in anyway. When it came to that part of his program, he still wasn't sure if it was a feature or a bug.

"Don't worry," assured Anderson, noticing the response. "I don't throw pity parties. I only bring up the point that you and I have killed men in service to our country. So, as soldiers, I think we can both dispense with the bullshit."

The frankness amused Carver, at least. "How's that?" he asked.

Anderson shrugged like it was obvious. "You run a security firm out of an office in the city. I run one on a wooded ranch in the hills. I'd imagine we're alike in a lot of ways. It's just we don't have anyone close to your skill or experience in distance shooting. Your work is hard not to notice. Quick bursts on multiple targets, tight groupings, impressive holster starts and off-hand control. You could give my guys a lot of pointers."

Anderson put up his hands as Carver was about to object.

"We didn't get into compensation the other day, but understand that I can pay you just as good or better than your corporate rates. My organization is flush with wealth, and it would honor me to share some of that hard-earned cash with a patriotic veteran who walks the walk. It's like you said, let the fat cats foot the bill."

It was actually Anderson who had alluded that, but Carver figured the quickest way out of this was letting the man finish.

"This is a training gig so it's easy money. You can set the hours and days. They can be as long or as short as you need. And I'd insist on taking a back seat to your more important clients, if any work does come up."

The way he said the last part, it was like he knew Carver didn't have a lot of opportunities. That was the problem with running a CIA cover firm that dealt in kinetics—there weren't always emergencies to quell. Even when there were, an abundance of other units better suited to such missions stood ready, often armed with more elaborate kit and higher security clearances than Carver's team.

In the security business, staying still was falling behind. Work kept you sharp. And it certainly didn't hurt to pick up civilian contracts now and then to give his firm the appearance of legitimacy. It wasn't like he could post "ONLY BLACK OPS ENTERTAINED" on the website.

"Listen," said Anderson, taking a breath at the end of his rehearsed pitch. "All I'm asking is you come down to the ranch and meet with my boys before you decide. See what you have to work with. Worst case is we have a beer, do some shooting in the private hills, and shake hands when we part ways."

Carver switched the rifle bag from one shoulder to the other and gazed back at the stalls of the outdoor range. Gun reports popped and echoed off the pavement. He wasn't hurting for income, though he wasn't against earning a little extra either. He had employees to pay and 401K contributions to match. Having a new place to shoot piqued his interest too, and it rarely hurt to nurture contacts in the local community.

No, there was no harm in a little consultancy gig, but something about the situation bugged Carver. He wasn't sure if it was Anderson or something else. He didn't even know what kind of organization he'd be instructing, or who or how many its members were. Maybe that was the precise problem.

Asking informational questions now would only solidify Anderson's hopes. Besides, anything the man said would be biased. As usual, Carver needed to do his homework on his own.

"I can't make any promises," he relented, trying not to sound optimistic, "but I'll look over my schedule and consider it."

"Music to my ears, Vince. Music to my ears."

They shook hands, Carver hoping it not be taken as a sign of a done deal, and the men parted ways. Anderson returned to the range and Carver to his truck. The fifth-generation Dodge Ram was a beast of a pickup, but it regrettably had not been put to good use lately. Cabins in the mountains and camping in the national parks were as far as he'd gotten. He didn't even have a boat to tow yet.

In the past, when Carver had worked domestically, he used vehicles with better passenger accommodations and ballistic protection. With the shuttering of his previous company, the fleet of Range Rovers had been liquidated, the assets filtered through a CIA buyout program that no doubt fed into someone's black budget. As the asset who had broken the case, Carver made a deal to vest out his equity in the corrupt company to found Kinetic National Security. The new operation amounted to a compartment of a department of his old firm.

But it was his.

The smaller the point, the sharper the thrust. And as the boss, it was his sole discretion where to direct it.

With the bags secured in the back seat, Carver started the throaty V6 diesel and headed toward the city. Although there was a municipal center with a couple of parks, San Jose wasn't a centralized area of notable destinations. It was more a series of residential sprawls, a giant unending suburb at the southern tip of the Bay Area, part of an even larger contiguous settlement running up both sides of the water all the way to San Francisco on one side and Oakland on the other.

It was fifteen minutes from the gun range to his office, but, as it was set to be a slow day, Carver made a detour to a boutique butcher and picked up a brisket, some potatoes, and fresh rosemary. He stopped at his apartment, secured the firearms, and rubbed an alarming dose of Santa Maria seasoning on the meat before he set it to dry in the fridge.

Dinner prep complete, Carver next steered the pickup to the office. It was 11 am. Staffing times were malleable and Shaw had taken the morning shift. Not that it mattered much. The old dentist's office was more or less a front. Kinetic National Security wasn't meant to attract walk-in business.

Which was why it intrigued him, as he pulled into the parking spot, to see a couple peeking into his office window.

The man was older than the woman. They carried themselves professionally, obviously not a romantic couple, and each had discriminating eyes and a sidearm holstered at the hip. Those were the small details. More prominent were the dark-blue windbreakers emblazoned in yellow across the back with "POLICE" and "HSI."

Carver's little venture had somehow earned the scrutiny of the Department of Homeland Security.

2

Carver gruffly unloaded and stomped toward the whispering couple. "Can I help you two?"

They nearly jumped to attention on the walkway. "This is government business, sir," declared the man.

Carver pointed to the glass door. "Yeah, and this is my business."

"Mr. Carver?" asked the woman.

"Yes."

"I'm Special Agent Guerrero. This is Special Agent Bentley. Homeland Security Investigations."

Bentley brandished the badge at his belt. It was gold with bright blue bands along the top and bottom. "We're with Domestic Operations out of the San Francisco office," he explained, as if that explained anything.

"What are you doing here?" asked Carver.

"A routine Homeland Security sweep." His accent was Jersey maybe.

"Is it routine to loiter outside peeping through windows instead of walking in and saying hello?"

To illustrate the point, Carver pressed the unlocked door halfway open. A small bell hanging above his head jingled to announce their arrival.

"It's just..." Guerrero swallowed, unsure how to proceed. Bentley grimaced and turned away so he wasn't elaborating either.

One look inside explained the hesitance of the special agents. Nick Shaw was planted against the lobby wall with crossed arms and hard eyes. His Beretta was holstered on his belt and his special forces beard was more unruly than ever. He had an intimidating presence, even to government agents.

"Knock it off, Nick," grumbled Carver, pushing inside. He let the door swing closed instead of holding it open for their guests.

"Does that mean I can't shoot them?"

"I wouldn't recommend it."

Shaw let out a disappointed, scratchy sigh. "They're trouble, Vince. You know it. I know it." He peeled off the wall and followed into the interior office.

Carver sunk into his Eames office chair and slid it backward so he could kick his legs out comfortably. He waited with his hands crossed in his lap.

"Do me a favor, Nick, and lock up your weapon. You know how it makes these types nervous."

His friend muttered under his breath and retreated down the hall. At the same time, the front bell jingled again, signaling that the two investigators had finally agreed on an infil plan and were presently clearing the lobby.

They entered his office as he assumed, with Bentley taking the lead. He looked about fifteen years his partner's senior, in his forties, hair mostly gray but a full head of it, gelled back in a dramatic swoop. He was fit, indicating he took his work seriously, and his hard, aquiline nose and strong jaw looked like they meant business. At the same time, he wore casual boot-cut jeans under his HSI-issue shirt and jacket. That meant he was practical and had been at this for a while.

Guerrero was in her late twenties, nearly his height but lithe, nearly in danger of getting lost in her jacket and neutral beige slacks. The bland attire seemed a way of not standing out, since she otherwise was not at all the tough-as-nails stereotype of many female law enforcement officers. Guerrero was soft and feminine, with plump lips, full eyebrows over hazel eyes, caramel skin, and frizzy dark hair only partially tamed by a ponytail, so that thick strands perpetually drooped to her cheeks. Carver couldn't get a read on her experience level. All he knew was he was immediately attracted to her.

"Special Agents Bentley and Guerrero," said Carver in greeting, as if they hadn't just met outside. "I must have missed you in my appointment book."

"That's because we don't need a root canal," snorted Bentley.

Carver looked around the office, bewildered. How did they know this used to be a dental office?

While he could immediately see Shaw was right about the crass New Yorker, there was still hope for Guerrero. The pair looked like they might solve the same problem with entirely opposite methods. Carver wondered if that made them a good or bad team.

"Yet here you are," stressed Carver, "in my office. I gotta say, the suspense is killing me."

Guerrero stood near the back of the room, taking in the scene with her mixed-color eyes. Bentley was too active for that. He paced along the wall examining the framed security credentials.

"We're looking into suspicious characters," he said ominously.

Now that he was inside the office, he dropped the "routine security sweep" act. Carver didn't like the surprise visit from HSI and decided to push back.

"You guys are a part of ICE, aren't you?"

Bentley's jaw tightened. Apparently he was the strong and silent type and didn't respond.

"Technically," answered Guerrero. "But don't let that structural reality misdirect you. When people think ICE, they think immigration. They think Enforcement and Removal Operations. We're a wholly distinct branch." Her eyes brightened. "In a few years, HSI might be its own top-level agency just like the FBI."

Carver didn't ask what we needed two federal investigative agencies for. The rest about the organizational mess was spot on. The Department of Homeland Security was a mishmash of multiple agencies all sliced, shuffled, and diced under one umbrella mandated after 9/11. It was like rummaging through the garage to find space to keep the old stuff. ICE was formed from the old Immigration and Naturalization Service, or INS, and the US Customs

Service. HSI investigators had come from both agencies. The federal government was the ultimate hoarder.

"But that ICE branding follows you around like bad BO," Carver pointed out. "Whether you call yourself the Customs Service, or Office of Investigations, or Homeland Security Investigations, you just can't wash off that stink, can you?"

Their faces hardened.

"Someone like the FBI rolls in, they invite participation from the PD. In this town the locals refuse to give you support."

"We're not looking for support," derided Bentley in a harsh tone. "We're only looking for cooperation."

Carver nodded. "Right. Suspicious people." He let that phrase hang in the air while he stared a hole through Bentley. To the special agent's credit, his gaze didn't shy away.

Guerrero stepped between them. She wasn't much in the planetary mass department but she might as well have been a total solar eclipse. "I think we're getting off on the wrong foot, Mr. Carver. Let's start over. I'm sure you're familiar with the president's 'Strength at Home' campaign?"

His eyes panned to hers. She had freckles where the light caught her cheeks, but it was her redirection of the conversation that attracted Carver's interest. It was clear she was the more strategic thinker.

President Alex Diaz was young, popular, and hungry. Strength at Home was his flagship initiative: investment in domestic industry to spur economic growth, enhance stability, and ensure future national security. In a time of hyper-divisive politics, it had refreshingly bipartisan support.

The purpose of HSI's visit turned over in Carver's head as he leaned forward. "President Diaz is coming to Silicon Valley to announce the technology arm of his initiative. He spoke to the East Coast port authority, the Heartland unions, and now it's Big Tech's turn."

Guerrero smiled. "That's correct."

"Great." Carver eased back into the Eames. "Kinetic National Security would be happy to offer our expertise in securing his visit."

Bentley scoffed. "Let's leave that to the professionals."

"Don't be an idiot, Bentley," said his young partner. "We both read the guy's file. He's legit."

Carver didn't think it was possible, but Guerrero was somehow even more attractive.

The senior agent nodded along, missing her rebuke. "That's exactly why we're here."

Carver frowned and waited to hear how that made sense, but Bentley continued his aloof bad-cop routine. He moved to the corkboard on the wall, probing for incriminating public materials. He didn't just want to hassle Carver, he wanted probable cause to justify it.

Various flyers and notes were pinned on display. He reached into a little plastic rack screwed to the frame and plucked one of the company's business cards from the stack.

"Providing top-end executive protection and investigations with special operations expertise," he read.

"That's a mouthful."

Carver was getting déjà vu. Bentley snickered and pocketed the card, shifting his suspicions to the next item on the corkboard: the menu of the taco joint three storefronts down.

"You mind me asking," started Carver, "why HSI is doing safety sweeps for the president instead of the Secret Service?"

Bentley only said, "Those overworked jackasses?" and kept studying the corkboard.

"Believe it or not," elaborated Guerrero, "HSI has more experience investigating threats from criminal and terrorist organizations. The truth is the Secret Service is overworked and understaffed. With protection as their priority service, they farm out investigative work to us."

The mention of the Secret Service obviously interested Shaw because he posted at the doorway to listen in. Not too long ago their team focused almost exclusively on close protection. The president of the United States was the father of all VIPs.

Bentley's tongue clicked and he spun on a dime, almost gloating. "You've been flagged for an incident involving gunfire."

Shaw shook his head and grumbled, "Hear we go..."

The agents pivoted to keep an eye on him. Bentley hooked his thumbs in his jean pockets. He had made some kind of decision and was going with it.

"We're keeping tabs on gun nuts, gun clubs, militarized security contractors... You know the type."

Carver frowned. "Can't say that I do. What gunfire incident are you referring to?"

"There more than one?" Bentley showed his teeth.

It took a lot more than cheap police tricks to ruffle Carver. His reply was measured. "Special Agent Bentley, you said you wanted cooperation. How can I give you that without telling me what you want?"

That point seemed to land. Bentley's interrogation tactics were confrontational by design. He probably enjoyed them. But Carver pegged him as pragmatic and that side won out. Bentley cut the crap and got to the point.

"Mesa, Arizona. You discharged your weapon on a public highway and in an airport."

"The shooting or shootings, however you wish to categorize them, occurred during the execution of my legal duties. The incident was investigated and cleared by the FBI and the local department. My team and I acted in a professional manner, in line with operational directives, in order to protect the lives and liberty of ourselves and our client, who would be happy to confirm our version of events."

Bentley nodded. "You do a lot of traveling overseas?"

This was the way it worked. The first questions were never the real ones. The trick was finding out where they led before you walked into an ambush.

"I do what's required to fulfill my obligations to the client," answered Carver evenly.

"You've been to China recently?"

"Taiwan, to provide close protection at a semiconductor

conference. I'm not at liberty to discuss details."

"That was Walter Lachlan again, right?"

"I can neither confirm nor deny my employment with him, per the NDA, but you know how this works. You're free discuss it with him, or you can subpoena me, but I'm required to take all legal avenues to protect my client's confidentiality until then."

Bentley snuck a sideways glance at his partner and scoffed. "Says the high-and-mighty security contractor after an espionage indictment."

"My old boss was indicted, not me. The rest of us had nothing to do with that. The old company folded."

"Long live the new company." Bentley slipped his hands all the way into his pockets now. Fully relaxed, meant to put Carver at ease. It was all part of the progression. "You seemed to come out of it okay."

"That's because I didn't break the law. I'm running my own business now. It's a clean operation."

"What about Europe?" asked Guerrero, tagging in to help a floundering Bentley, taking the lead at the end of the desk.

Carver's eyes met Shaw's before moving to hers. "I'm afraid you're going to have to be more specific."

She shrugged. "You've done a lot of work there, I take it."

"Is that a karambit?"

Her eyes flared. "What?"

He nodded to her waist. As she had neared, her jacket had opened and he'd caught sight of the small knife on her offside.

Guerrero followed his gaze, stunted by the left-field remark and unable to immediately reply.

"I have a similar one," he elaborated.

Carver pulled the Colonel Blade from his left side and placed the blacked-out knife on the desktop. Bentley and Guerrero stepped back quickly, the latter reaching for her gun.

When it was obvious Carver wasn't making a move, her hand moved from the gun to her knife. She pulled out a small bent blade of Damascus steel with a cherrywood grip. She didn't go so far as to place it on the table, but she held it for display.

"I thought you were going to make a joke about it," she admitted.

"Not at all. It's supposed to be reliable in a pinch. I like to say it's reliable in a punch."

"Bentley gives me a hard time about it."

Her partner pointed disparagingly. "Come on. The size of that thing..."

"No need to overcompensate," retorted Carver. "It gets the job done if I'm close enough to need it. Otherwise I use a gun."

Bentley didn't argue. It seemed to pain him, but he knew which of them had more experience killing with a knife.

Guerrero's lips twisted up ever so slightly. "Let's settle down, Mr. Carver."

"People who act neighborly can call me Vince. Are you neighborly, Agent Guerrero?"

He was hoping she would offer her own name in return, but she only blinked at him. He had her attention, at least. She stepped closer, to the side of the desk, and picked up the Colonel. "It's a nice knife," she remarked, taking a moment to weigh it against her own. She handed it back and he slipped it into the sheath.

Agent Bentley cleared his throat.

Guerrero stepped back and put her karambit away. "You do a lot of work in Europe, Vince?"

Carver pressed his lips together, wondering how to answer. Mostly he wondered if that little exchange had bought him a measure of camaraderie. "After the Army, I lived overseas for a stretch. I worked with a few private companies to learn the close protection trade. The civilian side of it, anyway." He nodded to Shaw hovering in the back. "That's how we met."

"And what was your business there last year, once you had already struck out on your own?"

Carver grinned. Homeland Security asking about his involvement in a disavowed CIA operation was a new one for him. This kind of thing never happened in the Army.

"Like you said, I'm running my own show now. Nick was working in Europe for a while after the indictments came down. I jetted over there to recruit him."

Bentley must have figured her questions weren't pointed enough because he came back in. "Any other recent travel you wanna tell us about?"

Guys in his position only asked questions so openly when they already knew the answer. Instead of calling him on that, Carver decided it was better to play along. To let the interrogator feel like he was the one in control.

"The team went to Mexico," Carver disclosed. "It was like a company retreat."

"Retreat, huh? What kinds of things did you all get up to?"

"Team-building exercises," said Shaw from behind. "Sack races, trust falls, that sort of thing."

Carver snickered. "It was more a vacation than anything else, agents. For the record, KNS had no official business across the border. And speaking of business, do *you* have any here? Or are we just jawing?"

"This is a friendly line of questioning," assured Guerrero.

"So this is what you call friendly. Too bad."

They locked eyes, and something seemed to sparkle in hers. Carver believed she had exciting ideas but wasn't in a position to discuss them.

He eventually sighed. "Why don't you level with me? Am I under investigation for something?"

"Not yet," said Bentley, as if it were a challenge.

"Then let's get serious. Homeland Security has no cause to harass my team. We're fully licensed. We haven't committed any crimes, nor do we plan to. But I'm always happy to cooperate with Uncle Sam as long as everybody maintains a conversation as adults."

The admonishment surprisingly earned him a few seconds of silence. Rather than squander that leeway, he quickly added, "So why don't you both humor me, and tell me why my little security firm rates a visit from HomeSec, and I'll clear everything right up."

Bentley set his jaw. "You got it, tough guy."

He went to the corkboard, ripped a small lined piece of paper from a pin, and slammed it on the desk between them. It was a note in handwritten ink with the name Lester and a contact number.

"This is the personal number of one Lester Anderson, who happens to run the local militia. As to why that's relevant, you might be interested to know that, just off the top of my head, they're on three separate watch lists for insurrection and inciting violence. And you're officially a known associate."

Son of a bitch. HSI was onto something after all.

3

Carver pulled the chair closer to the desk and the handwritten note. "Lester Anderson stopped in a couple of weeks ago. I run a security firm and he inquired about my services. I wasn't interested."

Special Agent Bentley sneered. "Yet his number is right here on your wall."

"As you've so graciously displayed, just about anyone can walk in here uninvited and fiddle with my corkboard. In this case, Anderson wanted me to think things over. In fact, in the spirit of full disclosure, I just ran into him at the gun range this morning. But maybe you already know that. He reiterated his offer to come down to his ranch."

Bentley's arms were crossed over his chest, unsure if he was buying it. Guerrero asked, "What services did he ask about, specifically?"

Carver sucked in a breath. Usually he kept client interactions confidential. This included *potential* client interactions. Then again, he took credible threats seriously. "Do you mind if I ask for an ID, Agent Guerrero?"

Bentley clicked his tongue, but Guerrero complied. She understood cooperation was just around the corner, even if she had to jump through a hoop first. They both knew she was legitimate. She strolled close and opened her jacket to reach the pocket. A waft of perfume hit Carver's face and his gaze strayed to her waist. Now he wondered if she was trying to play him right back.

"You can call the office, if you like," she said as she handed her ID over.

Carver didn't study it too deeply. It was real. Guerrero looked much the same as she did in the picture, a young wide-eyed special agent in an aggressive investigative team. "Where's the name from?" he asked. "It's nice."

"My family's Colombian."

He handed the ID back to her. "Here you go, Isla."

She took it without objecting to the first-name basis. Carver got down to business.

"This is simple," he explained, "and there's nothing here. Lester Anderson saw me shoot once or twice at the range off the 101 in Coyote. He asked me to train up his guys. That's as far as it goes."

"Really?" protested a still-skeptical Bentley. "So your nice, respectable security company—an honest outfit, as you say—is sharing air with radicals?"

"I'm sharing air with you right now."

"But why associate with them at all?"

"There was no association, Bentley. I don't even know who 'they' are. I've only met Anderson. He comes off as an okay guy. A vet. He said he runs a security firm like I do."

He chortled now. "A security firm. That's what they're calling themselves?"

"That's what the man said."

"They're a militia, Carver. They can slap on heels and a short skirt and paint their lips, but they'll still give you the same sloppy kiss."

Carver's gaze trailed to Guerrero. "Sorry, I got distracted by the part with the short skirt."

Bentley grunted. "What I'm saying is, if it quacks like an extremist militia, it's an extremist militia."

Now Carver wished he had gotten on that homework instead of prepping dinner. It wasn't that he doubted HSI's intel, not completely, it was that he preferred seeing these kinds of things for himself and coming to his own conclusions.

"Look," he said, "I'm not denying Anderson was here. I'm just saying we never had a professional relationship. I don't know anything about a militia."

"They go by S2," volunteered Guerrero. "It's a callback to the SS, among other things. People into these movements draw symbolism from wherever they can to attract a wide audience. S2 sees themselves as constitutional police with a mandate that transcends local authorities."

"They target ex-military types," said Bentley suggestively.

"What's their end goal?" Carver asked.

"What else?" countered Guerrero. "To bring down the federal government."

Bentley grinned matter-of-factly. "You can see why we're concerned."

Carver wet his lips and nodded back. "I didn't know

about any of this, obviously."

"Either you're lying," accused Bentley, "or you're not as professional as you think you are."

That raised Carver's hackles. He could have explained that he was going to look into them. He could have said he hadn't needed to because there was no agreement of employment. But the bottom line was HSI had walked in and put him against the fire, and Carver had been caught unawares. That never felt good.

"Thanks for the warning, agents," he said, voice measured again. "It should be a relief to everyone here that I turned down their offer of employment. I can't control whether I run into Anderson at the range again or if he decides to come into the office, but I can reassure him, and you, that I have no intention of doing business with him."

They both stared as if expecting more. He wasn't sure what they wanted, really, or if anything could possibly satisfy them. All he knew was that, given their mandate, they had more important things to worry about than him.

"So that's it then?" asked Bentley.

Carver shrugged. "You tell me."

"I think that's all," said Guerrero. "For now." She looked to Bentley for confirmation.

For a moment it seemed like a coin flip whether he would walk out or pound on this some more. Maybe the toss was lucky because he acquiesced. Bentley placed an HSI card on the desk and said, "Anything else comes to you, you tell us ASAP." Then, without waiting for a response, he spun on his boots and stomped to the front door.

"Thank you for your time," said Guerrero with a sheepish smile. She turned to go and Carver bounced out of the Eames.

"Special Agent," he called. She stopped and watched him grab a business card from the corkboard and offer it to her. "In case you need some assistance with security services."

She pursed her lips. "My partner has your card."

"This one's for you."

It took a few seconds, but the edge of her lip curled. She took the card, then stared at Carver's waiting palm.

"Networking 101," he explained. "This isn't a charity, it's a trade."

A dubious eyebrow went up. "You have Special Agent Bentley's."

"Like I'm going to call that guy."

She chuckled. She had a little snaggletooth and probably didn't like to smile because of it. Carver thought it was cute.

Guerrero reached into her jacket again. She moved slowly as he stood close, not unlike the seconds before a slow dance. Behind her, Shaw was shaking his head. She passed her card to him and froze as their hands touched. Their eyes snapped to each other like magnets, but there was a different kind of gravity brewing that could bend the path of light.

"Thank you, Isla."

"My pleasure, Vince."

"I'll call you if something comes up."

Shaw snorted and tromped away. Guerrero broke into a chuckle, covering her mouth and standing up straighter.

Her above-average height came up to his eyes, but she was like a twig next to him.

"Maybe I'll call you first," she said.

Her smile lingered a moment, and then she left the office.

Carver felt pretty good about himself as he saw her off from the lobby. Shaw let him have all of five seconds before raining on his parade.

"She just wants you close to dig for information," he pointed out, stopping shoulder to shoulder.

"Close is close."

"Not in this case it's not. There's no way you get into her pants."

"Do you have to be so crude?" Carver protested. And then, a beat later, "You really think my chances are zero?"

"Vince, if she sleeps with you, you have my blessing to give her the colonel's secret blend of herbs and spices. I just don't think it's gonna happen."

"Oh ye of little faith."

Shaw made for the door next. It was his lunch break. "As if my faith has ever stopped you before."

4

Plans are like train cars. When one gets derailed, the others catastrophically follow.

The locomotive powering this particular high-speed collision was any pretense of a side gig with the S2 militia. Because Carver skipped lunch and did his homework.

His first web searches treaded lightly, as he was worried about landing on the kind of FBI watch list that citizens into extremist ideologies find themselves on. But tangible, concrete information on the militia was hard to come by, and Carver's tepid digging grew more direct. The search sprawled into a meandering mess as he delved into warren after warren of twisted rabbit holes.

At the end of it all, Carver concluded that there wasn't a whole lot of credible information about S2 in the public domain. There was no official website. Most of the search results were either out-of-touch media hit pieces or offhand mentions in the dark recesses of the web. Even social media posts with mentions of S2 focused less on the organization and more on trivial subjects, like restoring old cars in Oregon, or strategies to cope with a long-term career as a corrections officer. The closest he came to a smoking gun was a post-capitalism subreddit, but there were no inciting calls to action.

Even the militia's history was in dispute. Some sources claimed the group broke away from the Atomwaffen Division, a neo-Nazi movement, after mass arrests of its founding members almost a decade prior. Other accounts stated that any overlap of membership was coincidental, and that S2 wasn't formed until years later. About the only fact the various sources agreed on was that its members had a presence in the Pacific Northwest, or Cascadia, which apparently extended into northern California.

Carver got the feeling S2 was more of a sympathetic club than a tight-knit group. They were hardly what he would call operational. Government criticisms without a list of demands, members without an official roster, and calls to unity without a leader. Trying to frame S2 in any specific light was sort of like asking a child to draw a leaf. Its color and shape got the idea across, but it was a far cry from the breadth of variety that existed in nature. S2 was only an idea.

But there were definite red flags. Agents provocateur had been arrested in larger protests organized by outside parties. They'd been confrontational with police. Here and there various S2 members, individually more than organized, were the belligerents in numerous encounters with authorities, many with minor legal ramifications. The incidents were haphazard but nevertheless provided a notoriety that worked in S2's favor. An image of unity against a greater power was slowly cultivated. Carver well understood the magnetism—and danger—of such a reputation.

At the end of the day, S2 had enough deniability and separation from any official breaches of conduct that they didn't rate Public Enemy Number One through Public Enemy Number Fifty. They were a group of rabble-rousers and malcontents whose accomplishments thus far amounted to the occasional minor headline. Perhaps they rated closer inspection from HSI, or perhaps they were the victims of media clickbait blown out of proportion.

Either way, Bentley's conclusion was a sound one. Kinetic National Security didn't belong in the same zip code as the S2 militia. Getting mixed up with their image and legal squabbles would be careless. And a detriment to his operations. For better or worse, any relationship that invited scrutiny from federal agencies wasn't tenable. Carver had a greater mission here, and OPSEC was the rule of the day.

So that train car derailed, along with other plans in tow. The next casualty was dinner. After spending the afternoon poring over the internet, there was no more time for the smaller pleasures in life.

Carver wasn't willing to cook brisket fast. Not having a yard, he already lacked a smoker or grill, but the least he could hold onto was roasting it low and slow in the oven. Anything less than five hours for his cut was a crime. And anyway, it would be better for sitting with the rub overnight.

So instead of hosting Shaw at his apartment, they detoured for a night on the town.

San Pedro Square Market was one of the only shining jewels in downtown San Jose. The oldest district in the city, a block-wide series of brick buildings was converted into a food hall complex framing a central courtyard that hosted live music. An eclectic but family-friendly troupe of fifty-somethings belted bluegrass tunes under strings of yellow lights. Spectators dined and danced, and kids attempted to climb a nearby tree surrounded by picnic tables. People with bottles of beer rested against the exterior walls, content to view the lively celebration from a distance.

Carver and Shaw sat sideways on a picnic bench drinking beers, having long emptied their hearty ramen bowls. They were far from a substitute for slow-cooked brisket, but little was.

"How could you *not* want one?" pressed Shaw, incredulous. "It's a mochi donut with Hot Cheetos topping."

Carver tried not to vomit in his mouth. "I'm sure it'll give you plenty of TikTok cred. In the meantime, I'm going to have an old fashioned for dessert like an adult."

Shaw huffed at the missed opportunity. He wasn't wearing his dark shades in the evening, but his ratty baseball cap was present and backwards. The thing was so tattered that any semblance of a logo had long worn off. "Fine," he said, raising his hand in invitation. "Drinks before dessert."

Carver curtsied and headed toward the bar. With the dense crowd, one of them needed to stay at the table to hold it. Carver cut through the masses like a ghost in plain sight. Instead of peace, though, he was on edge. This was a nice, happening, carefree atmosphere, but after the morning's events, it wasn't rubbing off on him. Music and a beer hardly overrode his training, and he was determined not to let down his guard.

He pushed inside one of the buildings framing the courtyard and headed for the short line at the bar. With the main attraction outside, it was easier to maneuver in here. A quick headcount tallied over thirty guests. Carver had taken in the environs in a fraction of a second, too fast for anyone to notice, first scanning for threats and then interests and anomalies. Someone holding a weapon or running toward him would be a threat, a group of young guys playing cards or pool might be an interest, and a man standing alone in a suit would be an anomaly. That kind of thing.

Carver sighed as he realized there was no hope of salvaging the night. In retrospect, it was a good thing he hadn't wasted the brisket.

The bartender waved him over when he was next in line. Carver powered through and ordered two drinks. Then, spotting a pair of premixed frozen-cocktail machines, he broke his routine and ordered a third. If he was going to be subjected to this, he was at least going to have a little fun.

"How was Mexico?" asked a woman in a stern voice.

Carver sighed again and halfway turned his head. "I wish I could say it was a surprise, Laney."

She arched an eyebrow and put her back on the bar. CIA Case Officer Lanelle Williams wasn't wearing her usual jacket tonight. Instead she was wrapped in a long-but-thin trench coat and wore a strange flowery hat that folded over the sides of her face. Definitely an anomaly. She had wanted to hide in plain sight, but the key to being a ghost was not trying too hard.

"I get it," she continued, unfazed. "You were in Tijuana. When in Rome and all that. I knew, working private security, you'd have access to a few firearms. I knew you'd be dealing with violent people. What I *didn't* know was that you'd get into multiple street shootouts, wreck a few vehicles, and upturn a fledgling drug cartel to boot."

"You can't blame me for the last one. That was family politics."

"I somehow doubt that, Vince. You're an enabler."

He shrugged. "Must be why you hire me."

"And what's that supposed to mean?"

"It means, if I'm an enabler, which of us am I enabling?"

Her cheeks tightened. "Is everything a verbal spar with you?"

"Not everything. Sometimes the sparring gets kinetic." Carver scanned his credit card and put away his wallet while using the touchscreen to select from one of a few generous tip options. "Incidentally, kinetic is also why you hire me."

Williams crossed her arms. "That's my Vince. Always good for a hot take."

He frowned as the bartender set a lager and a rye old fashioned on the bar. "Are you going to pile on too? I just had Homeland Security up my ass."

"Believe it or not, I noticed. That's why I'm here."

Carver's last drink was set before him. With a nod of thanks to the bartender, he picked it up and passed it to

Williams. It was a bright-red strawberry daiquiri in a plastic martini glass, replete with a spear of strawberry and honeydew melon.

She blinked evenly at him.

"Go on, I don't have three hands."

She grabbed the drink and Carver handled the other two. He headed toward the courtyard.

"I'm not going out there, Vince."

"Come on. We have a whole picnic table to ourselves, and if you don't sit with us somebody else will. No one likes strangers, Laney."

"You have company."

"Nick's not company."

She brandished the strawberry daiquiri. "Then who's this for?"

"That's yours. I clocked you the second I stepped inside."

Carver wore his shit-eating grin all the way back to the table with Shaw. They clinked glasses—theirs were real— and Carver said, "Get ready for this."

Lanelle Williams slinked to the edge of their table and sipped her frozen drink through a purple straw.

"This day just gets better," remarked Shaw.

"Whatever happened to the benefit of a doubt?" tempered Carver.

Williams decided the best way not to attract attention was to sit down and join them.

Shaw took a pull from his pint glass and wiped foam from his beard. "I can only assume you're here about our

HSI problem."

"Please tell us you can warn them off," added Carver.

"It's better that we don't," she said tersely. "Doing so would reveal the Agency's interest in KNS. Besides, occasionally being hassled by Big Government gives you cred in certain circles."

"Sure," bristled Carver. "Street gangs, extreme activists, anti-government militias—"

He stopped mid sentence. It was too much of a coincidence. The idea hit him so hard he couldn't even sip his rye yet. Instead, the realization sapped the energy from him and darkened his face.

"You set this up," he bristled, "didn't you?"

Williams accompanied her retaliatory smile with an angelic voice. "I can't help it if Commander Anderson believes you'd be an asset to his organization."

Carver shook his head and cursed. "I've been an idiot."

"There's your benefit of the doubt," chortled Shaw. "I'm not skipping my mochi donut for this." He abruptly stood and took his beer into the building opposite the one Carver had come from.

Williams scooted down the bench but Carver just shook his head again. He should have known. Anderson had hinted at Carver being highly recommended. It wouldn't have taken much, just a mention of a former special forces operator looking for work in the right ear or two, let it travel up the chain so Anderson "organically" hears it from his own men and "independently" decides to hire him on. That's how the CIA works. They bend you over, but only after convincing you it was your idea.

The case officer gave him a minute. She must have liked the fruity drink because she happily sipped while passively surveying the crowd. No one outside was in the least bit interested in them.

Finally, she said, "This is what we do, Vince."

"Don't I know it." He finally mustered a taste of his cocktail. "A heads up would have been nice."

"There wasn't anything there yet. You might not realize this, but most of my work is bureaucratic. A legion of files passes over my desk every day. We assess priorities. We put out feelers. We watch how situations develop."

"You're opportunists."

"Who isn't? We take what's given, and a few days ago access to S2 wasn't important."

"And now?"

She shrugged. "Now we'd like you to nurture inroads."

"Okay. But how much of a threat are these guys? I did some digging and found a lot of dirt, but nothing concrete."

"S2 lacks the presence on public networks to get into real trouble. They've participated in document-sharing of materials containing instructions on how best to attack electrical substations. This isn't just Anarchist's Cookbook edginess. We've tied them to the recent attacks on the Pacific Northwest power grid."

He frowned and took another sip, unsurprised that the CIA had a deeper well of information on the militia than the internet did. Those power grid attacks had been perpetrated by small groups shooting up hardware. The resulting damage and fallout were minimal. "I've heard about attacks all over the country."

Williams nodded. "The media does its part, but these things aren't entirely new. Electrical substations get hit by a hundred acts of vandalism a year. Bored hunters, disgruntled employees, metal scavengers. The numbers add up, and that's before you figure in twice as many weather incidents. But just because these vulnerabilities are common doesn't mean they're not serious. We have a double-digit number of critical high-voltage substations powering the American grid. With the right intelligence, surgical strikes can do real damage."

"So this is a coordinated effort by S2?"

"I wouldn't go that far yet. We've seen an increase in the number and complexity of attacks, but the efforts are, at best, loosely coordinated."

"Sharing techniques on the internet," he repeated.

"It's not much but it's something. Affiliated outfits in Washington and Oregon haven't accomplished a lot with the attacks, but we won't always be so lucky. Some of these electrical units are so specialized they need to be built to order. There aren't spares sitting in a warehouse. And it's always possible these have just been probing attacks so far. With an uptick of mobilized activity in your corner of the world, you can see our concern."

Shaw returned to the table somewhere in the middle of that. He was chewing the last of his donut so Carver didn't get to see it, but the powdered orange evidence was all over his friend's beard. Shaw took another slug of beer and wiped his mouth.

"I couldn't find a precise origin of S2," said Carver. "Are they a true homegrown threat?"

Williams raised an eyebrow. "As opposed to what?"

"A state-sponsored operation by a rival. Just spitballing, but Russia might be interested in funding the destruction of electrical transformers, spiking domestic demand. Every single one we need to custom build is one we can't use to repair Ukraine's grid."

"It's unlikely," she said. "There's no intel on foreign interference. Russia is good at amplifying these voices when they find them, anything to sow discord, but this movement was created on American soil. S2 is a domestic non-state actor filled with real, disillusioned people. Their circles legitimately believe if they bring down the power grid, they bring down the government."

"There are only nine meals between mankind and anarchy," said Carver.

She watched him blankly.

"Alfred Henry Lewis," he explained.

"No one knows who that is, Vince."

"You think it's true?" interjected Shaw. "The grid goes down for good, shipping and food supplies are cut, and after a few days society reverts to anarchy?"

"I don't intend to find out," asserted Williams. "But most intelligence agencies have run models and crunched numbers. A well-fed population is a sated one. If you remove that basic human need, it's not out of the realm of possibility that people devolve into self-serving animals."

Shaw hiked a shoulder. "Might be fun."

"Except there are no Hot Cheetos in the apocalypse." Carver shook his head. Prepping was one thing, but this was straight into Boogaloo territory. "I don't believe the theory. People have always fought over resources, but they've always banded together to share them too. Humans outperform all other species in part because we pool our efforts and work together. There'd be mass looting, it will be essential to have a gun, but society won't break down."

Shaw snorted. "Whatever, brother. I'm good either way."

Carver smiled. Operators like them didn't have a lot of attachments in the wider world. It made the calculus simple. It made them effective.

"Here's what I don't get," posited Carver. "If this militia is problematic, why not cut out the rot right now? Arrest them and lock up their finances."

Williams spat out a breath. "Getting to them or their money isn't easy. There's no centralized organization. We don't know if Commander Anderson heads the entire militia or just this branch. They're financed mainly by small donations. That means political capital and mention in the media cycle. Which means any action against them is scrutinized."

"Political capital?" scoffed Carver. "They want to instigate the apocalypse. It's a joke."

"They don't need to accomplish anything, they just need to claim they can. The more impossible the goal, the more appealing and galvanizing the movement."

"But if you tied them to the Pacific Northwest grid attacks, what do you need me for? Put them in prison."

Again, she hedged. "The evidence is circumstantial. Anderson has alibis for the previous incidents. We don't know that anyone at his ranch was directly involved."

Carver was starting to get it. If the evidence was a slam dunk, Williams wouldn't be spending her time in San Pedro Square.

"That's why I need your eyes and ears in there," she said. "You can bring us the evidence we need. You already have the invitation."

He took another pull of the old fashioned. In the scheme of things, this was a limited operation. He just needed to get onsite, do some shooting with the boys, and snoop around a little. He could even get paid on both ends.

"How do I reach you when I get something?" he asked.

The CIA officer shook her head. "You don't. HSI has marked you a person of interest."

He stiffened and scanned the crowd. He hadn't made anyone.

Williams let go a rare laugh. "They're not nineteen-forties private dicks, Vince. HSI isn't spying you on binoculars from a car down the street."

Carver chewed his lip and wondered what was wrong with binoculars and cars. No matter how advanced technology got, operational effectiveness was about boots on the ground. That was the difference between his world and the CIA's.

But then, the tech side of things couldn't be ignored. It

was all SIGINT these days.

"They're tapping my phone?" he realized, incredulous.

Williams simply shrugged. "They have access if they want it, Vince. I can't risk exposing myself like that. We're on US soil on this one. It's an added level of scrutiny, and I'm not even allowed to operate here. You need to go in without support, do what you do, and wait for me to contact you."

"That's all?" he huffed. "And right after I just told Homeland Security I had nothing to do with the militia. They'll think I blew them off."

Lanelle Williams stood and patted him on the shoulder. "Being hassled by the man is what we call cred, Vince. Just play it cool, keep HSI at an arm's length, and you'll come out okay."

"At an arm's length," he repeated sourly.

"You know I'm good for it."

Carver frowned at the half-empty daiquiri on the table and decided not to mention his inclination to ask Agent Guerrero to dinner.

5

It took a few days to get everything set up. Anderson was thrilled at the news, and what Homeland Security didn't know couldn't hurt them. Besides, they likely moved on to other concerns. It was almost as if Bentley and Guerrero and Williams were all a bad dream and Carver was taking a day trip, just driving to the ranch to enjoy the weekend.

But minutes from his destination, the conception vanished. There wasn't room for complacency where he was going. More than anything else, operational discipline was pivotal to success. Other aspects like training and planning were vital, of course, but it was discipline that assured their precise execution.

The ranch that served as the militia's base of operations was, unsurprisingly, in the same neighborhood as the gun range where Lester and Carver had met. Coyote was a small town on the southeastern outskirts of San Jose, with easy access to the freeway and surrounding hills. The countryside was wide open and barren in places, but wooded the further you got from civilization.

As Carver's pickup navigated the winding dirt trail on the last leg of the journey, Morgan said, "This better not be a boys club." She was sitting in the back seat with the gear. Not only was she usually in charge of everyone's kit, but she had the shortest legs.

"Of course it's a boys club," returned Shaw from the passenger seat. "How many incel white nationalists do you think are women?"

"Ugh. Do I have to pretend I'm racist?"

Carver smiled. "We're going to buddy up with whoever we need to in order to get the job done. For what it's worth, I get the impression these guys focus their energy on slamming the government. I didn't come across any pro-male pro-white dogma."

"It's not the type of thing you put in a brochure, Vince."

"Put it this way," offered Shaw. "When you work with us, it's a boys club. When you spend time with your husband and kids, that's a boys club too. You should be used to it."

Carver grinned at the thought of Morgan getting her nails done with her lady friends. She wasn't the spa type. Exhibit A were the gray clothes and drab brown ballistic vests they wore. Matching attire and equipment might be overkill for a casual day of shooting, but it would reinforce their presence as instructors and hopefully increase the trust extended to them.

"Speaking of your two little monsters," said Carver, changing the subject to calm his team's jitters, "how did camping at the lake go?"

"We had one bandaged foot after stepping on broken glass. Cleared some dry brush from around the campfire.

Saw a bear, too."

Shaw burst into laughter. "He didn't ask for a threat assessment. Vince was asking if you had fun."

She pursed her lips and considered. "Hunter growled at the bear to protect us. This little sausage of a dog is the last thing from scary, but her yapping sent that black bear running for the hills. The boys thought she was the coolest dog ever."

"You see?" concluded Shaw with an encouraging nod. "Now *that* sounds like fun."

Unlike Carver and Shaw, Juliette Morgan was a family person. Stories of her domestic life emphasized how they didn't have such connections. It also reminded them what they were fighting for.

"Heads up," said Carver. "This is it."

The pickup veered into a break in the trees obstructed by a double-height chain-link fence. The gate was open and waiting, manned by a young guy with a modified AR on a three-point sling. Carver buzzed down the window and heard a familiar whine in the distance. He gave a passing glance at the security camera sitting atop the fence post, then looked to the sky.

The kid approached nervously. "You, um, you from Connect... Connectic—"

"Kinetic National Security," said Vince. "Lester's expecting me."

The kid blinked a few times before he realized who he was talking about. "Sure is," he said. "Go on in." He waved down the road like there was any other way to go.

Carver nodded thanks and drove through. The kid in the rearview went to work swinging the fence closed. On the one hand, there was the semblance of security, but on the other it was pretty lax. Though clearly having been waiting for Carver, the kid was almost surprised to see him. They probably didn't see many strangers here.

The dirt road continued through sparse tree cover with occasional breaks, a whine still echoing off the canopy. As Carver drove, he kept leaning forward to check the sky through the windshield. Eventually, he fixed on the source of the rotor whine: a remote quadcopter. It was difficult to tell the size as high up as it was, but it wasn't a janky Target model. Carver scanned the terrain underneath the drone. The operator was a young woman in green camo. She was alone in the field and didn't register their passing.

In another minute they pulled into a small clearing fronted by a white-paneled ranch house. The building was the first in a series of houses, utility hangers, and barns. None of the construction was particularly modern, but it wasn't dilapidated either. Judging by several scattered residents attending to chores, Carver bet the militia members each contributed to keeping the grounds.

A few trucks were congregated under tarps some distance away. Seeing their host waiting to greet them, Carver simply pulled over where he was. It wasn't like they didn't have the space.

"Quite the welcoming party," muttered Shaw.

A pair of young men attended a waiting Commander Anderson. The first two held AR-15s pointed to the ground.

The commander only had a sidearm on his belt.

"Give me a minute getting out," instructed Carver under his breath. "I want your presence to grow on them." He climbed out of the truck and announced, "Looks like everyone's ready to go." As he hiked over, he noted their uncertain stares. "Is something wrong, Lester?"

The man winced. He wore a brimmed camouflage fishing hat and sunglasses to cut the glare, which made him difficult to read. The scruff on his chin ended in a pointed goatee that tweaked sideways with his lips. "It's Lester at the range, but Commander Anderson at the compound. We're not too formal here. Most everyone is on a first-name basis, even my Deputy Commander Sam Grafton. But as the ranking member of this complex I have a professional distance to maintain."

Carver nodded, no harm, no foul. "Understood, Commander."

"Nice truck," remarked the man in the middle. He was in his twenties and carried a military appearance, mostly impressing with his tall height.

"Still looking to match it to a boat," joked Carver. After sneaking aboard a pair of oligarch superyachts worth half a billion dollars, it was hard to find one that cut the mustard.

"Don't ruin it," said Anderson. "I've been on a lifetime of boats in the Marines. Trust me when I say the real action's on the ground."

Carver nodded politely and looked to the other two, who were about the same age. "Vince Carver."

"Holt," said the tall one. He wore a baseball cap over a

blond buzz cut and stood an inch over Carver.

"Chuck, sir," said the other. He was a squat guy.

"Nice to meet you boys," said Carver. "I hate to get off on the wrong foot, but I am here to teach shooting, and that starts with trigger discipline."

Holt was doing a model job with his extended index finger, but Chuck lazily rested his on the side of the trigger. He quickly corrected his grip, and Carver gauged three separate reactions.

Chuck had quickly fallen in line without complaint. He thought himself a good soldier. Holt glared at Carver and admonished Chuck. He was a hard leader. For Anderson's part, he had asked Carver to teach and didn't take offense at the instruction. That was a promising start.

The three militia members wore mismatched camo fatigues, Anderson and Chuck in dark green. Holt had flat tan gear and his cap featured a patch of a black-and-yellow American flag above the brim.

Carver nodded to it. "What's wrong with the red, white, and blue?"

Holt snorted. "Quite a bit, actually." His expression grew more defiant, like he was waiting to start an argument over it.

"Lay off, Holt," said Anderson. "I invited Mr. Carver here to talk guns, not ideology." His tone had the confidence of a natural leader. "Mr. Carver, can I have a word?"

No first-name basis for him, then. Anderson stepped toward the ranch house and Carver followed. Looking over the property, he had yet to see another security camera past the one at the entrance. That was also promising.

"Is something wrong?" he asked as they huddled by the white-paneled wall.

"You weren't supposed to bring friends."

Carver put on a show of frowning as he watched Morgan and Shaw collecting bags from the truck. Holt and Chuck kept wary eyes on them. Folks who gathered with guns in private compounds didn't tend to extend a lot of goodwill to strangers.

"They're not buddies," explained Carver, "they're associates. Your offer was so generous that I wanted to make sure you got your money's worth. To be frank, I still don't know how many people I'll be training. What I can tell you is that you're hiring the combined professional expertise of Kinetic National Security. They're part of the package."

Anderson's fingers combed down his mustache and beard. "It's just... You've probably noticed, but we rely on operational security here. Anyone coming to the ranch needs to be vetted."

Carver made an "ah" sound, as if he completely understood and sympathized. He also knew that Anderson had a soft spot for military veterans, and that he really didn't want to offend Carver after finally getting him on the ranch.

"I'll tell you what." Carver turned and waved Morgan and Shaw over. Holt and Chuck stiffened, and everybody converged looking a little jumpy. Chuck noticed Carver's gaze and checked his trigger finger again.

Shaw strolled up wearing his ratty backwards cap and

blacked out sunglasses. He gave the commander a nod and Carver introduced him.

"This is my main man, Nick Shaw. You're looking at an elite SEAL from DEVGRU who was instrumental in several high-profile operations which I cannot name. You hired me because I'm a good shooter. Mr. Shaw is a better sniper than I am."

Morgan stood beside him, brown hair curved to her chin, green eyes focused on the boys club.

"Next up is Juliette Morgan. She served Special Reconnaissance in the Army Special Forces. She's a logistics wizard and gets the team what it needs."

Anderson and the others nodded in greeting. They were too impressed with the team's credentials to ask followup questions.

"I've worked at various security companies around the world," continued Carver, "and Mrs. Morgan and Mr. Shaw are the top choices to fill out my staff. They're trained experts, dependable contractors, and—even better—good people. I trust them with my life."

"Okay, okay," relinquished Anderson, not wanting to make a scene and probably wanting to look in control in front of his soldiers. "I don't mean to get into anything. I'm sure you two will be a great complement to our training regimen. Thank you for being here."

Carver nodded. "So how do you want to get started?"

"I figured I'd show you around my neck of the woods first." Anderson waved everybody on and started walking around the main house. "This is HQ. It's my residence but it also has a war table where I meet with my officer core."

"Deputy Sam?" prodded Carver.

"Yes, along with Holt. He's an XO. There are two others."

They stepped around HQ into the back, where several other buildings formed a central yard. They walked by several fire pits and long benches and firewood stacked above their heads.

"This is the cafeteria," said Anderson, pointing out the long building they walked along, then signaling the barns across the yard. "That's the workshop and the bunker over there. We keep them centralized as safe houses in the event of an attack. You'll notice all the other structures form a perimeter. The building at the back is the barracks."

"Your men sleep here?" asked Carver.

"In stints. It's not a regular thing but you never know when the need will arise. S2 is, above all, a safe haven for our members."

"Safe from what?" asked Morgan.

"From anything that comes our way. We're supplied to support forty soldiers for near on two years."

Carver's team shared a glance. That was a lot of militia members, though he assumed that number was more of a future ideal than a current reality. Nonetheless, he could already see how serious Anderson's operation was.

"The small range is right there," said the commander, pointing out the shooting lanes past the building perimeter. "It's a good start, but we have longer targets set in the hills."

"Impressive property," said Carver.

"We do what we can."

As they headed over to take a look at the range, the barn door of the workshop opened. A woman with red hair nearly jumped with surprise at the sight of their group. She shared quick words with some people inside and they shut the large door. The woman took a breath and stomped toward them.

"Commander," she said sternly, "you didn't say anything about hosting multiple guests today."

They stopped as they waited for her to catch up. "This is Mr. Carver's team," Anderson explained.

"And which one is Mr. Carver?"

Carver's immediate impression was that this woman sassing the commander was his wife. She halted before them with hands on hips and her head at a lean. Unlike the others, she wore a plain black shirt with mom jeans.

"That would be me, ma'am," he answered.

She extended a hand and they shook. "Deputy Sam Grafton. I'm in charge of security around here. Uninvited guests aren't supposed to wander the compound. Isn't that right, Holt?"

The young man seemed almost twice her height, but he withered under her glare.

"It's fine, Sam," assured Anderson. "Mr. Carver is here at my invitation. We hired his company, and his company is welcome. They all served."

Her eyes sharpened. If they were married, there was no love lost between them.

"Have you seen Lorelai?" Anderson asked her. "I was hoping to introduce them." He turned to Carver and said,

"She's a slight thing, but she's a fighter."

Sam's head lolled from one shoulder to the other. "You know she's all over the place, Commander."

Carver lifted his hand to his chest and piped in. "About yea high, blonde hair, and wearing a cap?"

"That's her," said Anderson.

"I saw her north of the driveway piloting a drone."

Sam's head jerked toward that direction. "That girl's always playing with toys," she complained. "Holt, would you mind collecting her? Tell her the commander's instructors are here."

"Sure thing, Ma," said the boy. She gave him a disparaging glare and he quickly amended it to, "Deputy." He was relieved to trudge away.

"Family," chuckled Sam with just a hint of Texas in her voice. "God bless them." She huffed and searched Carver's team with her eyes. "I'm sorry, but I don't think we're set up for you all at the moment."

"It's not a problem," reassured Anderson before Carver could reply. "I figured we'd start informal. Warm up over here, drink some beers, and get to know each other first. How's that sound to everybody?"

"Sounds good to me," answered Shaw for the group.

The commander nodded. "Chuck, grab a cooler of cold ones and meet us at the range. We've got shooting to do."

6

The open-air firing lanes were spacious and equipped with the basic necessities for everyday use. It made Carver wonder why Anderson bothered with the public range at all, but he figured it was difficult to recruit on private property. Anderson had met Carver on the public range, and that was exactly the point.

A small stock of crates with firearms and ammunition sat snug against the near wall. Anderson mentioned it having been taken from the vault for training. The rifles were an assortment of common AR-15 models, mostly FN 15s, PSA PA-15s, and Smith & Wesson Sport IIs.

As the weapon of choice in the United States, AR-15s and their accessories were ubiquitous. It was easy to blend in with them, especially in the right circles, and since they were here today to train those circles, Carver's team was armed with the same system. They unbagged a set of BCM Recce-16 MCMRs. They were largely unmodified firearms for the masses, with government-profile 16" barrels and ergonomic pistol grips.

"Nice weapon," remarked the commander. "If you don't mind me asking, why go with Bravo Company over another premium manufacturer like Daniel Defense?"

"It doesn't make much of a difference in my book," answered Carver. "I suppose it comes down to which furniture you prefer." When talking clean and simple, the Recce-16 was a favorite of Carver's. It was a workhorse more than a match gun, and that suited him fine.

After a little more shop talk, Anderson opened up the session with an FN 15 and a tight grouping on a paper target. His military experience was apparent in his stance and performance, though he complained of a nagging shoulder injury.

"I took shrapnel running COIN while clearing a building in Fallujah."

"Friendly?" asked Shaw.

Anderson chuckled at the assumption. "Sounds like you know military. We were clearing insurgents block by block. When the Hajis got frisky we would take down the whole building. Sometimes the pressure blowout from one central satchel charge of C4 was all it took. Usually it wasn't so easy and we met resistance. There was a miscommunication under fire. A junior Marine let a frag loose early in a direction that surprised us. I recovered then, but I'm not so young anymore, and the pain comes back in waves."

Shaw clinked his beer bottle to Anderson's. "Pain means you're still alive, brother."

"That it does."

Carver rapped his left arm. "I took two rounds in nearly the same spot. I know what you mean."

"Afghanistan?"

"I'm not at liberty to disclose the when and where."

"You spec ops guys must have stories, but I understand they're not the kind you tell." His eyes tracked a hawk gliding over distant hills. A curt sigh cut off his repose. "Shitshow on every continent, right?" Anderson made sure his weapon was clear and set it aside. "Men like us, our eyes are open to the cruelty of the world. Some people take it for a holy mission, but that's horseshit. You're either someone who can take it, or someone who can't."

Chuck was already waiting with his weapon, and the shooting attracted a few more militia members. Carver made a point to stop and personally welcome each one. First was Trent, who had long, disheveled hair. He'd completed basic for the Marines before receiving a medical discharge. He didn't elaborate why. One of the other XOs, Victor, also came round.

Holt returned with Lorelai in tow. She was shy, not saying anything when they shook hands. Barely drinking age, and not short, really, but she looked it next to Holt and Carver. Her hair was light with a tinge of strawberry. It was hard to tell how long it was wrapped under the military cap.

Introductions out of the way, it was Carver's turn to go through a mag. He figured modeling form and execution was a nice opening salvo. He also wanted to start off with a good impression, so he bypassed the 50-yard lanes and jumped right to 100. His grouping was tight and far outperformed the commander's at twice the range.

"What did I tell you!" crowed Anderson without a hint of embarrassment. "Can this man shoot or what?"

A few of the guys cheered, Lorelai actually clapped, but Sam wore an expression of boredom over crossed arms.

"Not bad," remarked Shaw. "Not perfect, but not bad."

"Glad I have your approval, Mr. Shaw."

The exchange earned a few chuckles from the captive audience. Anderson was right about shooting being fun. These guys seemed okay, at least socially. More importantly, they were starting to build a rapport.

"What about your stance?" asked Holt. "I mean, target practice is one thing, but shouldn't you stand at an angle in a live-fire situation?"

Carver cleared the shooting lane and said, "Show me."

The young man shrugged like it was nothing and moved into position in the 100-yard lane next to Carver's. He angled his body so it was almost fully bladed to the target. "Like this. You know, to make yourself a smaller target against return fire."

Carver nodded approval as a teacher would. "I don't see anything wrong with that." Then he pivoted to the growing crowd of militia members, keeping this about the group and not the man. "Stance really depends on your personal preference, comfort, and training. When it comes down to it, if you shoot better one way, stick with it."

"But what about incoming fire?" Holt pressed.

Carver turned back to the student. "When firing from a defensive strongpoint, I want as low a profile as possible. But when you're not dug in, when it's you and a tango sharing space, military doctrine for special operations forces is to square up with the enemy so as to present maximal armor." Carver stood straight and used his hand to display various impact points against his ballistic vest. "In close protection, this has the added benefit of obstructing lines of fire to any principals behind you. But, there's no always-on answer. Optimal strategies depend on context. Remember: combat is about adapting to the situation at hand."

"Ideally quicker than the other guy," chimed Shaw.

There were more laughs. Even Holt smiled, and Carver suspected he had purposely put him on the spot to challenge his authority. But not everybody was having a good time. In the back of the crowd, now fifteen strong, Sam argued with Anderson. Their voices were sharp but hushed enough to be discreet. Carver removed one of his earplugs but it didn't help.

Suddenly sensing the crowd's attention, Sam threw up her hands. "You always come around in the end," she admonished. "You'll see." Deputy Commander Grafton stormed away toward HQ.

She was going to be a problem. Sam was a seasoned woman who didn't like hosting Carver's group and didn't mind getting in her commander's face. What was worse was that those opinions were entirely right. Anderson had invited foxes into the henhouse, and Carver did pose a threat of infiltration. The question, in turn, was what did S2 have that was worth hiding?

Anderson's gaze moved back to the training. Carver didn't want to appear overly interested in militia politics so moved on without skipping a beat.

"Holt, since you're already in place, why don't you

demonstrate next?"

"In the hundred or the fifty?"

"Whichever you like."

Holt nodded, fitted muffs over his ears, and took aim from the hundred. His first two shots were wide. It looked like nerves. But he hit center target next, and the rest of his mag besides one had excellent aim.

"Nice shooting," lauded Carver.

"Took a minute to warm up."

"That's why we practice. Who wants a go next?"

A whispery voice said, "Me." It was Lorelai.

She went to the stock and looked over the rifles for a minute, ultimately opting for a Sport II. Pulling it out of the box, she immediately swept the barrel over the crowd. Carver leaned away and grabbed the weapon to angle it down.

"Sorry!" she hurried, as if she had been chided for the same thing many times before. She was nervous too.

"It's okay. I don't need to tell you, but every weapon is always loaded, even when it's not. That goes just as much for professionals as it does enthusiasts."

Holt muttered under his breath, and Carver wasn't sure if he was more mad at him or Lorelai.

She moved to a 50-yard lane, visibly uncertain after her flub. "Shoot with your body straight, you said?"

"Sure, if that's comfortable. Stock to your shoulder." He adjusted her left hand to give her more control of the barrel. "Is that too much of a stretch?"

She felt it out. "Nah, it's okay."

"Good." He handed her muffs and a mag and said, "When you're ready."

She took a long time to set up. She worried about her feet. She worried about her breathing. Then, in a complete turnaround, once she started to shoot she was in a rush. She went through half her capacity without taking the time to aim, and her paper target had only received two hits.

"Slow down," called Carver a few times. "Tighten those elbows."

She finally heard him and paused long enough for him to give more instruction. At her level, he stuck with the basics, working on her aim along the sights and relaxing her trigger pulls. The next ten tries were a mess and she was getting frustrated, but Carver calmed her down and she salvaged the final shots. Three hits on the outer rings of the target, and all five hit paper.

Lorelai was relieved when the mag clicked empty. "Well that was crap," she groaned.

Carver smiled. "Actually, it was a good demonstration that improvement can be immediate when you focus on your training. We're not Al-Qaeda out here painting a target with lead and firing AKs into the sky, are we?"

"Hell no, sir," said Chuck.

Carver nodded at the group. "Suppressive fire is one thing, but shooting—real shooting—is more about restraint than release."

"He's right," said Victor, the other XO observing. "I've been over this with you, Lorelai."

"Maybe you're a shit teacher," quipped Holt.

Victor huffed. "If you don't mind, Mr. Carver, may I?"

Carver waved him on. Allowing prospective students to teach revealed a lot about them. In this case, Carver was less curious about the shooting and more interested in where Lorelai's attention went. This was a camp of, what, twenty guys? Lorelai might be the only prospective female among them.

As Victor went over technique with Lorelai, Anderson converged on Carver's shoulder.

"You'll need to excuse her. The girl's mother didn't want her around guns growing up. But she's hard-nosed. You'll see."

Carver pivoted his attention from training to commander. "She's your daughter?"

"My pride and joy," he beamed.

"What does her mother think now?"

The expression of joy ended with a sigh. "She's out of the picture, I'm afraid. But I respected her wishes. Lorelai's here by choice, if you're asking. She tried the normal life. It didn't work out..."

Lorelai was avidly watching Victor shoot. With Carver occupied, Shaw had stepped up to assist. Meanwhile Anderson only had eyes for his daughter.

Carver was getting the sense that half of his shooting instruction was meant to focus on her. Sure, the rest of these boys could do with training, but Lorelai required special attention. As far as the CIA operation was concerned, this created an opportunity to get close to the Andersons. Especially with the Graftons, Sam and Holt, being antagonistic toward them, retaining support of the commander was invaluable.

Victor did a pretty good job. The XOs were probably XOs for a reason. That said, he was a little cocky for Carver's taste. Though he hadn't quite matched Holt's showing, he acted above it all, going so far as to ignore Shaw's coaching tips. That was a sign of someone who'd reached their capacity to learn.

"Trust me," Victor protested, "I'm better at range."

Shaw shrugged. "You can't walk if you can't crawl."

"What's that supposed to mean?"

"It means what I said."

Victor's face hardened and he took a step toward Shaw, who was stone behind the hat, sunglasses, and beard.

Morgan slipped between them. "The testosterone's a little hot, folks. We don't need to take it any further than that."

"Please don't get in his way, ma'am," ordered Chuck, defending the XO. His rifle was in hand as if keeping guard.

"This is our house, lady," warned Victor.

"Cool it!" screamed Sam, stomping from nowhere to the head of the group. Despite her very public exit, she had been keeping an eye on things. "I won't tolerate fighting in the compound."

"It's okay, Sam," said Anderson. "They're just boys flexing their muscles."

"It's not okay, Commander. It borders on insubordination."

Carver didn't say anything as he watched the deputy pull

her XO off the line, but she was absolutely right. Calling someone Lester or Commander wasn't the prize of respect, it was the ability to keep soldiers in line. As the boys rejoined the crowd, Anderson must have sensed this, because he changed the subject.

"I understand your misgivings, boys. I do." He stepped forward. "We're all fighters here, but that doesn't mean we have to fight. We're competitors too, aren't we?"

He got some nods.

"So hows about a friendly competition? It seems Kinetic National Security needs to earn your respect. What better way than to pit our best shooter against theirs?"

His soldiers joined a heated chorus. This was what they were here for.

7

Anderson was a smart enough guy. He had to know his people didn't have a chance. That was why Carver was here in the first place. The shooting contest was a de-escalation method that simultaneously gave his boys what they hungered for. It was a chance for both sides to prove themselves. And, ultimately, a way to get them to start listening.

"What will it be?" Anderson asked, turning to Carver for approval.

Carver nodded.

The commander turned to the range. "Mr. Shaw, I believe Mr. Carver nominated you for the role with his earlier statements."

The Kentucky boy with sun-reddened cheeks nodded. "And who's your best shooter?" he asked.

"Ten years ago that would've been me, but I'm sorry to say my shoulder pain aggravates my stance."

Sam's hands went to her hips. "Go on, Holt. Make a name for yourself."

Holt swallowed, nonplussed at the prospect of being pitted against a former Navy SEAL.

"Now, Sam," tempered Anderson in what was probably an orchestrated slight, "your son has an excellent eye and outstanding shooting discipline, but if we're in a match, you know Chuck has him beat on the targets."

The remark surprised Carver after the trigger-discipline incident. But Chuck was an avid learner. Instead of taking offense at being corrected, he took the advice to heart.

He was a devoted soldier too. He hadn't stepped on his friend's opportunity by speaking up, but now that the spotlight was firmly on him he didn't balk.

"Yes sir, Commander."

Unlike Holt, he showed no trepidation at going up against Shaw.

"Then let's see it," declared Anderson.

The group set up a series of targets. Each man would get a 50-yard shoot and a 100-yard shoot, and the points from each round would be tallied into a grand total. Once everything was ready, the militia gave their shooter space.

Chuck started with the fifty, measuring each fire. He was more consistently accurate than Holt, fired with confidence rather than cockiness, and began tallying an impressive score.

"You boys government, ain't ya?" asked Trent.

An older man with long greasy hair of wild brown-and-gray streaks, Trent probably hadn't bathed in days. His eyes were curious though. Unlike his militia brethren, he was more interested in Carver than the ongoing competition.

"If you mean former military," countered Carver, "I think that describes a lot of us."

"I don't mean that." Trent leaned close. "I'm asking if you're part of the machine."

Their eyes locked. It was an odd question, and out of nowhere. Then again it probably didn't mean much. This was a fringe militia prepping for an age of lawlessness. Paranoia came with the territory.

"My security company handles private contracts. My clients are—"

"Part of the capitalist machine!" concluded the man. "But those days are crumbling. I know you can feel it. You just need to look around."

"He's not wrong," said Holt, moving closer to them. "Environmental destruction, wide-scale depletion of vital resources like water, timber, and arable soil. That's overpopulation combined with famine."

"Social unrest," added Lorelai. "Political unrest." She was eager to be part of the conversation and showed a little more ivory now that she had his attention. "A growing class divide."

Trent nodded with his cohorts. "It's no coincidence we're seeing a worldwide spread of armed conflict and disease. If you haven't noticed, we've entered a period of capitalist decline. The end of an era. You do see that, don't you?"

Carver glanced from the shooting contest to the suddenly devout militia members around him. Anderson waited a few feet away, listening but pretending not to. Staying out of it.

They were feeling him out.

"I'm not sure about all that," he hedged, not wanting to appear too willing, "but I do know this is a different world than the one I grew up in."

"Damn straight!" punctuated Trent. He was already claiming victory.

"You ask me," said Holt, "we need to take control of our destiny."

Cheers erupted in the crowd. Chuck had apparently scored one of his best targets yet. He was on such a roll that he forewent taking turns and moved straight to the hundred lane. Shaw watched patiently without objection.

"Is that what we're doing here?" posited Carver. "How does practicing shooting change our destiny?"

"It's about preparation," explained Sam, once again joining in from an unexpected angle. The woman was everywhere. "I'd expect a man of your impressive military credentials to know that."

Carver nodded to concede the statement.

"Corporations are absconding with our wealth," continued Trent. "Big Tech is converting our lives to data. They can't sell us but they can reduce us to numbers and sell that. It's a form of slavery."

"The politicians don't help," asserted Holt. "It don't matter if they're red or blue." He pointed to the patch on his cap. "That's why my flag doesn't carry those colors."

Carver considered the strange band of conspirators, on the same page but of different books. Their ideologies were similar enough to be compatible even while they said different things. So far they weren't so much about right or left. It anti-government, anti-corporation, and anti-control. That was a lot of overlap to work with.

Victor hadn't shared his thoughts. He was wrapped up in Chuck's performance. Anderson was pretending to be. Lorelai grinned, just happy to be there. When Carver met her gaze, she looked away. Sam was like Carver, in the thick of it and taking it all in.

"There's nothing wrong with being patriotic," countered Trent, proving that even among a single S2 cell there wasn't unanimous agreement. "The government is ineffectual, but the people are the problem."

"The government *is* the people," countered Holt.

"Exactly my point. We change hearts and minds, and we have something worth saving. Anyone who served this country realizes that."

"You weren't mentally fit to serve this country."

Trent shot him daggers. "Boy, you better show some respect."

The crowd cheered again, interrupting the challenge. Chuck's performance had been scored and he did a pretty good job on the long target. It was better than Holt's, and combined with his excellent short target, he had set an impressive bar. The celebration was contagious and broke up their discussion, which was probably for the best before it got out of hand. Shaw turned to the crowd and put both hands up in an animated shrug, like he had his work cut out for him.

"You've outdone yourself, Chuck!" praised the commander. "Best foot forward when it counts."

"Yes sir."

Anderson was clearly pleased with his nomination. Sam glowered a little at Chuck's success, but Holt had no hard feelings. He patted his friend on the shoulder in congratulations.

"Mr. Shaw," announced the commander after the crowd settled down. "I believe you're up."

"Actually," called out Carver, "I'd like to change the plan." He took his place at the front and nodded to Chuck. "That was great shooting, soldier. I admit to being surprised. You should be proud. But we all know it's not exactly fair to pit you against a DEVGRU sniper, is it?"

Chuck was about to object, but Carver continued.

"If you lost, you'd say, yeah, but he's the best of the best. And you'd be right."

"Don't try backing out," called Victor.

Carver put a hand up to calm the crowd. When they silenced, he said, "My purpose here is to teach you that you don't need to be a Navy SEAL to apply your training to the target. Now, I grant you, Mrs. Morgan is overqualified for the job too, but she's the one with the least range time among us, so..."

Juliette Morgan rolled her eyes. "You're going to put me on the spot, aren't you?"

"I believe he already did," chuckled Shaw. No skin off his back, he passed his prepared rifle to her.

"Come on," complained Victor. "You're just setting yourself up for an excuse." A few other militia members grumbled at the bait and switch.

Carver grinned. This was exactly what he wanted.

"Fall in line, soldiers!" ordered Sam. "The challenger is his to name. Why don't we see how Mrs. Morgan does instead of bitching about it?"

For once the deputy was on his side. Or she was on the side of giving the woman in a boys club a chance, at least.

Morgan took position at the 50-yard mark. The Recce-16 popped at even intervals like a metronome. Aim, breathe, shoot. Aim, breathe, shoot. Experience in the field tempered her nerves against anything the audience could bring. As rounds expanded already existing holes in the target, the crowd gasped. Morgan finished with a tight grouping that resembled Chuck's but ultimately outscored it.

The real difference was on the long target. Whereas Chuck's performance significantly degraded at twice the range, Morgan's shooting was machinelike. Another tight grouping at center mass, with few strays outside. It was a resounding victory before bothering to tally points.

Chuck's eyes were dinner plates. Even the deputy was noticeably impressed. But Victor's face twisted.

"You trying to embarrass us?"

"It's supposed to display what hard work and training can accomplish," answered Carver.

"This isn't a bullshit game." He stomped forward. "What is this bitch gonna do when her ass is really on the line?"

Morgan showed her teeth and placed the rifle on the table. "Put your money where you mouth is, tough guy."

Victor converged on the line like he was going to

outshoot her. Instead he slugged a half-smirking Morgan on the cheek. She fell as the crowd yelled. Morgan planted her boot in the dirt to spring back on her attacker.

Normally, Carver would let this play out. She wasn't as big as Victor and was behind the eight ball after a sucker punch, but he had faith that she wasn't down and out.

That said, this was a situation that could quickly get out of hand. If brawls were how these boys responded to being outshot by a woman, what would happen after she kicked someone's ass?

"How do you like that?" Victor crowed. "You want some more?"

He kicked, but Morgan, still low to the ground, lifted a boot to intercept his. She was waiting for him to expose himself so she could take him down. Before it got that far, Carver latched his arms around the man from behind and lifted him off the ground. As he pulled him away, the XO tried to ram the back of his head into Carver's nose.

Carver deftly avoided the blow and threw Victor forcefully to the ground.

The XO rolled away. "You piece of shit!"

He came at Carver now. An angry charge. Not seeing any other option, Carver pulled away from a wild swing and then decked Victor. A single connection to his jaw knocked him out.

Chuck stepped forward, gripping his gun. It wasn't pointed and was likely empty, but blood was in his eyes.

"That's it!" cried Anderson, running before his men and batting them back. "Fall in line!"

Frantic outbursts erupted from the crowd. Jeers, taunts, laughs. Nobody went against the commander, but it was curious that Sam stood in the back with her arms crossed letting this play out. After her repeated enforcement of discipline, she was almost daring the men to defy the commander now.

Morgan dusted off her pants, and Trent hurried to check on Victor. The XO was starting to move his head back and forth as the world came back to him. The crowd was still rowdy.

"I said that's the end of it!" screamed Anderson, pulling the sunglasses from his face. His eyes were bloodshot, and they commanded respect when they needed to. Amid some grumbling, his militia fell in line.

Victor hopped to his feet too fast and almost fell again. Embarrassed, he glared at Morgan. "This is what happens when you put bitches in the military."

"I couldn't agree more," she replied, staring back.

He blinked in a daze, slowly coming round to her insult. Then his eyes flitted to Lorelai. He'd shown her his true colors. It was hard to come back from that. He spun around and stormed to the barracks. The rest of the militia waited awkwardly, not knowing where to go from here.

"I think it's time to call it a day," said the deputy from the rear.

"Sam's right," conceded Anderson, patting Chuck and Holt as he walked by. "Things got a little hot today. Understandable with egos on the line. Now that we've shaken all of that loose, we can break for the day and start the real training tomorrow on the long targets. If that's okay with you, Mr. Carver?"

He hiked a shoulder. "No harm, no foul."

"Good. I'll walk you to your truck."

They collected their weapons and headed out. The crowd broke into smaller groups, jawing excitedly over what had just happened. Carver hoped the majority of the guys could see Victor was out of line.

"I had wanted to make an impression," confided Anderson as they separated from the pack. "I wasn't expecting one so big."

"If you wouldn't mind, Commander, please impress upon your men the importance of not attacking my team. We're trained warfighters who won't always be able to hold back. Victor got off easy."

"I bet. He won't be a problem tomorrow, I promise you that."

They reached the truck and loaded up. After Carver started the engine, Anderson lingered at his open window.

"You know, Vince, that kind of assertiveness was impressive. We could use more men like you. Plainspoken doers instead of double-talking dreamers."

Carver smiled, not unlike how he had the very first time Anderson asked him to train his men. "How about we start with the long targets and go from there?"

The commander nodded, tapped the roof of the pickup, and stepped back to let them go.

8

"Here we go," announced Commander Anderson.

No armed escort today, they finally made it to the deep rear of the complex where the hills encroached. There was no fence line or other indication of how far the property went, and maybe the country was too wild for it to matter. An organized militia platoon of about twenty-five waited for them in the field, all the familiar faces and several new ones. Fortunately for Carver, Deputy Grafton wasn't one of them.

It was a hot, dry day, and a table was set up with bottled water. No beer this time. A pair of dark-green Polaris Sportsman ATVs with hitched tandem-axle trailers contained today's arsenal. Carver happened to know for a fact those vehicles and wagons weren't cheap. The crates, too, were new supply. For a backcountry militia of a few dozen, they were surprisingly well equipped.

"Looks like you were holding out on me," said Carver, admiring the front-forward tractor profile of the all-terrain vehicles. "I didn't know you had Silicon Valley seed money."

The commander laughed it off. "That's not so far from the truth. Instead of one investor, we're crowd-sourced. A lot of little donations from a lot of little sources. Power to the people."

That lined up with the CIA brief. S2 was a political entity that solicited donations. With a twenty-four-hour news cycle and a bombardment of rhetoric on the social media bullhorn, today's fringe movements have no shortage of funding. There's a saying about fools easily parted from their money. The deeper realization is that the whole world is a circus, and it's the clowns who are cleaning up.

A stoic-faced Victor made a beeline to them. "Mrs. Morgan, may I have a word in private?"

Her gaze flicked from Victor to Carver and back. The man was neither happy nor angry. All things considered, that was ideal. "Sure thing," she replied.

They distanced themselves from the group so Victor could get something off his chest.

"Is he apologizing?" Shaw asked under his breath.

"I do believe he is."

They seemed to be doing okay, so Carver dug into his soft case.

"Actually," said Anderson, "let's put the Recces aside for a change. I want everybody using the same kit today."

Carver returned a sideways grin. "There weren't claims of unfair competition due to superior hardware, were there?"

"Nothing of the sort. I was thinking about some of your tips yesterday, about slowing down and going back to basics. Now, not all of my men need it, but it wouldn't hurt a one of them to review it."

Carver couldn't agree more. And if the focus on the basics gave Lorelai the foundation she needed, all the better for Anderson.

"We'll shoot whatever you have," said Shaw.

"Good to hear," said the commander, already leading them to the metal boxes on the wagons, "because we're taking a trip down memory lane."

He swung the crates open one by one, revealing the communal arsenal. In stark contrast to yesterday's set of modern AR-15s, this was a cache of wooden-stocked SKS rifles.

Carver picked up one of the dinosaurs. They were in great condition for their age. Not the newer Chinese models, these were of Soviet origin. Used, with scratched wooden rifle grips. Fixed bayonets folded under the barrels. All identical. The cache included cases of 7.62x36mm cartridges in 10-round stripper clips for easy loading into the firearm's internal box magazines.

"These are something else," remarked Carver. The feel of the carbine in his hands evoked memories from home. The SKS was a capable weapon for hunting but almost quaint nowadays.

"Zero bells and whistles," Anderson said with pride. "You shoot one of these, it's just the gun and the man."

Back to basics, indeed.

"Give me a second to gather the troops." The commander hiked to his group, leaving Carver and Shaw alone with the cache.

"Crates of SKSs and old Soviet ammunition..." muttered

Shaw suggestively.

Carver nodded. With the kind of funding S2 apparently had access to, the Soviet stock threw him for a loop. The rifles themselves weren't rare. The eighties and nineties saw wide proliferation of old Soviet surplus across the United States.

In fact, Carver was sure that was the point.

"Plentiful and untraceable," he said.

It made him wonder what other surprises S2 had in their stockpile.

"Mr. Carver."

They turned to see Victor waiting. Behind him, Anderson and the collected men headed over.

"I don't need an apology, Victor. You gave it to the person who did." Carver offered his hand. "If you treat my team with respect from here on out, we can pretend like it never happened."

Victor was surprised by the attitude for a second but quickly recovered. "I appreciate it, sir." He met Carver's firm grip.

Carver turned to the converging group. "Okay, everyone. Happy to see the turnout. Today we'll be hitting long targets from a rest. This simplifies some aspects of your shooting stance but introduces others. Because we have a sizable crowd today, we'll be splitting into groups. Mr. Shaw and Mrs. Morgan will take their places on my right and left. Feel free to line up with whichever instructor suits you."

Victor looked between them. "This is probably for the best," he said, lining up with Shaw. Carver chuckled and dipped his head in agreement. Victor had embarrassed himself; at least he was being a good sport about it.

Chuck was too. After having been bested by Morgan, he lined up with her. Anderson stuck with Carver. At first, Holt lined up with Shaw, but when Lorelai hurried into Carver's line, he begrudgingly followed. His expression wasn't just a little annoyed. Carver detected jealousy.

After a few minutes and some reshuffling to even out the groups, they were set. A short walk took them to prepared nests in the hillside, spaced about fifty yards apart. Carver watched Shaw and Morgan take their groups away before turning to appraise his.

Holt was his best shooter. He knew Anderson, Lorelai, and Trent. The other four were fresh faces: a middle-aged husband and wife team, a skinny kid in his twenties, and an old vet in his sixties who couldn't be more at home with the wooden rifle.

First thing Carver did was reintroduce himself, have each of them explain their experience level, and make sure everyone understood the basics of the firearm. After that they took turns shooting.

Starting at two-hundred yards, they focused on prone shooting. The stations were set up with a mat and a dirt pile to accommodate a sandbag rest. The old man was a good shot. Holt lost a bit of his edge with the rifle grip, but he was an avid study.

"You're picking it up," Carver told him.

"It's simple enough," he agreed. "It's just a little outside my comfort zone, if you know what I mean."

"Same here. It takes getting used to, but you're a natural. Did your mom teach you to shoot?"

Holt turned away from his sights to look at Carver sharply. He was about to say something but seemed to reconsider. "The deputy has other strengths."

The kid was obviously defensive so Carver continued the lesson without pushing.

Lorelai proved eager to learn, and her nerves weren't as pronounced in the more intimate group.

"You're not going to shoot straight if you can't steady your wrists," instructed Carver.

He grabbed her trigger hand and displayed how wobbly it was. Lorelai blushed at the simple contact, and when Carver searched for another sandbag, he noticed Holt attempting to disguise his glare. These guys were territorial out here.

"Try this," suggested Carver, putting a small bag under her wrist for support. "Feel it out, back and forth, getting it into a shape that feels good. That way you can relax your wrist. Don't look at me, look at your target. The rifle should be an extension of your arm. You feel that?"

She adjusted and nodded a little too abruptly. Carver calmed her down and made sure she was in position before she pulled the trigger. It was slow going, but she was learning.

Trent was a bit out of it today. Uninspired shooting, no zealous conspiracy talk. He was unsettled and distracted and clearly not at his best.

Commander Anderson, too, was not going to shine

today. Shoulder pain prevented him from getting into a proper prone position. Instead he fired from sitting, which was enough of a disadvantage. Past his first clip his aim wavered. Unlike Trent, the commander was aware of his limitations and accepted them. He was only here to support his soldiers.

After a couple of productive hours behind the long guns, the militia broke for chow. They cleared the weapons but kept them at the stations for later use. Morgan and Shaw reported solid time with their groups, and everyone headed back to the central courtyard.

The cafeteria looked the same as every other mess hall in existence. Long tables, a stack of trays and plates heading off a food line filled with hungry guys. Holt sat with Chuck and openly flirted with Lorelai. Carver took his beef stew to a side table with Anderson and they got to talking. Halfway through lunch, Trent blew up at his table. He stomped out of the cafeteria.

"What was that about?" asked Carver.

"It's just the boys are pent up," he explained, playing it off.

"It's more than that. Trent seems a little off balance today."

The commander sighed at the undeniable truth. "He has better days and worse. Trent deals with depression. You know, he says the military was the best thing that ever happened for him, and he barely had a chance to get started."

Carver nodded. He believed Anderson genuinely felt

sorry for the man. "That can be hard, uprooting your life to start training, and then again when you become a civvy."

"It hits us all. I myself struggled with the decision to retire. It's a different life out here."

Carver finished his stew, letting the commander talk. But instead of volunteering information, Anderson pried.

"What about you?" he asked. "You get out on your own terms?"

Carver took a long breath to really think about it. "It wasn't my plan. Bad intel got a friend killed. I almost lost an arm." His scars stung just thinking about it. "But it was my decision to leave. You could call those my terms."

"Good for you." Anderson bit down in thought. "That kind of life is a mission. You give pieces of yourself until it no longer makes sense. Then, hopefully, you have enough pieces left to keep together."

Carver nodded. "So what's your new mission? With S2?"

The commander chuckled hoarsely. "Nothing nearly so noble, if that's what you mean. We preach safety in numbers, preparation, family. Truth is, it's about brotherhood more than anything else."

Carver wasn't sure if he was dubious or disappointed. The commander either wasn't super radicalized or he hid it well. Either way he was convincing. That wasn't at all what Carver had expected.

"Anyway, I have to hit the head."

Anderson took his tray to the front before heading to HQ. Carver dumped his tray and noticed Holt scolding Lorelai about something or other. He considered getting involved but thought it might do more harm than good. The two were alone now, Chuck being gone, and they could work out their disagreements in private. He passed by Morgan and whispered in her ear.

"I'm doing a little snooping. Run interference if necessary."

She nodded affirmative and he headed into the central yard. A couple of people were around, but most were either still in the cafeteria or had temporarily retired somewhere more private, like the barracks, which didn't have windows except for the ceiling-height skylights. That gave him tentative privacy. Checking his watch, everyone still had a good half hour before heading back to the targets. That called for an innocent stroll of the grounds.

His first inclination was to check the barns across the way, the workshop and the bunker. Carver was pretty sure someone had mentioned the vault being inside the bunker, and more than anything he wondered what the militia had in their possession. As luck would have it, the bunker door was halfway open.

Carver strolled with aimless rhythm in broad daylight, just a man looking around and getting sun. As he directed his approach along the opposite wall, a shrill whine emerged from the workshop. He crept close to the heavy door and reached to inch it open. Before his fingers touched the wood, it trembled at the release of the interior latch. He stepped back as the door swung open.

"Mr. Carver," exclaimed Sam, taken off guard.

The sound of machinery cut out, but not before Carver

identified it as likely belonging to an angle grinder. He peeked past the deputy to fulfill his curiosity.

Sam filled the door. "What are you doing here?"

He gave up his attempt at inspection and said, "Looking for you, actually. We missed you at the range this morning. I was wondering if you'd make it out for the second half of the day?"

Sam licked her lips, taking time to decode his motives. She pushed outside and shut the door, giving it a double knock. Someone inside slammed the metal latch shut to lock it up.

"The workshop's off limits," she said tersely. "This isn't a public facility and you can't go wandering wherever you like."

"I'm sorry. I just heard those noises and—"

"I'm not interested in what you think you heard. And I'm not interested in shooting today. But I am a stickler for the rules, Mr. Carver."

She was a hard woman, and he clearly wasn't going to gain an inch of ground. He was about to apologize again when a gunshot rang out, close enough that they both ducked.

"Get off!" someone yelled, and then another gunshot. A scream of pain.

Their eyes fixed on the half-open bunker door. Carver drew the SIG on his waist and stepped forward. He stopped suddenly when Trent emerged with crazed eyes, pistol in hand.

"What did you do, Trent?" he asked.

They both raised their guns.

"Stop it!" cried Anderson, sprinting from the front yard. "Stop it!"

Sam didn't have a weapon and glued herself to the locked workshop door. Carver, luckily, had chosen to wear his vest for the second day in enemy territory. He could see Trent's hands shaking from here.

"Put down the gun, Trent."

"He shot me!" cried Chuck.

Trent flipped his gun to the doorway as he stepped further away. Chuck limped out. His camo pant leg was drenched in blood.

"You're in on it!" shouted Trent. Then, turning to Carver, "You're all in on it!"

Anderson slowed to Carver's side. "Trent! Buddy! Put down the gun."

"How could you do this to me, Commander?" His eyes shone with glaze. "I'm a patriot! You know that."

Anderson nodded, hands forward in a signal of calm. "I do know that, Trent. I do."

"There are all kinds of ways to serve our country. Being loyal is one of them."

"I know that." Anderson's voice was soft and precise.

Trent fixed on Sam, and the gun followed. "You did this to him!"

She was trapped, caught dead to rights. "You're not yourself today, Trent," she admonished.

Carver took a step forward, aim never wavering. "You need to put the gun down, Trent. This isn't a game."

"Don't shoot him, Vince," cried Anderson. "He's had a rough go of things. We talked about that."

"That's why I'm giving him a chance."

Trent's weapon swiveled between Carver and Sam. He was coherent enough not to point it at his commander, which indicated he might be open to reason.

Sam trembled. Carver bit down. He understood Anderson's point of view. He really did. And he had no idea what had transpired between Chuck and Trent inside the bunker. But the fact was, the man was waving a pistol around like a lunatic. If it came down to it, the safest option was to put him down.

Holt and some others rushed into the yard. "He shot Chuck!"

Morgan and Shaw each had their pistols on him. This sideshow was quickly becoming the main event. Every added spectator and weapon only increased Trent's anxiety.

Carver took another step forward, wincing as he drew the gunman's aim. "Trent, Chuck needs medical attention. Let me get him out of here."

"Put your gun down first."

"You know I can't do that."

"You better do it."

Carver gritted his teeth.

"Be reasonable," appealed Anderson.

Chuck was bleeding. He unlooped his belt to fashion a tourniquet. Trent spun his weapon at the snap of leather, and Carver lunged. It was a risk, but it paid off. Instead of firing, Trent attempted to pivot back to the incoming threat. Carver barreled into him first, pushing the handgun up during the tackle.

The pistol fired into the sky as Trent landed face first. He didn't give up the gun. It fired again. This time the bullet peppered the cafeteria wall.

Carver wanted to twist the man's arm behind his back, but the gun posed too much of a danger. Instead, Carver yanked Trent's wrist backward. The bone snapped. He tossed the gun away, then holstered his own weapon, all while controlling Trent's arms behind him.

"You're all in on it!" he berated, dirt-filled spittle caking his lips. "This is a government op! I'm not crazy!"

Anderson recovered the pistol and hurried a hand to Carver's shoulder. "That's enough, Vince. You got him."

Trent's taut muscles gave out as he deflated into a sobbing mess. Carver relieved him of his knife and made sure he had no other weapons before releasing him. He stood and backed away, allowing Anderson to comfort him.

Sam and Holt rushed to Chuck's side. They helped him with the tourniquet before each hefting a shoulder and hurrying him to a truck. He was going to the hospital.

Anderson met Carver's eyes in a grateful exchange. Trent climbed to his feet, wiping his face and only getting more dirt on it. "You of all people," he said to his friend, crestfallen.

The commander shook a bewildered head. "You need help, Trent."

"You want me dead, more like."

"What are you talking about?"

"You know it. You know it or you don't want to know it."

Anderson sighed.

Trent leaned into him. "I'm not stupid, Commander. People dismiss me, they talk behind my back, but I know what black ops look like." His gaze locked on Carver. "And I know a killer when I see one."

Trent made for the front yard. Shaw had his gun ready and moved to intercept him, but Anderson said, "Leave him. Please."

They quietly followed Trent to his truck and watched him speed away.

"That's twice," noted the flagging commander. "Two days, two incidents, and two examples of decisive action. I'm starting to feel like we'd fall apart without you."

Carver searched Anderson's face for a hint of deception or manipulation. It troubled him to not find any.

9

Carver cracked a beer and peered out his apartment window into the blackness. He wanted to confer with Williams and had no way of reaching her. The threat of surveillance by Homeland Security seemed diminished, but the CIA was nothing if not careful. She still hadn't made contact.

He left his phone on the kitchen counter, locked up, and went for a nighttime walk around the block, bottle in hand. The movement stirred his blood and helped him think, but his true purpose was giving the case officer every opportunity to reach out. Rounding the block, he ticked through the usual counter-surveillance procedures. Nobody was on his tail, friend or foe.

Which was unfortunate. He needed an updated capability assessment on the militia. How coordinated of an operation did the CIA really think S2 was? Because the large stock of weapons, the brand-new ATVs serving the old property... Something was a little off.

Why Anderson, on the other hand, seemed relatively normal—that was another puzzle to figure out.

But Carver was running black out here, and he had no way of initiating contact with Officer Williams. What was the point of intelligence work when there was no intelligence to be had?

The despair of the situation lasted through a whole swig of beer. Then there was no more room for it. This was what Carver had signed up for. In a lot of ways, this lack of contact, this lack of *oversight*, was his preferred modus operandi.

Gathering intelligence was the op. It was Carver's sole purpose at the militia compound. Morgan and Shaw were there to back him up. As an operator, he wasn't exactly high and dry.

And he had already completed his first objective. He'd earned the trust of Commander Anderson. Deputy Grafton was another matter. He could either try to change her mind, avoid her, or outplay her with the commander. As far as Carver was concerned, the options were wide open until they weren't.

Until then, it was back to business as usual, full steam ahead.

With or without the CIA.

* * *

The next morning, the team arrived at the compound to find a white Chevy SUV parked front beside two Santa Clara County Sheriff's vehicles. They were empty, with one car running the strobes without the siren. Carver approached Deputy Grafton and a few others waiting outside HQ.

"What's going on, Sam?"

"Just the usual government snooping," she said with a derisive snort. Despite playing cool, she seemed on edge.

Carver moved to the side of the house to check the yard, where Lorelai caught up with him. Nobody was searching the grounds. They returned to the deputy.

"You get this a lot?"

Sam rolled her eyes. "Only every other month. I wouldn't worry about it."

Holt exited HQ with the sheriff in tow. Lorelai's eyes widened when she saw him. "Is it true what they're saying?"

"Lorelai," snapped the deputy, "I want you in the workshop today."

The girl flinched at the brusque instruction before turning to Carver, realizing the downside. "But the commander wants me to practice shooting."

"Not today, girl. We appreciate your dedication, but you need to put the team's needs above your own, first and foremost, and the team needs you in the shop. You can shoot another time."

Lorelai blinked quickly but couldn't come up with an objection.

"Go on, now," said Sam.

"Yes, ma'am."

Lorelai cast a longing look at Carver before heading back to the yard.

Sam positioned closer to Carver's ear and said, "That girl wants to stick with Holt every second of every day. As a mother, I love the sentiment, but she has responsibilities that shouldn't be interfered with."

The deputy's stern glare did not go unnoticed.

Another police officer exited the house with Commander Anderson and a pair of familiar faces, Agents Bentley and Guerrero of Homeland Security Investigations.

"Well if it isn't our favorite security contractor," remarked Bentley in snide surprise.

Carver grimaced.

"You know him?" asked Holt, even more surprised.

The special agent planted hands on hips and swiveled from one man to the other, thoroughly amused. "Oh, we go way back, don't we, Mr. Carver? In fact, we were just in your office the other day, weren't we?"

Eyes hardened around him.

"Not by choice," was all he said in his defense.

Carver knew how bad this looked. Sam was suspicious by default, but now even Commander Anderson's face was painted with concern.

Guerrero had an opinion too. She brandished a thick eyebrow like a weapon. "Since you don't appear to be kidnapped, we can assume being on S2 property is your choice. You mind if we ask what you're doing here?"

Without time for a good answer, Carver went with apathy. He scoffed, hiked a shoulder, and said, "It's a free country." And then, to turn the tables back around, "What brings Homeland Security to this neck of the woods?"

Bentley crossed his arms defensively, gobbling up the bait. "We're assisting an investigation. Guess you were wrong about us not having local support."

"They got no jurisdiction," complained Holt.

"The sheriff's office does, kid, and they're tapping us in a support role."

"Meaning," added Sam, "that you saw an opportunity to nose in on our business, and you took it."

The two stared defiantly at each other.

"What's the investigation?" interjected Carver.

Bentley flashed a Jersey smile and pranced toward him like a peacock. "You might know something about it, as a matter of fact. You were our next person of interest."

"In what?"

"Sometime last night, Trent Dillinger ate a shotgun."

Sam's eyes fluttered at his colorful language. Holt and the commander bit down, having already been apprised of the news.

Special Agent Bentley tactlessly pressed his advantage. "We hear there was an incident yesterday involving you?"

"It didn't involve him," insisted Anderson. "Mr. Carver just helped talk the man down."

Bentley held up a finger. "I'd like to hear his side of it, if you don't mind. Carver?" The special agents stepped away from the group and he followed, mind racing.

The hardest aspect of undercover work is aligning all the moving parts. It doesn't only involve keeping your story straight, it means maintaining all the various fictions interlocking together like well-greased gears. And the more unnecessary lies you add to that contraption, the more points of failure you introduce to the machine. If even a single one of them breaks down, everything comes to a grinding halt.

In light of that danger, Carver explained his interactions with Trent just as they had gone down, in as simplified terms as possible. He was here to teach target shooting. It was good money, he told Guerrero, though she wasn't interested in the reasoning. He went over how Trent seemed unstable in general but especially so yesterday, and the weapon going off, and talking him down.

"Did you see him fire the weapon?" she asked.

"I didn't. Just heard the two reports. Anderson said it was Trent's private weapon."

Bentley nodded like he was bored. "He already provided it as evidence."

"What happened to Trent?"

Guerrero shrugged. "Near as we can tell, he went home, popped a lot of fentanyl, drank a lot of Jack, reclined in his easy chair, and blew his head apart. Powder burns and other evidence backs up a suicide."

It was brutal. It was also more than a little suspicious.

But any speculation was just that. Conspiracy theories around suicides were common. By definition, taking one's own life is esoteric and unthinkable. Sometimes it was more comforting to reach for the easy conspiracies.

What stood out about Trent was that he had felt betrayed. Something or someone had caused him to question the militia, to even question his friendship with Anderson, a man who by all accounts had genuinely cared for him. While a hit like that could certainly drive one to suicide, Carver couldn't rule out foul play.

"After Trent left in his truck," asked Bentley, "did you see him again?"

Carver shook his head slowly, staring blankly in the distance. "No."

"Did you visit his residence last night?"

"No."

"Are you aware of anyone doing so?"

Carver turned sharply to him. "Is there evidence that someone was there?"

"An abundance of evidence," complained Guerrero. "We have techs going over the scene, but, even though Trent lived alone, he hosted a number of visitors in recent weeks. DNA from a glass or cigarette butt can tell us who was there, but not if it was last night or last week. At this point we're attempting to isolate anyone who wasn't in his regular circle of friends."

Not very illuminating, unfortunately. "Me and my team have never been there," he stated for the official record. "I don't even know the location."

The officer in the background shook hands with the commander. The sheriff tipped his hat, and they headed to their vehicles. Apparently, this visit was little more than a notification.

"I think we have what we need," said Bentley, more than a little annoyed. "But if I find out you had anything to do with this, or that you're holding out on us, I *will* burn you."

The lights of the squad car turned off. With the officers loaded up, the militia spectators focused on Carver's cooperation with the HSI agents. It was a disastrous final impression.

Carver fixed a glare on Bentley. "You don't have enough fire," he threatened.

Bentley's eyes narrowed. "What's that?" He took a menacing step closer. "You think you're some kind of badass or something?"

Here it was. Carver had to see it through.

"You don't want to find out the answer to that, Special Agent." Carver matched the man's approach and got an inch from his face.

"Piece of shit!"

Bentley pounded his hands into Carver's shoulders, shoving him away with surprising strength. Carver barely avoided stumbling.

Bentley took another step forward and Carver backed off.

"That's right!" gloated the special agent. "You don't want a piece of this."

Guerrero put a soft hand on her partner's shoulder. He looked at her and spun away, storming back to the Chevy.

"You better get yourself in gear before I haul you in for obstruction," he warned. He climbed behind the driver's seat and slammed the door.

The Santa Clara squad cars idled past, pausing at the perimeter to wait on HSI. Carver ground his teeth. His anger was real. Backing down didn't come naturally to him, especially to such a punk on a power trip. But the stern faces of Anderson, Sam, and Holt assured him he had done the right thing. Instead of cooperation, their lasting impression was now one of official overreach and abuse. Or, as Williams would put it, cred.

"What are you doing?" admonished Guerrero, still lingering. She was sly. She could tell something was up.

"I just don't like threats," he said. Which was true enough.

"You didn't call."

"My business with the militia isn't really—"

"I'm talking about a personal call." Isla Guerrero's hazel eyes searched his face. "I didn't expect you to take a back seat on this."

"What did you expect?"

She hiked a small shoulder in a large jacket. "I expected a man of action. Was I wrong?"

Carver bit down in the presence of the militia. "No."

Guerrero nodded. "Good. Then you shouldn't expect I'm your average girl who likes to wait. So consider this me asking you out. This new thing will keep me busy through dinner, but I'll be in the downtown lobby lounge of the Signia at ten. What are you doing tonight?"

Carver cocked his head slightly. "I guess I'm having a drink."

"Good answer."

Special Agent Guerrero, more business than pleasure, turned without another word and joined Bentley in the SUV. As they pulled out, the sheriff's cars continued toward the gate, and thirty seconds later they were all gone.

The date was sudden and not at all how he'd expected it

to develop, but he wasn't complaining. Shaw, on the other hand, wouldn't let him hear the end of it. His opinion was that Guerrero was only interested in pumping him for information, and this development only reinforced that position. She hadn't taken the plunge until there was visual confirmation of him cavorting with S2.

So was it business, or was it pleasure?

"What was that about?" asked the deputy as he returned to the group. Morgan and Shaw, who had been waiting by the Ram, also joined them.

"I don't know anything about Trent," swore Carver.

Sam eyed him sharply. "I mean about you being friendly with Homeland Security?"

"I didn't see you drawing battle lines," he returned. But he needed to set their minds at ease. He sighed. "In full disclosure, Special Agents Bentley and Guerrero stopped by my office last week. There's some thing with the president and they apparently think it gives them the right to hassle private citizens."

"Bastards," said Holt.

"They're asking about us?" checked Anderson.

"They saw your name and number on my corkboard," Carver explained. "They gave me a hard time about associating with S2. Any idea why that might be?"

The militia members went tight-lipped. Anderson shook his head. "You know how it is with these government types."

"Hassling private citizens," added Sam. "Like you said."

Carver nodded along with them. "Right. Anyway, that

was before I decided to work with you. I told them we had no association, then the next week they see me here. They thought I lied to them and were suspicious. It was just a misunderstanding."

"It was more than that," returned the commander. "You were a second away from being arrested."

"Bentley's an asshole. He's got no cause."

"Damn straight. Though I gotta admit, it was nice to see your pushback."

"I was the one who got pushed, but thanks."

Anderson jutted his lips out as he worked over a thought. "I also appreciate that you didn't shoot Trent yesterday in the yard. He had his demons, but he was a good man. You showed restraint by giving him a chance. It's a shame he didn't give himself one."

Sam shook her head. "Lord help that poor soul, wherever he is."

"That's right." Anderson scratched the back of his head, surveyed the ranch, and said, "How much can I trust you, Vince?"

Carver hadn't expected the abrupt conversational turn. "Well, I'm aware we don't have history. We don't know each other well. But I say what I mean and mean what I say."

The commander nodded agreement. "I believe you do. Which is fortunate, because I've got a problem."

Morgan and Shaw expertly faded into the background, not wanting to interrupt where this was going.

"Problem?" asked Carver.

"Trent shooting Chuck is a double whammy."

"Is Chuck okay?"

"He's fine," said Holt. "I just visited him in the hospital. They're gonna keep him another day, at least."

"He needs to keep off his feet for a while," translated Anderson. "Which means we're two men down."

Sam's eyes narrowed. "Commander, no."

"What would you have me do, Sam? Chuck was our best shot."

"Holt can pick up the slack. A change in personnel is too big a risk."

"So is moving forward two men short."

Carver traded glances with Morgan and Shaw. This was happening fast.

The deputy huffed. "Lester, I respect—"

"It's Commander, Deputy."

She gritted her teeth. "*Commander*, we've barely known Mr. Carver half a week."

"Nonsense. I've been seeing him on the range for some time. Besides, you can tell a lot about a man in times of crisis. Words are hollow, but actions are solid. And I think he's earned the benefit of the doubt."

"Sir—"

"I've made my decision, Sam," he said sharply, making it clear there was no further room for debate.

Surprisingly, the deputy didn't have a rejoinder. There was a first time for everything.

Anderson pulled Carver aside. It was only a few steps. Enough to signal that the discussion was private, but not enough to actually make it so. Sam watched on hotly.

"We've got a good thing going here," Anderson confided, "and I don't intend to screw it up. I wonder if you'll consider staying on with us longer?"

Carver glanced at his team and frowned. "Doing what?"

"You'll be a consultant."

"Commander, that's hardly a job description."

"No, it's not. Come with me to HQ and I'll get you up to speed." Anderson ignored Sam's scolding look and told the group, "You all wait outside."

Carver nodded the okay to his team. Shaw mentioned that they'd be in the yard and went that way with Morgan. As Anderson led Carver to the front door, Sam and her son muttered in hushed voices. Their glares suggested displeasure with the development.

Anderson wedged open a stubborn wooden door and said, "Come inside, Vince. It's just you and me so we can speak plainly."

"Sure thing, Lester."

The peek inside HQ didn't reveal a state-of-the-art command center. The building housed Anderson and his daughter and many hallmarks of domestic life, most notably clutter. Most available surfaces were stacked with paper or used plates and coffee mugs. But the function of the living room was very different from most homes. There was no sofa, no TV. Just a large central planning table accompanied by only three chairs. Built-in shelves were filled with books, while the opposite wall was decorated with metal filing cabinets, dented from a generation of wear.

"Your war room," concluded Carver.

"You'll have to excuse me," mumbled Anderson as he opened a filing drawer and dug through haphazardly stacked documents. "I had to tidy up for the police."

The commander settled on a large map which he unfolded and placed on the table. Carver quickly identified the Northern California Bay Area. Three locations were marked with a red sharpie. From those central points, blue lines extended outward like nerves into neighboring areas.

"Targets," said Anderson.

Carver leaned close to examine the locations. The cartographer hadn't seen fit to label them, but the affected areas offered an educated guess as to what he was looking at. A pit formed in his stomach.

"These dots don't look like much," explained Anderson, "but these three substations bear two-thirds of the load of Silicon Valley's electricity. Without them the local power grid completely collapses."

"That seems like wishful thinking."

"It's not. Smarter men than me have raised alarms about the vulnerability of the power infrastructure. It's not protected like it should be."

"Protected from what?"

"Bad actors."

Anderson watched Carver's reaction for a pause. They were both at opposite sides of a fine line.

"This is what you want my help with?" he asked the commander.

A nod. "It is."

"To what end?"

"To audit the security at the sites."

Carver snorted. "This is why Homeland Security is up my ass about you."

"They're playing their role, just like we all are."

"What's that supposed to mean?"

"Not what you think, Vince. I assure you. You asked if I had a secret benefactor, and I do. It just so happens to be the United States government."

The news staggered Carver away from the table. This was the last thing he expected. He worked his jaw and said, "If this was a simple threat assessment, you wouldn't need me training your soldiers. You wouldn't need replacement shooters."

Anderson's face tweaked as he realized his dilemma. He winced and nodded in resignation. "You're right, Vince. I'm not lying, but I'm only telling you half the truth. I wanted to avoid it until I knew you were on board. You're too smart for that so I'm going to level with you. But this is strictly confidential, understand?"

Carver gave an unwavering nod.

"Do you know what a red cell is?"

Carver frowned. Anderson wasn't talking biology. "Government black hats, more or less, but instead of hacking, their actions are more kinetic."

"Exactly right. Kinetic is a good word. Red cells test domestic defenses by infiltrating friendly targets, and they do it on the down low. Our mission is not just to assess threats to these power stations, but to carry them out."

"As in, take the grid down. Isn't that illegal?"

He shrugged. "Illegal, yes, but also sanctioned. We have an executive employer hiring us for top secret work. It's legitimate, it's noble, and we're not hurting anyone. On the contrary, we're bolstering national security by exposing flaws."

Carver was doing mental somersaults trying to make sense of it all. If this red cell was legit, which was a gargantuan if, it was unknown to Homeland Security as well as the Central Intelligence Agency. Then again, maybe testing those agencies was the point. Stranger things have happened.

Carver grumbled at a realization. "Is this what sent Trent off the deep end?"

"Trent didn't know."

"But did he walk in on something he wasn't supposed to?"

"It's impossible. Chuck hasn't been read in yet. Only my deputy and XOs are aware of this action, and only in the broad strokes. Besides, Trent trusted me. He was a good soldier."

Carver worked his jaw. Trent certainly hadn't looked the trusting type yesterday. Though, as crazed as he was, he had never pointed his weapon at the commander. That counted for something.

"Come on, Vince. You must have had a dozen missions like this before. Black ops. Need to know. Only difference is this one's on American soil." Anderson offered an open hand. "What do you say? I could sure use the hand of a skilled operator."

Carver glanced at the map, then at the waiting man. "This is important to you, huh?"

The commander dipped his head. "Believe it or not, it's my whole world."

Carver allowed an audible sigh before taking Anderson's hand. "Lester, you can rely on me."

10

The downtown Signia fit the bill of trendy upscale hotel within the budget of a humble government employee. Across the street, on a strip of green with the cumbersome name *Plaza de César Chávez*, a live band played a funk rock set under the stars. Next door, dramatic spotlights painted the stonework of the San Jose Museum of Art. Foot traffic was scattered at this hour, with even the event at the park sparsely attended and rapidly dwindling down.

This didn't rate as a hot spot, but it was centrally located as well as the perfect place for Special Agent Isla Guerrero to bunk down for a few nights instead of making the drive back to San Francisco.

Carver parked a block down and walked into the street entrance. He was greeted by a dim lobby with swooping arched curtains and alcove benches lining the hall. A group of candied-up women posed for selfies with cocktails and giggled as he passed.

The hallway split two ways to lap around the centerpiece of the room, a huge lounge in a recessed floor, leaving the front desk forgotten somewhere out of sight. Carver descended stylish steps with blinding bands of white light into a space framed by curved booths and wood columns. The wraparound bar rested under a high ceiling supporting the weight of an elaborate metal framework that suspended dozens of LED bulbs.

It took Carver a second to identify Guerrero sitting alone at the bar with her back to him. He converged on her side, angling to slip onto the low-backed barstool.

"Hope I'm not late."

She turned, hazel eyes lighting up and a smile stretching the kind of lips most women painted on. "Look at you."

She was remarking on Carver's light-blue button-up over his nicest pair of jeans. He was admiring her in turn, completely dumbstruck at the sight of her. Whatever opening line he had on deck suddenly fled his brain.

"You clean up well," she said with a smirk. "I'd have never guessed."

Carver canted his head. "And you look... like your jacket hides a lot."

Guerrero now wore her hair out of the ponytail. Thick, dramatic zigzags framed her face and tickled her long neck. She had changed into a black top with spaghetti straps that snuggled tight against soft cleavage. She bounced with laughter.

"I do my best to hide my assets. Hey, eyes up, mister." A playful finger on Carver's chin redirected his view back up to her face.

"Sorry, I've been trained to directly assess threats."

She sat up straighter. From the high barstool, it put her lips just at eye level. "Are you claiming to be under duress at the present moment?"

Carver cleared his throat. "I'm in the middle of an ambush, that's for sure."

The bartender swung by. Guerrero's martini was full, so Carver only ordered for himself. His usual rye old fashioned. He adjusted the stool closer to his companion and sat.

First dates have a weird energy, and those initial moments can predict how the rest of the night goes. Carver and Guerrero traded flirtatious glances brimming with fire and possibilities. Ten seconds in and his blood was burning.

"So what was that today, with my partner?" she asked. "You don't seem the type who tries to impress the cool kids." Guerrero lifted her glass and watched him expectantly as she took a sip.

He had realized that she picked up on his play. Deception rarely works when one expects it. Carver didn't want to lie to her, but he could hardly confess all his secrets.

"You know their type," he hedged. "They wouldn't trust me one bit if they knew I was having a drink with you now."

Her head shook in confusion. "Why do you care about their trust at all?"

He sighed. "I owe you an explanation, Isla. Look, I was straight with you when we first met. Lester Anderson, at the time, was just some guy I'd run into a couple times. He wanted to hire me, but I had no plans to go through with it."

"So what changed?"

"That's a tough one. But I'd be lying if I said you and

your partner didn't play a part in it."

She snorted. "Meaning we warned you off so you had to charge right in to prove that nobody tells you what to do?"

"That's not my problem. I was a soldier and the son of a soldier. I've been told what to do most of my life." Her eyes held his in rapturous interest. He chuckled. "It's more like, when Homeland Security asks around, it makes me wonder why. I make my living in security. It's a job hazard."

"The private sector's a different animal."

"You might be surprised by the overlap."

She chewed her lip a moment and said, "So our concerns about national security are your concerns too."

"That's the nutshell," said Carver, keeping things both vague and truthful. "I figured, if I saw anything strange, I could let somebody know."

"So what is this to you, undercover work?"

Hammer, meet nail. Carver eagerly turned to welcome the bartender bringing his drink. He thanked him, picked up the glass, and agitated the large block of ice. Sniffing the cocktail before taking a sip was a ritual that thankfully bought Carver some time.

Guerrero's ensuing laugh suggested the question was a joke. Just in case, to set her mind at ease, he elaborated.

"That's the long of it. The short is that Kinetic National Security is between clients, and my team could use the work. We're just shooting targets."

"Fair enough."

As a peace offering, she lifted her martini. Carver gently tapped his rocks glass to it, and they partook. Afterward it was smiles, but hers was dabbed with gloom.

"And did you?" she prompted.

Carver studied her a long moment. "Did I what?"

"Did you see anything strange? Out of place?"

"It's hard to say. We're mostly in the field shooting or chatting in the cafeteria. I'm not into the whole doomsday-prepping thing, but besides that they seem pretty low-key. They certainly aren't breaking any laws that I've seen."

His statement carefully reserved room for that to change in the future.

Guerrero set her drink down, crossed one leg over the other, and set her hands in her lap. "If you want my opinion, I see S2 as the biggest potential threat in the area. I'm trying to get the local ASAC office on board."

"ASAC?"

"The Assistant Special Agent in Charge. He's an old-school guy. Has a reputation for doing things slow and by the book. But if you ask me, I think he has a chip on his shoulder against the newer generation of agents out of the full-fledged San Francisco SAC office."

"Office politics at their finest. You almost make me want to re-enlist."

"Stop," she laughed. "This is important. I need to get the ASAC probable cause, and that has me combing through S2's financials. It's a lot of work and Bentley thinks I'm crazy, but I'm convinced there's a trail of dark web activity."

"Evidence?"

"A *suggestion* of evidence."

Carver grinned. "You sound like someone I know."

As she ruminated on her latest investigation, Carver wondered about Anderson's role as commander of a red cell. Actual government employment helped explain why the man seemed pretty rational. He wasn't a radical that wanted to upturn the social order, even if his organization attracted the type. When it came down to it, it didn't matter whether his people genuinely wanted to stick it to Uncle Sam or if they were just following orders. They would serve Anderson's purpose, he would protect them, and everybody walked away happy.

But that assumed Anderson's government contact was on the up and up. The claim sounded nice, but there was no way Carver could take it on faith. He was determined not to be sunk by bad intel once again.

He absentmindedly rubbed the scars on his upper arm before catching himself. If Anderson's mission was legitimate, it exposed vulnerabilities by exploiting them. In a backwards kind of way, notifying the authorities worked against the interests of national security. The thought was enough to wrap his head into a pretzel.

"Now you're distracted," bemoaned Guerrero. "I think I preferred you staring at my boobs."

He chuckled. "Sorry, but you started it with all this shop talk."

"What's on your mind?"

"That you're just using me for access to the militia."

Her face went red. "Oh my God, you're right. I'm so sorry." She put a hand on his and squeezed. "That's not what this is about. I swear."

Carver took another sip of his old fashioned and shifted a little closer to his date. "I was hoping you'd say that."

Her eyes sparkled. She leaned close and said, "New rule. No more talking about work the rest of the night. No government agencies, no security contractors, and absolutely, positively no militias."

Carver jokingly frowned. "Are you sure there's anything left to fill the time?"

Her gaze never wavered. "You tell me."

He kissed her. It wasn't a long, drawn out, sappy display of public affection, but it wasn't a shy peck either. Carver felt an animalistic urge with this woman, and she responded in kind.

When they broke away, she asked, "Do you have someone special?"

He smirked. "That's sudden."

"Not sudden. Up-front. I'm not asking to be your girlfriend, I'm just making sure you don't have one."

Her directness was refreshing. Carver decided to reciprocate. "I don't have anyone now. With my history, my line of work... I don't know. Things tend not to last."

"Same here. It is what it is." She canted her head. "I actually like it."

"That's unexpected."

"It's true. I'm single and I have nothing to be ashamed of."

She finished her martini and signaled the bartender for another. Carver added his finger to the request before taking another swig to catch up.

"I don't care what people think," she continued. "I'm a practical person and seek intimacy where I can. Today we're sleeping together, next month we're with somebody else. Those expectations will never let you down."

"As long as you don't pretend to be something you're not," he agreed.

Despite believing every word she said, he was amazed she was already taking sleeping with him as a given. It was those initial moments of a first date. Either the spark was there or it wasn't, and this felt like the electric chair.

"Not that I'm trying to talk you out of anything," he said, "because I know where you're coming from, but, I mean, look at you. You're beautiful. You must change your phone number a lot."

She returned the rare shy smile, like she was just a tad embarrassed. "I'm not saying that's *never* happened... But that's why transparency is important to me. It clears things up."

"You couldn't be more clear without signing a contract in triplicate," he joked.

"Stop. You're making me sound like a lawyer."

"A sexy lawyer."

She shook her head instead of dignifying that with a response. "Did you grow up in California?"

"Bend, Oregon. I only moved out here for that thing we're not supposed to talk about."

"My parents are Colombian, but I grew up in Miami. Doral, to be specific."

"You miss it?"

"I miss the coffee. The family parties. But I don't miss the scene. I had to move away to be taken seriously."

"Why's that?"

She shrugged. "Everyone saw me as arm candy."

"No large unflattering jackets in Miami, I suppose."

She laughed. "That must have been it... One way or another, I had to get out of there."

He held his glass up. "And look how far you've come."

"It's a work in progress," she said. "I'll be ASAC one day. And maybe, by the time I'm old and gray, Special Agent in Charge."

"The American Dream. Is that something you believe in?"

"I wouldn't work for HSI if I didn't. Same with you, I imagine. You were special forces. That has to come with a sense of duty and pride. Unless you're just really good at killing."

"Those aren't mutually exclusive," he pointed out. "But you're right. I believe this country's worth fighting for."

She admired him a moment. "Strong and sappy. My kind of guy."

The next round of cocktails arrived and they continued the idle chat. Their longing gazes grew more intense, more demanding. Instead of holding their chilled drinks, their hands searched for warmer contact. They tugged at each other, mentally and physically and emotionally.

"Are you happy you came?" asked Guerrero.

"I like you, Isla. I like your taste too. This bar is stylish. But maybe it's time to take our drinks upstairs."

"Check please."

Carver went for his wallet but she shot him down. He insisted but when the check came she scribbled her room number and signed it and that was that.

He stood and pulled his chair away to give her space. "I guess I'll get you next time."

She grabbed her martini and said, "I want you to worry about this time first."

He watched her walk away for a moment and shook his head. He grabbed his old fashioned, thanked the bartender, and followed her to the elevator.

The room was nice, newly remodeled but not large. They kissed inside the door before she excused herself to the bathroom. Carver set their drinks on the TV stand. The room was neat and didn't appear heavily lived in. Guerrero didn't leave a lot of clutter and probably worked a lot. Carver assumed her gun was in the safe.

She came out of the bathroom freshened up. Focused now, serious, and maybe a little nervous. She met him at the foot of the bed and they embraced, kissing long and hard. There was no one around to tell them they shouldn't.

She rubbed his arms and chest and undid his buttons, peeling off his shirt and delicately draping it over a chair. Carver gruffly kicked his boots across the room and they embraced again.

"It's not that I don't trust you," she whispered. "It's that I don't have the emotional energy to decide if I should."

"You sound like a spy."

She chuckled. "I just think women are more intentional

than guys."

Carver nodded, as if accepting the challenge. "How's this for intentional?" Then he threw Isla Guerrero onto the bed.

114

11

"Field trip!" bellowed Anderson to the crowd gathering before HQ. He clapped his hands to move people along. "Let's go, let's go! No time like the present!"

Carver and his team had just arrived for the morning. Either the militia had been waiting on them or they'd completely abandoned the idea of training.

"What's going on, Commander?"

Anderson rapped Carver on the shoulder. "Change of plans today. We're doing a little scouting. I want to bring the troops in on what we talked about yesterday."

Carver's eyebrows crawled up his forehead. He supposed it made sense, now that they'd agreed to be full militia consultants, that their roles would transition away from merely teaching shooting. He just hadn't expected the change to be so sudden.

The S2 crew was ready. Dressed in drab greens, browns, and blacks, they held packs and canteens and other gear. Notably missing were any firearms. No slings, carries, or holsters.

"We're going offsite?" deduced Carver.

"Yes we are. That means no weapons. We're focusing on

recon and have no intention of accidental engagements." The commander turned to the group and raised his voice for a last reminder. "Leave your phones behind. No tablets or unapproved smart devices on ops. We'll have three teams, two trucks each. This morning we're all starting in the same place."

Interested murmurs swept through the group. Anderson was right about them. They were good soldiers. Ignorant about where they were going or why, they were nevertheless eager and willing to get a move on.

The bulk of the militia headed toward the line of trucks parked on the far side of the yard. Carver and his team returned to the Dodge Ram to secure their sidearms. They had to separate their weapons from their gear. Deputy Grafton approached behind them.

"And here I was hoping you wouldn't show today."

Carver glanced at her sideways as he dropped his phone on the seat. "Why would we not show, Sam? We're consulting on this op."

"You think we need you," she replied, hands on hips.

"I think help can't hurt."

"Anything can hurt, Vince." He turned at her sharpened tone. "You're part of the group now. First-name basis from here on out. Don't expect any more special treatment."

"Yes, ma'am."

Holt trudged up. "You boys are on my team," he said. "Before we get started, let's make sure we understand each other. I respect your experience, I welcome your input, but I'm the one leading this op. Got a problem with that?"

Shaw apathetically hiked a shoulder. "You're the XO."

Sam smiled like a snake with a full set of teeth. "Keep a close eye on them, Holt. Show them the ropes."

"Will do. With that said, lock up your truck. You're riding with us."

Carver frowned. "It would be easier to follow."

"No can do," cut in Anderson, approaching with his daughter. "These new trucks are GPS beacons, broadcasting your location straight to the authorities. Dumping your smart phone but taking your smart car isn't very smart at all. We're staying low tech so as to remain ghosts."

The line of waiting trucks consisted of well-used pickups from the seventies and eighties. Carver had to hand it to them, Anderson was serious about OPSEC. If electrical substations were attacked, a digital record of militia cars visiting the targets in the prior weeks would surely raise red flags. The best way to defeat location history was to not record it in the first place.

"Lorelai," added the commander, "you're coming with us too. I know you have a different role, but I want you to see this. You should get a handle on what the field looks like."

Sam opened her mouth to object, but Anderson didn't let her get that far.

"She can skip a day, Sam. She'll be back piloting with you tomorrow." Anderson met Carver's eyes, dipped his head, and twirled a finger in the air in military parlance. "Let's get a move on."

The deputy held her tongue, but she communicated a

warning to her son with a glare. Lorelai, oblivious to the subtext, happily skipped alongside them to the trucks. For Carver the meaning was clear: Holt was now their babysitter. Just what they needed on an undercover op.

* * *

As they drove, Carver quickly zeroed in on their target destination. Not only did he have the benefit of having seen Anderson's map, but he knew the area well due to his frequent runs of Coyote Creek Trail. Spanning San Francisco Bay through Coyote Valley, a series of county-maintained parks hug the 101 freeway. One stretch where the creek thins, off-limits to the public, houses energy infrastructure facilities.

After passing a smaller energy center on the left, the large complex making up the Metcalf Transmission Substation sprawled over dusty brown land across the street. The convoy hooked left down a little-used dirt road heading away from the substation and parked a few minutes out of sight. A short hike on foot over rocky hills led them to a vantage point overlooking the first small energy center. Across the Monterey Highway, the main substation loomed large.

"This is as close as we're going to get without drawing undue attention," said Carver.

"No way," said Holt. "This is too far to see anything."

"It's the highest point of elevation with direct line of

sight. We move forward and we might be seen from the highway. Also, any descent would mean we can't see through the trees along the creek that's between us and the target."

Holt bit down. He wanted to refute the assessment but had no ready reply.

"Calm down, folks," tempered Commander Anderson. "This is the first stage of recon. It's a decent spot to take a look at what we're dealing with. We're not locked in if we find something better."

Holt swallowed his objection and turned to the substation.

"Soldiers," addressed Anderson, "we have a mission to protect the sanctity of our United States energy infrastructure. We will carry this out by auditing several government facilities. Everyone here, with the exception of my daughter, is a field operative."

"If you don't mind me asking," chimed in Victor, "why are all three teams at the same location?"

"This is one of three facilities we'll be scouting today. I wanted to first address you as a collective, to get everyone on the same page about the importance of our mission. This current target is for Holt's team. He's down Chuck and Trent, so Vince, Nick, and Juliette are standing in for them. Holt has been briefed and knows what to do, so I want you all taking notes that you will apply to your targets later. XOs Victor and Davie will lead the other two teams."

"I have a question," said someone in the group. "Are we gonna shoot shit up, sir?" Sniggers broke out among the men.

"We just might," snapped Anderson, immediately cutting off their mirth. "The first stage of this mission is recon, but if the feds give us the green light, we will return with a set of untraceable SKS rifles and attempt to take down the grid."

"Are rifles really the best we got?" asked someone else.

"The purpose of the operation is to expose vulnerabilities to small arms. The government wants to know how much damage the average Joe can do."

One of the older guys asked, "Are they really going to activate us?"

Anderson nodded. "The call may come tomorrow. It might be next month. For all we know it may be never. That is not up to us. But what we can control is our level of readiness if called. The when doesn't concern the soldier, only the how. This is not a joke, men, it is a patriotic duty. Are there any other questions?"

The standing soldiers returned quiet resolve.

"Good. Our first objective is to identify and monitor the staff, security, and any other possible obstacles to a successful mission."

Carver's team was already surveying the target with binoculars. The energy center on their side of the highway was a small administration complex. This was where the majority of employees went about their daily duties. At this time in the morning there was light activity outside, but a line of parked cars indicated the presence of people onsite.

The large substation across the street was less about

people and more about equipment. A couple of engineers in the yard looked to be testing or repairing a small piece of machinery. Aside from them, a pair of security guards wandered the lot.

"Contractors," reported Morgan. "Vanguard Security. I see two at the target."

"And one here on the nearside," added Shaw, watching the energy center.

Anderson approached. "I bet you know all about how they operate."

"They're middle of the road at best," said Carver. "Vanguard provides access control but no real defense. That perimeter is way too large for two men to adequately defend. They do have sidearms, but the worst damage they'll likely inflict is calling an alert over the radio."

The commander frowned. "What kind of reinforcements would they have on hand?"

"Reinforcements? None. Unless one of them has a hero complex, these guys are trained to look tough first, duck and cover later. This is a low-security environment. Government facilities like this don't have a quick reaction force. If there's any trouble they can't scare off, they'll call the local sheriff's office."

Shaw checked the sight line from a few spots before settling on one. He dropped to his knees and unzipped his bag.

"We need to identify their automated alarm setup," said Morgan. "These systems will be monitoring deviations to normal operational parameters."

"Already taken into consideration," relayed Anderson. "There's a telephone exchange at the base of this hill just off the highway." Carver pivoted the binoculars to the point in question. "Right before we go live, we'll cut those lines, disabling communication between the energy center and the transmission station. Any automated security checks and hardwired alarms will be effectively neutralized."

"What about cell transmission?" she asked.

"Not present at this substation."

It was clear the commander had already received limited intelligence about the site.

"Who else is on our team, Holt?" asked Carver.

The XO waved three other guys forward. "Johnny, Steve, and Beau."

Carver looked them over and wasn't especially impressed. All three were in their late twenties, out of shape, and hadn't been present for training. Johnny was wiry, with tattoos along both arms and looking like he partied too much. Steve seemed disciplined enough, but had let himself go, balding and overweight despite his young age. And Beau was just a guy. Not athletic in the slightest. He hadn't been in a fight in his life.

"Okay," he decided, "Juliette can cut the phone lines. Immediately afterward, she will proceed one klick north along the highway. That's where the police will be coming from, and she can radio us as soon as there's a response."

"Hold it," snapped Holt. "This is my operation. I'm calling the shots."

"I'm just offering advice," tempered Carver. "The final

decision is yours. I figured you'd want your men up here for the shooting."

The XO snorted. "Are you kidding me? This has got to be two thousand feet out. We're not shooting SKSs from here."

"Four hundred and fifty meters," corrected Shaw, looking through a spotting scope mounted on a tripod.

"You see?" he said. "That's past its effective firing range."

Shaw harrumphed. "You read that on Wikipedia, kid? The Simonov can hit four-fifty no problem."

Holt scoffed uncertainly. Shaw pulled away from the scope.

"Listen, we're not shooting dimes over here. We're also not hunting buck that'll run after your first miss. We're popping large stationary targets from a resting high ground. Anyone here can pull it off."

Anderson let Carver's team deal with Holt. "Lorelai, what about you and Beau? Any concerns about flying in from here?"

The girl shrugged. "I don't see what would stop him. The guards might notice the bird, but they couldn't do anything about it."

"Piece of cake," agreed Beau.

"We're using a drone?" asked Carver.

"Sure," answered the commander. "One per site. We've modified the auxiliary switches to drop a custom payload. Attacking from the top gives us a few options we don't have with guns, increasing our damage potential and lengthening the downtime of the grid."

"Project Sundown," joked Johnny. He shared a laugh and a high-five with Holt.

"Is this necessary?" protested Carver. "Drones raise our profile and can be traced."

"I hear you, Vince," said the commander, "but this isn't a suicide drone. It will go home with us so there'll be nothing left behind to trace. Even if one crashed, the supply chain is airtight."

"We can accomplish the mission without it."

"The drone stays," asserted Holt.

Anderson dipped his head. "I appreciate you thinking about exposure, Vince, but I have competent people working on this. The mission is to expose common, accessible vulnerabilities. Drones are perhaps the most overlooked component of modern warfare, and any Tom, Dick, and Harry can buy one online and mod it for attack. These are our operational parameters."

Carver didn't like it. Drones were an extra element to worry about, one he had less control over, even if he couldn't discount the added punch they provided. But everyone was set against him and he had to live with it. "Understood."

Holt smiled ruefully, happy to win a showdown with him.

Shaw trudged to Carver's side. "I say we set up a few nests in advance, spaced out, aligned with our targets."

Carver nodded. "Commander, what *are* our targets?"

Anderson moved to the edge of the hill and took a knee.

"This location is the path of the Bay Area's main 230kV transmission artery. The substation drops the voltage to smaller 115kV lines that lead out to a host of distribution stations for local connections. Our plan is to target the substation transformers. They're the most expensive points of failure, and the most difficult to replace." He pointed out the large boxes arrayed within the property. "We fill every one of those things with bullets and we're talking millions of dollars in damage."

Carver stifled a wince. Once again, it seemed like overkill. This time he didn't say anything.

"Let's do as Nick says," ordered Holt. "I want shooters setting up as if they had their guns on them today. The rest will monitor the employees and security to see if we can pick up a schedule."

As the teams got to work, Carver pulled Anderson aside and spoke in a hushed breath. "Commander, are you sure you want to cause quite so much destruction? Are we proving a point or are we inflicting long-term damage?"

"It's only a lesson if it's painful," he said sternly. "People take potshots at these stations all the time. We're not going to make a statement unless we take this as far as we can."

"And your contact? Are they DoD? They have the authority for this?"

Anderson clenched his jaw, avoided the details, and simply said, "We have it."

He started to walk away but Carver hurried into his path. "Lester, I know this is a weird question, but how can you be sure about that? I mean really."

The commander bit down and avoided eye contact.

"Who's your man on the inside?" pressed Carver.

Anderson's cheek twitched. "Vince, you and anyone else cannot know that information. Trust me when I say this is way above your pay grade. This is for your protection as much as mine."

He brushed past Carver to further coordinate with the men.

12

Over the next hour, Carver and his team made several tactical recommendations to improve the plan. Much of it was basic OPSEC and military procedure. Despite most of the militia first hearing about the objectives today, it was apparent the broad strokes had already been worked out by Anderson's government sponsor. They were entering a plan in motion.

Though the scout team was successfully advancing their objectives, Carver grew worried at the size of it. A convoy of trucks parked off-road, give or take twenty soldiers loitering in the hills... It was too visible. Carver shared his concern, and Commander Anderson rounded up the other two teams to walk them through the next two sites.

"You want me to come with?" Carver asked. "Or you could take Nick or Jules along?"

"No need," replied the commander. "This is your target, and I don't want to split your people up on short notice. You're in charge of those two. Finish up here and you're done for the day."

"Copy that."

"Lorelai doesn't need to go up north with us. She'll stay

here and return to the compound with you."

"You got it."

Anderson rolled out with the other two teams. While it would have been nice for Carver's people to get eyes on the other targets, it wasn't necessary. He already knew the broad strokes and specific locations. There was work to be done here in order to earn their worth as consultants. And as far as his worth to the CIA, fewer eyes now meant more opportunities.

From a cargo pocket, he palmed a tiny covert camera. He took discreet pictures of the summit, the nearby energy center, and the substation across the street. He waited until Holt was distracted in a conversation with Johnny and Steve before snapping pictures of them too.

"What are you doing?" asked Lorelai, navigating the rocky terrain over to him.

Carver casually slipped his hands into his pockets. "Just doing a final scan to make sure we're not missing anything. It looks like everybody's on top of their assignments, but you can never be too careful about outside factors. How do you feel about the plan?"

She stared wide eyes at him. "I'm nervous. But only a little. Holt's a pretty good XO. And I feel safe with you watching over us."

"There's nothing to worry about."

He put his hand on her shoulder to steady her. She talked a good talk, but she had shaky legs just being here. Looking into her eyes, he realized she was more nervous about him than she was about the op.

"Lorelai," called Holt, brow hardening. "Come over here a sec."

She swallowed and said, "I'll see ya," with a sheepish smile. She headed over and Holt shot him daggers.

Carver took a breath and surveyed the scene. Morgan and Shaw had hiked back to the truck to return some equipment as well as get a feel for the surrounding terrain. They didn't want any surprises either.

That left Beau sitting by himself watching the energy center while snacking on an orange. Carver wandered that way.

"You're gonna pick up those peels, right?" he asked.

Beau spit out some fibrous material and said, "Of course." He quickly gathered the scattered remains so they wouldn't leave evidence of their presence.

Carver looked to the distance. "So you're on the drone team?"

"I'm your pilot for Sundown."

There was that word again. "Project Sundown?"

"Oh, it's nothing. Just a joke with the guys."

Carver nodded, hearing but ignoring the statement. "Is that what we're calling this?"

For a second, Beau looked like a deer in headlights. Then he snickered. "Sure. You know, we're turning the lights out."

"I get it. It sounds like a few of you have known about this op longer than the others."

"Um, that's right. Not much longer, but Sam says drone prep takes practice."

"The deputy's part of the drone team?"

Beau tensed.

"Is she leading it?"

"I never said that."

"Sure you did, in so many words. The thing is, Johnny was joking about Sundown too, and he's not on the drone team. I was under the impression that only the XOs knew about the op in advance."

Beau pushed to his feet looking at the ground and the sky—anywhere but at him.

"Whoa," tempered Carver. "No need to be evasive. We're all on the same team here. Right?"

He had pushed too hard. Beau said, "I'm not supposed talk about it." Then, before Carver could stop him, the kid hurried to rejoin the group.

It was a known unknown at this point that Deputy Grafton was working on a separate project in the workshop. Heading up the drone team accounted for some of the secrecy, but not all of it. Lorelai and Beau were operating in the open here so there was something more.

He had to dig deeper. Johnny and Steve wouldn't be too cooperative. Holt was likely to be more tight-lipped than Beau, and he was overly protective of Lorelai. Getting solo time with her was going to be tricky.

"Hey," called Shaw, returning from his walk with Morgan. Seeing Beau with the group, he hurried over. "Beau was supposed to be watching the energy center." He peeked through his glass and checked the offices. "Damn it, we might have a problem here. The Vanguard employee is

MIA."

Carver lifted his binoculars too. Beau hadn't been gone more than a minute, but before that he'd been more preoccupied with his snack than the energy center. There was no telling how long the security guard had been missing.

"Car's still there," reported Shaw. "He's on foot."

"Same two guys are across the street," noted Carver. "We're one tango down."

They checked with Beau, but he didn't remember the guard going inside. That was the most likely explanation, a bathroom break or something. But after waiting fifteen minutes and him still being a no-show, they started to worry.

"We're done scouting," decided Carver. "We should pack it in for the day."

"Sure thing," agreed Holt. "Let's head back." He slugged Beau's shoulder for killing the party.

The group hiked down the far side of the hill toward their trucks, bickering. Beau accused the others of not watching the guards either, and Holt said that's because it was his job. It turned into an argument and the XO shoved Beau aggressively.

"Be nice, Holt," begged Lorelai, pulling him away.

He brushed her off and lifted his hand before realizing who it was. Despite Holt holding back, Lorelai spooked and tripped backward onto the ground.

"Lore..." he started.

She turned to Carver and reddened. Lorelai jumped up

and called Holt a prick.

"What did you say?"

"I said you're a conceited prick! Want me to yell it louder?"

He stepped into her. "You better watch it, Lorelai."

"Hey!" snapped Morgan, stomping over. "Knock this off. We aren't clear yet."

Lorelai bit down. Though she had looked ready to explode a moment ago, she reined in her voice. "You know how I feel about being manhandled, Holt."

"Nobody was manhandled by anybody," he insisted.

"Except maybe Beau," chortled Johnny.

Holt didn't laugh along with Johnny and Steve. He offered Lorelai a conciliatory hand. She took it halfheartedly before seeming to reconsider. She huffed and tried to spin away. He gripped her tight. She pulled.

"Let go."

"I just wanna talk."

"Let GO!"

She slapped him hard. Molten lava spread over his expression. "You little—"

"I said that's enough!" shouted Morgan, walling between them.

Carver approached and Lorelai ran and clamped onto his side, trembling.

"Oh, so you're gonna run to him now?" called Holt.

"I'm scared!" she cried.

"Scared? I never hit you once in my life, but you flinch away like I'm a criminal or something."

She buried her head into Carver. "You know I don't like that."

"Like what? Your ex-husband? He got what he deserved, didn't he? I'm not a woman beater!"

Lorelai just sobbed. The drama was so sudden and fiery that no one really knew what to do. Holt threw his hands into the air and stomped ahead, cursing, with Johnny and the others in tow.

All this time, Carver had just thought of Lorelai as an inexperienced kid. Instead, she had history in what sounded like an abusive relationship. No wonder she was so gun-shy around men.

He did wonder what Holt meant about her husband. Anderson had said Lorelai tried living the normal life for a while until it didn't work out. Something big enough had finally convinced her to break away from that toxicity, move in with her dad, and join the militia.

"It's okay," said Carver, knowing he couldn't offer more than lip service. Morgan came up and spread her arms, and Carver thankfully handed the girl off.

For her part, Lorelai welcomed the female companionship. Carver nodded thanks as he and Shaw moved on, leaving the two to trail at their own pace.

"This is better than a *telenovela*," mumbled Shaw as they marched.

It may have been callous, but this wasn't the time nor the place for an emotional outburst and resolution of feelings.

It took about ten minutes to get back to their vehicles. Instead of descending the final slope, Holt and the guys ducked behind withered hedges at the ridgeline. Carver and Shaw, sensing unease, hustled forward.

Beau set on them with frantic eyes. "Shit, what are we gonna do?"

At the base of the hill, their missing security guard, using both hands to shield his eyes from the sun, peeked into the driver's window of Holt's pickup. After a moment, he pulled away and gazed down the dirt road, lazily chewing gum. Failing to see any explanation for the parked vehicles, the guard rounded to the second truck.

"This is a problem," grumbled Holt. "We need to take care of this." He drew a pistol from inside his military jacket.

"What are you doing?" snapped Carver.

"It's just a precaution."

"You're not supposed to have a gun here."

They stepped away from the ridgeline. "This is my command, Vince. And it looks like I was right to bring a little insurance along."

"How is shooting a security guard going to help us?"

"He could identify us if we don't."

"He hasn't seen anyone. Look at him. He hasn't even checked the plates. He's just snooping." While Carver argued with Holt and the others, Shaw remained on his knees to keep eyes on the guard. It was the best course of action for now. "Let's just observe from a distance and make sure he doesn't note the plate numbers."

"And what if he does?" asked Johnny.

"We'll figure it out if it comes to that, but as long as he

doesn't see us, there's nothing for him to identify."

"What if he calls it in?" asked Beau, frazzled.

"He hasn't yet. That's a good indication that he's not suspicious. This is public land and the trucks could belong to hikers. No laws have been broken so there's nothing to call in. And even if he does get on the radio, the second he steps away we can jump in the trucks and disappear before backup arrives. No harm, no foul."

Beau swiveled to his XO for confirmation. It sounded plausible, but he wasn't looking for tactical options as much as reassurance from a familiar face. Steve and Johnny needed more convincing too.

"It's best to stay out of his way," Carver assured them again. "Let's not give him something worth remembering."

Holt adamantly shook his head. "Think about it, smart guy. If we get the green light to go ahead with the op next week, he'll remember the trucks then. He'll report what he saw. It only takes one little detail to screw us."

"And what do you think killing a security guard's going to do? They'll start an investigation. Increase security. You'll be blowing the op before it begins."

The XO scoffed. "It's not ideal, but the guard's the bigger threat right now. He's a loose end. I'm not going to jail over this."

He turned to the ridgeline. Carver moved to stop him, but Holt spun and pointed the pistol at him.

"Don't even try it!"

Carver stopped and bit down. Shaw approached, but Holt backed away and pointed the gun at him too.

"I'm warning you two," he said gravely.

"The commander doesn't want anyone hurt," asserted Carver.

"I appreciate the advice—"

"It's not advice, it's an order."

"Uh-uh." Holt's gun centered on Carver again. "I'm the ranking officer here. A casualty is unfortunate, but it's my call. Now stand back or it's insubordination."

Carver grimaced. The stupid kid wasn't really a soldier, he was just pretending to be one. He was play-acting, and it was going to carelessly get people hurt.

But under the threat of the pointed weapon, Carver didn't have a choice. He took a step back.

"Good. Now you too." Holt pivoted to Shaw.

The only movement from the SEAL was the sneer on his face.

"The XO gave you an order," declared Johnny. He went in for a shove, but Shaw planted a fist in his face and Johnny hit the dirt.

"Nick," warned Carver curtly.

The boys were getting hot, about to throw down here and now, but it wasn't the right time for this. Shaw met Carver's gaze. After a tortured scowl, he finally backed away too. Everyone stared hard for a moment, but the argument was over.

"Good," said Holt, lowering the gun. "Stay put while I deal with this."

The XO peeked through the hedges again. The security guard faced away from them, hands on hips, trying to decide what to do about the abandoned trucks. Holt quietly descended toward him.

Carver worked his jaw. Well-intentioned operations did sometimes incur civilian casualties—that was an unfortunate truth of war. But this? This was an American on domestic soil protecting a minimal-security government facility. Carver couldn't envision a scenario where he allowed this to happen.

Unfortunately, Holt was the only one with a firearm.

A chuckle escaped Carver's lips. *Holt was the only one with a firearm.* Johnny and Steve and even Beau were standing tough watching them, but their only leverage had just walked down the hill. The three of them possessed no means of enforcing their will on Carver and Shaw.

"What are you laughing about?" demanded Johnny with a rueful smirk.

Carver grinned. "Nick, if they so much as try to stop me, make it hurt."

Shaw's glare was statuesque. "Copy that, boss."

Carver walked to the ridgeline and let out a guttural, "Hey!"

The security guard spun and Holt, halfway down the hill, hurried the pistol behind his back. Everybody on the ridge ducked so only the two of them were visible.

"Yeah, you!" called Carver again, barreling toward and waving at the waiting guard. "Thank God we found the trucks! We've been out here for hours!"

After a jogging descent that bypassed Holt, Carver tripped at the base of the hill and ate a faceful of dirt. The security guard stepped away, startled, hand on his belt hovering near his radio and his gun. Carver rolled onto his back, laughing hysterically.

"Guess I took that too fast! Sorry, I'm not much of an outdoorsman." He pushed to his feet with strained effort. It was difficult for a person with Carver's frame to not appear menacing, so he slouched and hammed up his role. "Please tell me you have something to drink."

The guard was wary of getting near him, but his hand relaxed.

"Wait! Never mind." Carver tried the door of Holt's pickup. It was locked.

The security guard watched him pointedly. "Sir, what are you doing in the area?"

Carver tried the door a few more times. Holt converged, pistol still behind his back.

"Would you mind?" asked Carver.

Holt ground his teeth. He was angry, and there was a decent chance he might still pull his piece, but with two sets of eyes on him, he held back. The best Carver could do was continue playing his part and hope Holt went along.

"Come on," Carver pleaded. "I'm dying of thirst."

Holt pulled the keys from his pocket and tossed them over. Pretending to be drunk, Carver made sure his reaction was adequately insufficient. The keys bounced off his chest and hit the floor before a delayed swipe impotently whiffed the air. He laughed, picked the keys up, and unlocked the truck.

"Sir," said the guard more sternly.

"Hold on, hold on."

The easiest way to scare a security guard was to go right at them. By contrast, keeping your attention somewhere else took the pressure off them. Carver wasn't a security threat, he was an annoyance to get rid off. He dug into the cooler and turned to the guard as he twisted off the cap of a beer bottle.

"Want one?"

"What?"

Ignoring the guard's response, Carver took a swig. When he was done he tossed the bottle cap to the dirt. "Free beer, dude. You in or out?"

"Sir," warned the unamused guard, "you can't be out here. And you can't throw your trash on the ground."

"Sorry, force of habit."

Carver moved to the man's side to pick up the cap. The guard watched him before turning to study Holt. The XO conspicuously kept one hand behind his back, but Carver wasn't sure the guard was attentive enough to notice. Either way, no one was looking at the helpless drunk for the time being. Carver upturned the beer bottle and knocked it across the back of the guard's head. He dropped to the ground like a sack of potatoes.

Holt pointed his gun now, but Carver ignored him. The threat had passed. Carver emptied the remainder of his beer over the unconscious guard. Pulling the man's radio from its belt holster, he wiped the bottle down and stuck it in its place.

"What the hell was that?" demanded Holt. The

adrenaline was still running high but there was nothing to do with it.

"I took care of the problem without killing him."

With the guard down, the rest of the group hurried down the hill.

"He's gonna wake up in a minute," pointed out the angry XO.

"And we'll be long gone. He won't have his radio so there won't be a quick response. After he thinks things over, he'll figure he got assaulted by drunk douchebags instead of stumbling on an organized operation. With any luck he'll be so embarrassed by the whole thing that he won't mention it to anyone. In fact, do you have a pen?"

Holt's brow furrowed. "A what?"

"A pen."

The others loaded into the trucks. Carver found a felt-tip pen in the center console and drew a twirly mustache on the sleeping guard's lip.

Shaw yanked the pen from him. "If you're gonna do it," he admonished, "do it right." He added a pointed goatee on his chin.

Johnny cracked up as Shaw handed the pen to Holt. The XO wasn't amused, but he apparently decided that the situation was acceptable. They shut the truck doors and sped away as the dazed guard began shaking his woozy head.

Hopefully the man would only require an aspirin. At any rate, he was certainly feeling better than dead.

As they sped around a sandy ditch, Carver wiped and tossed the radio. They had successfully neutralized the threat to OPSEC without the loss of innocent life, and they had done it with style. Despite Holt's angry sulking, Carver couldn't help but smile.

13

Shaw burped as he shoved aside a destroyed platter of carne asada nachos. "It's not smoked brisket, but it'll do."

"It's a shame about the brisket, all right?" Carver leaned back against the hard wooden booth bench.

With Morgan at home with the kids, Carver and Shaw decompressed in a ratty Irish pub. They were in a dark spot at the back with a view of the door. For the first half hour they managed not to discuss the militia, but, even in a dingy corner with the Pogues blaring in the background, reality had a way of door breaching with a sledgehammer.

The waitress set down a fresh pair of beers and scooped Shaw's credit card from the table. Carver was cutting himself off at two and Shaw didn't drink alone.

"You believe this red cell business?" his friend muttered as the waitress walked away.

"I don't even know if Lester believes it. But it does explain him not being an anti-government fanatic."

"That's just as easily explained by him being a mercenary, doing it for money."

Carver dipped his head in acknowledgment and they clanked bottles.

After a couple of gulps and some rumination, Shaw said, "I will admit he seems like an okay dude."

Carver picked at the label on his beer bottle. "I was almost expecting a cult situation, but somehow the commander's the most normal out of all of them."

"Well, you know that environment attracts a certain sort."

The waitress briefly returned to drop off the check and the card. Shaw signed and left it on the edge of the table. It was a slow night but the waitress was constantly moving.

"Speaking of trouble," said Shaw, "it's going to come to a head with Holt and his crew."

"I know it, but the real player is Samantha. She's been suspicious of us from the jump. I'm convinced she's hiding something. We need to get into that workshop."

"To get eyes on the drones? Maybe Jules can cozy up with her. Do some feminine commiseration."

"The deputy won't fall for anything so overt. Besides, even Commander Anderson is giving you two a short leash. He trusts me, but he's repeatedly made it clear that you both should stick to my side."

Shaw grumbled and took a drink. "What about that poor girl?"

"Lorelai."

"She's an in. She has a soft spot for you."

Carver sighed. "I get the feeling she's been through enough."

"You say that like she's out of the woods, but she's not. If she's hanging with this crowd, she's in the thick of it. I don't know how her father allows it."

"Don't you think that's a little harsh? She's a grown woman, Nick."

"She's in over her head and has no business with this crew."

Carver attempted to fold back the crumpled edge of the beer label he'd been peeling. Why did he feel the need to defend Anderson? The commander wasn't the careless type, even if he was playing with fire. Carver could only assume he had his reasons.

"Damn it," he said, double-checking his watch for confirmation of the lost time. "I should have another woman on my mind." He took one last swig and set the half-empty bottle down. "Sorry, I need to go."

"You know what I think about that too," muttered Shaw.

"Save it, Nick. I'm a big boy."

Shaw pointed the tip of his bottle at Carver in warning. "Watch yourself, brother. If you don't, I will."

"I know." Carver rapped Shaw on the shoulder and walked out.

* * *

Carver's pickup pulled into a marked spot across from the park, but the car following him passed, turned the corner, and lingered at an open curb. Carver trekked across the concrete plaza, illuminated by streetlights but still a little grainy on the phone screen. The camera clicked several times as he entered the hotel lobby.

The only reason someone who lived in San Jose would go to a hotel in their own city was to meet someone.

It was risky to go inside and take a look, but it had to be done. There was no cause for Carver to suspect anything. It was just a matter of being careful...

* * *

Carver and Guerrero lay naked in bed, his back propped up on a stack of pillows and her on her side, running fingers up and down his muscular arm.

"How did you get these?" she asked, tracing lightly over the scars on his bicep.

He glanced at the reminders of the fateful day that changed the trajectory of his life. In many ways, the tragedy had made him stronger. But strength, he knew, wasn't always worth the price.

"A good friend and I were were deep in an op, deeper than we had any right to be. But the intel took precedence. Duty overrode good sense." He clenched his jaw. "I took a couple of bullets. Almost lost control of my arm."

"You were lucky."

"My partner wasn't. He only caught a single round, but that one was enough." Carver's face darkened.

"I'm sorry."

"Don't be. I learned not to take faceless orders anymore. All our training sculpted us into perfect machines capable of infiltrating non-permissive areas, capable of assessing hard courses of action. But, in the end, our directives came from some spook in a cubicle somewhere. It's sort of a paradox, isn't it?"

"What's the alternative?"

"To use our capabilities to call the shots that sit right with us. To not be blindly compelled to walk into ambushes that make our skin crawl from a mile away. My friend died because some analyst fresh out of graduate school didn't do his homework."

She watched him with large eyes. "What good is an army if everyone does their own thing?"

"That's not what I'm saying. Your average grunt isn't as informed as even the lowest-tier analysts. But investigators need to be trusted to apply their skills in the field." He turned his head to appraise her dimpled cheeks. "Take your position, for instance. You and Bentley are the boots on the ground. You walk the scenes, talk to the players, identify the dangers. Having to rubber stamp every one of your judgment calls has to hold you back. Wouldn't it be better to skip that part?"

"It would be *easier*," she corrected. "At the loss of accountability."

"Not at all. None of us get a free pass. If we screw up, we pay the price. That's how the world works anyway. We might as well be honest about it."

Guerrero sighed and rolled to her back. Carver liked how her hair fell over her face. "You have such laser focus all the time," she affirmed, "but it's just not reflective of government work."

"Slow and steady wins the race, huh?"

"I admit, your philosophy appeals to me right now. It's taken a week to get S2 on Homeland's radar."

Carver couldn't make out her expression except for a tweak of her lips. This was the first she had mentioned the militia tonight. He wondered if she would pry into his interactions with them. For now she was content to stare at the ceiling.

It was him who pushed the subject.

"The other night you said Bentley thought you were crazy for looking into the militia's transactions on the dark web. Did you find the proof you were looking for?"

She snorted lightly. "Let's just say the local ASAC is coming around."

They lay in silence, neither pressing nor elaborating. Carver wondered where this was going. Even though Guerrero was upfront about her expectations, a part of him felt slimy that their cross purposes had to meet in the bedroom. It would have been one thing if she were a heartless government drone, but he suspected he was starting to like her.

He sighed and sat up. She quickly put her arm around him. "What are you doing tonight?"

He frowned. "I don't know. I..."

"I was thinking..." she hurried before trailing off. She pursed her lips, smiled, and said, "I was thinking you might want to stay here. Relax a little."

Carver didn't know if he felt better or worse, but he

forced a smile. "That would be nice."

They fell asleep nestled in each other's arms and desires.

****

Carver lightly toed into the bathroom so as not to disturb Guerrero, but the water was only on a minute before she tapped at the door. They showered together, her standing away from the faucet to keep her hair dry. She soaped him up and he returned the favor, neither ruining the moment with words. As they stared deeply into each other's eyes, he pressed her gently against the steamed glass, and they made love.

They dressed by the bed, and Guerrero seemed bothered by something. Carver was sure he hadn't said anything callous. Fortunately, she didn't keep quiet about it long.

"When are you going back to the militia complex?"

Carver fixed the watch around his wrist. The honest answer was that he didn't have a training schedule anymore. He was a consultant now, a stand-in for a full-fledged member of S2. There were no shifts, so to speak, but he was expected to check in.

He decided to keep it simple and said, "I was planning on passing by in a bit."

She tied her hair behind her neck and approached. "Would it be suspicious if, just today, you didn't?"

His cheek twitched. Despite his best efforts, it was a crack in his facade. "What aren't you telling me? What do you have against these guys?"

"Personally? Nothing." She said it matter-of-factly, with a shrug. "They're a security risk to the president's visit. My job is to investigate any outliers."

"By asking me not to go in today?"

She huffed and rested her palm on his chest. "I did find something, Vince." Her eyes were on her hand, not him. "A dark web marketplace. I can't talk about it, but HSI is paying them another unannounced visit. And this time we're not assisting the sheriff's office."

He blinked. "You're raiding the compound?"

She turned away. "I didn't say those words, but you and your team should find an excuse not to be there. Just for today." She turned back to him and finally met his eyes. "For me."

Carver wet his lips and swallowed, unsure what to say or do with this information. Why would she tell him this? It was possible she was playing him, testing him, observing his reaction.

His cynical instincts about her motivations brought on a wave of guilt. Which in itself could be a manipulation.

"I'll see what I can do," he said. "But I might not be able to avoid it."

"Vince..."

"I'll be careful. I won't get in Homeland's way. You have my word."

She pursed her lips, mulled it over, and nodded. "Okay. I'll walk you out. I had an incident with the coffee maker yesterday that I don't want to repeat, and there's a nice cafe on the corner."

They gathered their belongings and exited, making it halfway to the elevator when Special Agent Bentley turned into the hall. He froze in his tracks mid chomp into a freshly opened power bar. Guerrero stiffened, pulled away from Carver, and said, "Special Agent."

He hurriedly swallowed. "Guerrero... this guy?" His Jersey intonation came on strong. "Are you kidding me?"

She sighed. "Bentley, I'd appreciate if we kept our personal business personal."

"Come on now. This is beyond personal."

"How so?"

"You know—"

He clipped the statement short and looked at Carver. Then he wrapped the power bar and slipped it into his pocket, breakfast officially ruined.

"I was just coming to talk to you," he told his partner. "There's been a development."

Guerrero rubbed her neck and turned to Carver. "Rain check?" she asked timidly.

"Sure thing." And then, mimicking her dry greeting to her partner, "Special Agent."

She rolled her eyes in a failed attempt to disguise her amusement. That was good enough for Carver so he left them behind for their a stern discussion.

In the elevator, Carver wondered if Guerrero had somehow gotten into trouble. But there was something positive to be gleaned from the interaction. Bentley's surprise at seeing them together had been genuine. That meant she wasn't getting intimate with him as part of the investigation, not without the knowledge of her partner. That was something, at least.

He strode through the lobby, now well lit and well trafficked. Guests with suitcases waited by the front desk, and the bar area was empty save for a party taking advantage of a booth to rest. The sky outside was so bright it took half a minute to adjust to the glare. Across the street, a string of birthday decorations was being hung for a party.

Completing the quick hike to his truck, Carver stopped short upon seeing the envelope under his windshield wiper. For a brief second he thought it was a parking ticket, but he speedily determined the envelope wasn't government issue. He snatched it without fanfare and climbed into the pickup, waiting until the door was shut and his sunglasses were on to unassumingly scan the immediate area. Looking without looking like he was looking.

Nobody in the open was concerned with his business, but the surrounding buildings were flush with windows. If his truck was under professional surveillance at this precise moment, it would be impossible to tell.

14

The envelope was unmarked and sealed with a self-adhesive strip. In the off chance a fingerprint could be recovered from the sticker, he ripped open the side of the envelope and pulled out a folded napkin that, upon inspection, was unused. In the corner was the colorful logo of a local mochi donut chain, where "ASAP" was scrawled in messy black handwriting.

Carver tossed the message onto the passenger seat and drove off, keeping an eye out for pursuit. This was the side of surveillance that favored the quarry. The onus would be on anyone following to take action, and that was a risk when tailing a trained operator. No cars stuck to his six. By all accounts he was clear.

The drive back to San Pedro Square Market was short, even with the additional turns to throw off pursuers. He strolled through the coffee shop into the food hall interior and located the same donut booth Shaw had talked up. Scanning the breadth of the cafeteria, he spotted the back of the maroon jacket at a tequila bar on the opposite wall. At this early hour, a metal shutter was rolled down to the countertop, and Officer Williams was alone. He joined her.

"Didn't take you for the dessert type, Laney." He placed the donut napkin on the counter and sat on the stool beside her, facing outward to watch for unexpected visitors.

She sternly swiveled her seat to face him, unconcerned with surveillance. "Which part about staying away from HSI was difficult to understand?"

"You having me followed?"

"I'm not the only one. You had a tail last night as you entered the hotel."

His head turned to her. "Who?"

She sighed. "My guy wasn't on to it in time. He let them slip away before he realized the possibility."

Carver frowned. "So it's only a possibility now?"

"If you want to take that chance. Possible threats are threats waiting to be actualized. But you know that already —you work in security." She looked around. "I assume the envelope was a reminder of OPSEC and you made sure you weren't followed here?"

He worked his jaw. If what she said was true, he deserved that. "I wasn't followed here."

She nodded. "Are you sleeping with Agent Guerrero?"

"Is that your business?"

"It is now."

The CIA officer enjoyed her badgering, but Carver had long learned that it was pragmatic. It was her way of unraveling problems. Williams was figuring things out, not twisting the knife deeper once it was in there.

"There was a spark when we first met," Carver explained dryly. "After you reached out, I decided against following up. But then HSI showed up at the S2 compound with the sheriff's office. She knew I was up to something. I couldn't ignore her anymore."

"What does she know?"

"Nothing. She's just feeling me out. And I'm feeling her back."

"In more ways than one." Her lashes sharpened at him. Instead of disdain he detected respect.

"No. It's not like that. I didn't think there was anything there."

Williams arched an eyebrow. "Meaning you found out there is?"

"You tell me. She uncovered a dark web marketplace related to S2."

"Related how?"

"I don't know."

"How heavy is she riding you?"

Carver's face sagged. "Is that another joke?"

She smacked his shoulder. "Get your head out of the gutter. I don't want this to be a problem. She could compromise you if you aren't careful."

"She's not leaning on me about anything," he assured. "An odd question here or there, but I haven't given her any information and she hasn't pressed."

Williams took a long, inward moment to review the information. "Okay," she finally said with a self-satisfied nod. "I think you've managed everything right so far. You might need to throw HSI a bone to keep them playing on your team. If she fed you information once, she might do it again."

"Throw her a bone?"

"Okay, it *is* funny, but you know what I mean. Make yourself useful to keep her around. Then she can be useful to you too."

"I'm surprised you're taking this so well."

"Look, Vince, I don't articulate this a lot, but you're more than a tough nut with good aim. There's a reason I trust you with so much leeway. You've shown good judgment so far. Use it to decide what's necessary to share with HSI without compromising the op. The techniques are no different than your undercover militia work."

Carver didn't say anything. The thought of treating Guerrero as an asset bothered him. He understood keeping secrets—standard OPSEC had been drilled into the core of his being long ago—but the HSI agents weren't pawns to position at will. Even more unsettling was the cool confidence of Williams discussing the subject. Carver wondered if she was working him too, if she was so far up her own ass that she couldn't be straight with anybody.

Mostly he wondered if that would one day happen to him.

"You've been inside a few days," she pivoted. "Tell me my faith in your abilities is justified. Tell me you have an idea what these doomsdayers are up to."

Carver scanned the food hall as he spoke. "It's more than an idea. S2 is well stocked. They can afford shiny new toys and my expertise, yet put me to work training their soldiers on an old stockpile of untraceable Soviet SKS carbines."

"Legacy throwaway weapons. It's a means, but not a motive or a crime."

"That's where this comes in."

Carver pulled a folded gas-station map from his back pocket and handed it over. Williams peeked inside just enough to see several locations marked across the Bay Area. "These are electrical substations."

"Three of them, to be hit simultaneously with gunfire and improvised drone payloads in order to cause maximum catastrophic damage."

"You're talking massive and sustained power loss."

He nodded. "It's a professional operation. Most of the militia soldiers are amateurs, but Anderson has them organized into capable teams. And he's operating with legitimate intelligence."

"When is D-Day?"

Carver hiked a shoulder. "That's the thing. We might go active tomorrow, next month, or never."

"He's not telling anyone."

"I don't think it's up to him. Anderson has a boss. It might be more accurate to say he has a handler."

Williams narrowed her eyes, enhancing the streaks of violet eye shadow. "You think he's attached to a foreign service."

"It's more complicated than that. At least how he tells it. He's waiting to be activated himself, but the entity supplying his intelligence and funding is domestic."

She stared at him a whole minute before blinking. Then it felt like another minute before she said, "Explain."

He nodded unevenly, uncomfortable with this next part. "This is where things get tricky, because I don't know what to believe."

"Try me."

"Before I do, I need to ask a question, and I need you to be honest with me."

Williams waited without making any promises, which was fair enough. Carver went ahead.

"Does the CIA have a relationship with Commander Anderson?"

His case officer scrunched her eyes. "I don't understand."

"It's not a hard question, Lanelle. Is or was Lester ever an asset for the CIA or another American intelligence agency?"

Her mind was racing. "He... Where is this coming from?"

"Why aren't you answering the question?"

"Because it's preposterous. Commander Anderson doesn't work for the CIA, the FBI, or anybody. He never has. The man is completely unassociated with the intelligence community. He doesn't have access, he's never had access, and I'm struggling to determine where you're going with this."

"I have your word?" He looked her dead in the eye. "Because this is the type of thing I need to know to put my life on the line. And the lives of my people."

She didn't shy from his gaze. "Vince, barring the roundabout method of you entering Commander

Anderson's atmosphere, there's absolutely no deception in my management of this operation. I gave you the sum of the Agency's intelligence, with the disclaimer that our intelligence is incomplete. *We know* there's something *we don't know*. That's the mission: to find out what that is."

He studied her a moment. "Okay," he said, satisfied. "I'm choosing to believe you. You know why? Because I'm a good judge of character, and I don't think you're lying. But therein lies the rub, because I don't think Anderson's lying either."

"Please tell me he's not claiming to be CIA."

"He's light on specifics, but he says he's part of an official red cell operation run by someone in the executive branch, possibly the Department of Defense. Anderson claims the strikes on the power substations are sanctioned by the government in order to achieve national security goals."

"Bullshit."

"Sure sounds like it. But a military operation does a good job explaining why the CIA and Homeland Security are chasing their tails. If this is an internal security concern and it's not you guys, who else could it be?"

"It could be *bullshit*, Vince. A half-assed justification to take a payout while fooling yourself into thinking you're doing your patriotic duty."

Carver grimaced. "I've considered that, and I could be way off, but the guy doesn't strike me as the type. Everything about it screams that Anderson is being straight with me. Unusually so, as a matter of fact."

"And that doesn't set off alarms?"

"The guy is either playing me to perfection or I've earned his trust completely. For better or worse, Laney, I have to believe it's the latter. He's shown me too much already. Which isn't to say I believe the red cell business, but I'm not ready to accept that the whole thing is a Lester-special shine job."

The CIA officer took in a long breath as she considered his points. "Operations resembling red cells *do* have a legitimate historical basis, but their scope is usually exaggerated and romanticized. What's important is that they have, at times, existed. But something about this is wrong."

Carver canted his head. "Like I said, it's hard to believe."

Instead of allaying her fears, her frown deepened. "I don't like when facts don't line up, Vince. It means somebody's missing something. That's a very dangerous position for you."

"So give me a way to contact you if something goes sideways."

"It's too risky. You've already picked up a tail."

"It was one slip. I have the larger picture in focus."

"No you don't. You need to hear me in no uncertain terms, Vince. The Agency cannot play as fast and loose as you do. Especially not domestically. Independence is the appeal of your service."

"I thought it was my results."

A small upward curve almost broke through her frown.

"Is there something you're not telling me?"

Whatever hint of a smile there was disappeared. "This

operation," she said slowly, "it isn't official. I'm not supposed to be talking to you. My bosses are still uncomfortable about your actions in the Black Sea."

"You're not thinking of pulling me, are you?"

"It's a consideration," she said.

"Come on."

"We're not there yet. Your intel is valuable, but this could burn us. I don't want to get you killed."

"I'll mitigate all possible threats."

She held his eye. If he had said he was on top of things, she would have shot him down again. Instead, he was coming at the problem tactically. Nothing in life was guaranteed. It was what made even the most inane sporting contests exciting. But the edge always went with the team that was most prepared. That was something Williams could digest, even if it didn't sit well.

"I'm not sure I agree with your assessment of Commander Anderson," she added.

"The tail wasn't him."

"They don't trust you."

"The commander does."

She snorted. "Fine, if you're so sure. But is the commander in control?"

That one stopped Carver for a second. He had no good answer for that question, but it was worth looking into.

"Do me a favor," he said. "Do background on Samantha Grafton. Has a son, Holt. She's Anderson's deputy commander and their relationship is at times rivalrous. She heads up the drone team."

"Is she a problem?"

"She's savvy. Sometimes I feel like she sees right through me. Does that count?"

Her scowl signaled the affirmative. "When's the next time you're meeting them?"

"That's another thing we need to talk about. I'm supposed to swing by today, but Agent Guerrero strongly suggested I don't... HSI is raiding the S2 compound."

"What, because of dark web transactions? That's not good."

"They might find something."

"We don't want to blow up the red cell business for paltry weapons charges."

"There could be more than that. The deputy's been at some secret project in the workshop. I haven't been able to get eyes on whatever they're customizing."

"You mentioned an improvised drone payload."

"Could be, though I haven't identified it yet."

"A high-quality quadcopter can be repurposed to drop frag grenades and mines."

"I don't know. That makes sense, it just doesn't sit right. It doesn't explain the secrecy. Sam's people are in the workshop nonstop. No one else can enter."

Williams worked her lips. "And your assessment is that this project is significant?"

Carver leaned onto his knees and sighed. "One of their guys, Trent, just killed himself."

Williams rolled with the pivot as adeptly as ever. "You believe there's more to it than suicide?"

"I don't have a scrap of evidence, but the timing is awfully suspicious. The afternoon Trent was last alive, he had stumbled on something in the bunker. There's some kind of vault or armory in there. He wasn't a stable personality on his best days, but he got real emotional about something he saw in there. He was angry with Anderson. He felt betrayed. It's possible he walked in on something he wasn't supposed to."

The news troubled the CIA officer. Her face grew more stern with every sentence. "If there's a special payload being used in these attacks, we need to find it."

"Can you call off the raid?"

She twisted her lips. "I can look into it. Loosely. But it's probably best we keep our fingerprints off this."

"If we're still insisting on that level of deniability, then—given what we know—my options are limited."

"I agree. You can't mysteriously not show up the day the compound is raided. Even having nothing to do with it, your op would be compromised then and there. If the deputy already doesn't trust you, this would take it over the edge." Williams mulled it over. "Try not to do anything that stands out. The raid is about the militia, not you. You're just another hapless recruit."

"And HomeSec will leave me alone?"

"I can't speak to their intentions. But don't worry if you get arrested. I'll take care of you."

He swiveled to her. "Into the breach then?"

"It's the only way to understand the full scale of this plan," she asserted. "That gives us three priorities. First is the date of the attacks. We know that and they'll be trivial to stop. Second is the identification of the payload. It's impossible to make an accurate threat assessment without it."

"Either or both of those problems might be neutralized by Homeland Security in a matter of hours," pointed out Carver.

"That's very possible. A raid might uncover these answers, but we have a deeper mission that cannot be compromised. Our third priority is to ferret out S2's mysterious sponsor."

"Problem is, if the commander gets swept into federal custody..."

"Then the individual behind this red cell will disappear."

Carver grimaced. Every hunter knew there was such a thing as moving in for the kill too fast. "There's an exception to that scenario," he countered. "If Anderson tells us what he knows."

"It's a last resort if we're forced into a corner, but if we go there and he refuses we're out of options."

Carver swiveled away from her, watching the floor darkly. "You're right. He doesn't seem the type to save his own skin." He snickered inwardly, but it came out loud and bitter. "I can't believe I'm saying this, but I almost like the guy."

"We're not here to protect the militia from HSI, Vince. We might need to in this case, but don't confuse your priorities."

"I got it," he griped. "Date, payload, and sponsor. Piece

of cake."

"I can't stress strongly enough how vital it is that we uncover the mastermind. They're potentially a far larger problem than the Bay Area power grid. I don't buy this Department of Defense business."

Carver slid off the stool to stretch his legs. "And what if the red cell is legit?"

She shrugged. "Don't let the thought discourage you. If they're a genuine red cell, then all countermeasures are fair play. Their job is to prove we're not ready, and ours is to prove them wrong. You understand?"

"I think I do."

"And are we, Vince?"

He looked at her. "Are we what?"

"Are we ready for them?"

15

Carver debarked from his pickup to see Lorelai approaching. She waved and he waved back, prompting her to smile and hasten her gait. Opening the truck's back door, he recovered the SIG from his range bag and holstered it to his belt where it would be plainly visible to law enforcement.

Considering the innumerable ways today could go wrong, he had given Shaw and Morgan the day off.

"Howdy, Vince," said Lorelai as she converged, military cap smartly tying her hair in the back. She didn't have a gun.

"How are you today?" he asked warmly.

"A little uneasy, if I'm honest. You wouldn't happen to know what's going on, would you?"

Carver eyed her quizzically and was about to ask for details when Holt rounded the building with his guys.

"The prodigal son returns!" he called. Holt held his AR across his chest on the way over.

"What's with the sarcasm?" Carver asked Lorelai.

She shrugged. "Don't know but he's sure acting weird."

Holt peeked into the Ram's windows. "No sniper team today, huh?"

"Sorry to disappoint," Carver replied. "Shooting's not on

the schedule today."

Holt rapped Carver's shoulder with misplaced familiarity. "But you decided to come in and check up on us anyway, didn't you?"

Carver swiveled his head to the spot Holt had touched before resuming eye contact. Lorelai wasn't wrong about something being off, but Carver couldn't afford to show his hand before he knew what everyone else was holding. Better to play it cool.

"I'm part of the team," asserted Carver, "aren't I?"

Holt chuckled, standing close to amplify his one-inch height advantage. "Of course you are. I'm just surprised you showed up without backup."

Lorelai squeezed between them, using considerable force to clear space. "What's gotten into you today?"

Holt's eyes didn't leave Carver. "Lorelai, stay out of this."

Her hands planted on her hips. "Or *what?*"

He turned to her. "Get out of here or we're gonna have a talk later."

She bit her lip and her face went red.

"It's all right, Lorelai," said Carver before she exploded. "Holt's not going to have a talk with you, is he?"

Both men stared hard. Carver doubted Holt would be as confident without Johnny and Steve. Maybe he would. He was certainly somewhat capable. Even more to the point, he had a high opinion of himself.

"Don't forget what Sam said about going against your own people," Holt warned. Lorelai's eyes hit the ground, and Carver wondered which of the Grafton's had a bigger hold over her. "Now go on before you need to explain yourself to the deputy."

Her eyes scrambled between the available faces, searching for a rescue.

Carver nodded. "It's okay. We're just going to talk."

She swallowed, thought a second, and almost turned to go. Then, at the last second, she gave Carver's hand a squeeze. Holt ground his teeth, and she spun away without meeting his gaze. Holt bored holes into her as she receded toward the house.

Carver plastered an easy smile across his face and turned to fuming man.

"Real magnanimous of you," grated Holt.

"You get that from your word-of-the-day calendar?"

"I guess you're the smart one, huh?"

"No, but I do have some advice. Lorelai's a nice girl, but she strikes me as the type that holds things in until, one day, she doesn't, and all the pain and bullying comes out at once in a single vengeful stroke."

Holt bit down and blinked. The statement caught him strangely off guard, and maybe something else. Maybe it hit a little close to home. "Forget Lorelai," he said.

"You're right. I'm here with news. I need to speak with the commander."

"You can tell me. I'm an officer."

Carver idly shook his head. "You and the deputy and the other XOs can join us. I don't have any secrets from S2."

Holt turned to his friends and nobody said anything for a

moment. Then he backed away and said, "Okay then. I think I saw the commander in the yard. Let's go talk."

Carver pushed past Steve and Johnny, hurrying to stay on his flank as they marched to the rear of the wood-paneled building. The boys were nervous and unsure of themselves. The last time they were at odds, he had effortlessly outmaneuvered them. This time things were a little trickier. All three wore rifles in a sling.

They rounded the building to evidence of past activity. The cafeteria tables had been moved to central positions in the yard. Some guys chopped wood and a woman tied balloons to chairs.

"You throwing a party?" asked Carver.

"Didn't you know?" laughed Johnny. "It's my birthday."

Carver gave the man a sideways glance. The party favors didn't distract from the more important details he witnessed, like the Sportsman ATVs parked at hand as if recently put to work. Notably, the doors to the bunker, workshop, and barracks were wide open. Samantha Grafton exited the workshop and made a beeline for them without locking up behind her.

"I didn't know you were stopping in today, Vince," she said, slightly out of breath.

"And I didn't mean to intrude."

She regarded the hasty setup. "Oh, this is nothing. Johnny wanted to keep it small, but you and your team are part of the militia."

"No team," remarked Holt. "He's alone."

"That so?"

Carver surveyed the yard again. Victor spotted their grouping and headed over with a few members of his team. The woman with the balloons paused her work to watch. So much attention on him except from the man who mattered.

"The commander here?" he asked. "I have news."

"That's good," returned Holt, "because we need to talk."

Carver nodded. "So where is he?"

"Let's hold off on that for a sec. I have something to address first. In front of the group."

Holt spoke loudly, purposely attracting the attention of everyone in the yard and then some. A man from the barracks walked to the doorway to see what was going on.

Carver frowned. He pivoted to Johnny and Steve looking way too cocky for this not to have been planned. His alarms were going off ten times over, but he steeled his nerves. There was no way he was in immediate danger. He wasn't sure whether Sam was in on this or not, but even Holt wasn't stupid enough to attack him in front of everybody. It was too public, even amongst friends.

"That's fine," said Carver, "but why not have Commander Anderson join us? Like I said, I don't have secrets."

"You would say that, wouldn't you?" Johnny stepped in his face, skinny meth addict that he was. He snorted and sucked his teeth, swirling a loogie over his tongue.

"If anything comes out of your mouth," warned Carver, "your face will hit the ground before the spit does."

Johnny froze, unsure what to do with the ball of mucus that had aborted its flight plan. He twisted his cheeks in distaste, cleared his throat, and fought swallowing it down.

Holt pulled him out of the way before he choked himself. "Laugh it up, Vince, but we'll see who's laughing in a minute."

"We will if you ever get to the point."

His face hardened. "Fine. Is there anything you want to confess?"

"Just that I have urgent news for the commander. Is this you getting to the point?"

Carver turned to Samantha expectantly, but she was just as clueless as he was. This was Holt attempting to take charge.

"Enough with the games," commanded the deputy. "If you have something to say, say it."

Her son deflated. "Fine I said. Our friend Vince is compromised." Lorelai and Anderson exited HQ from the back door as Holt held his phone up in the air. "I have pictures of him meeting with feds."

All eyes snapped to Carver. Samantha, Anderson, and even the balloon lady understood the severity of the charge, but Holt vocalized it anyway.

"Vince Carver is a traitor."

"That's bullshit," hurried Carver, knowing he had precious seconds to appear aggrieved lest everybody believe the accusation.

"Pictures don't lie, my friend."

"If you have proof of me betraying you, I'll shoot myself in the head. That way you don't have to stage a crime scene like you did with Trent."

Holt's face went from angry to dumbfounded to enraged, all in the span of a second. His reaction was so visceral that Carver knew he was gearing up to deck him before Holt's brain did. Carver sidestepped Holt's fist, shoving the man aside, but he was far from clear. Steve latched onto him, probably assuming he was trying to run.

Carver threw a low punch into his kidney, but pulled away from the follow-through as Johnny attempted to slam the butt of his rifle into Carver's head. By twisting away, the weapon only grazed his skull and slammed into his shoulder instead. The heavy blow shoved him to a knee.

Holt spun in a fierce rage as others pointed their weapons. Carver considered pulling his. Surrounded by ten hostiles at close range, he was sure he could take at least three of them out. Going down the ranking of cocky pricks would have been easy. But there was no scenario where drawing his weapon would end bloodlessly.

He held off.

"Everybody, stand down!" shouted Anderson, running into the fray and shoving Johnny aside. Samantha pushed down her son's rifle and repeated her commander's order.

"He's working with the feds!" insisted Holt. "That is if he's not a fed himself."

"That's ridiculous," snapped Anderson.

"Is it?" Holt slinked forward. "How much do we really know about our friend Vince? Think about it."

"It *is* ridiculous," insisted Carver with ice in his veins. "I did my duty as a soldier. Lord knows I've worked for them enough in the past, but now I work for myself."

Anderson nodded, if a little unsteadily. "You see?"

"Look at the proof if you don't believe me," said Holt, brandishing the phone. The crowd closed ranks again. This time all eyes were on the small screen. "I followed him to a hotel last night."

The first images showed Carver walking across the plaza and into the Signia. Carver tried not to react at the amateur getting one over on him. That was especially hard when the photos moved indoors. Carver was easily visible sitting beside Agent Guerrero at the bar, arm around her waist. The final picture was of them entering the elevator together.

"That all you got?" challenged Carver, indignant.

"It's quite a bit," Sam shot back. "Because I see, *at best*, a security breach. At worst..." Her face darkened.

Anderson grabbed the phone and swiped back and forth before turning to Carver, face ashen. The mood of the crowd was turning.

"Just hear me out," said Carver.

"You should have mentioned this, Vince," said the commander.

"I was about to." He turned to Holt. "I told you what, four times since I got here that I wanted to talk to the commander. I have urgent news, and all you're doing is wasting time."

Anderson's brow sharpened. "What news?"

"No, no," cut in Holt. "Don't try to weasel out of this. I expect you to explain yourself."

Carver hissed. "Look, normally I'd break your jaw for

following me. I consider that an extremely disrespectful move against a fellow S2 soldier. But we don't have time for this bullshit right now so I'll tell you like it is. Yes, I was with Agent Guerrero this morning. I told you that she visited my office before—"

"And just what the fuck are you doing in a Homeland Security agent's hotel room overnight, Vince?"

Carver laughed incredulously. "Has your daddy never told you how babies are made, son?" Carver mimed holding Guerrero's waist before his and pumping his hands up and down. "Do I need to explain the mechanics of what we were doing in there?"

A few of the guys who'd been friendly with Carver chuckled, Victor among them. Holt's face reddened. Lorelai just stared at the ground, probably trying to unsee that. Carver hated for her to think he was an asshole, but he needed the guys on his side here. The alternative was a bullet.

"I don't know if you've noticed," Carver continued, "but Special Agent Guerrero, fed or not, is smoking hot. She's young, and she's lonely, and she knows what she wants."

More grins joined his side. It was a small win, but the deputy and commander still showed concern. Holt and his guys hadn't softened at all. It was time for the big guns.

Which Carver didn't feel great about. The locker-room talk in front of Lorelai was awkward, but his next betrayal was more difficult to stomach.

"I haven't just been having fun," asserted Carver, voice unintentionally picking up gravel. "I've been keeping my ears open. For us."

A spark of something lit up in Anderson's eyes.

"HSI is gearing up for something big. I don't have the full details, but I'm pretty sure they're going to raid us."

That was twice he repeated the word "us." He had to get them in the mindset that they were a team, that the enemy was someone else and they were in this together. Not only that, he had to move this along or it was all for nothing.

Carver broke away from the group. It was easy in their stunned state. He marched toward the workshop as Sam and the others hurried to keep up with him.

"Where do you think you're going?" she demanded.

"Don't you get it? They're going to be here soon. We need to move fast."

Holt jumped in his way. "We're not done with you."

It didn't take an Oscar for Carver to look annoyed. "You don't understand, I'm trying to keep all of us out of prison. The feds are on to us. They've identified the dark web marketplace." Sam was appropriately shocked by the last comment, so he turned to Anderson next. "We need to burn the maps, destroy any traces of contraband, or they'll use the full force of the law against us. And the workshop. If you don't want HSI to see what's inside, we need to clear the workshop right now."

He brushed past them again, hopped up the steps, and barged inside.

The workshop was empty. Not only of people, but of anything else. There was only a sturdy table, a bench, a few scattered stools, and the strong smell of industrial cleaner.

16

The stunned silence seemed to drag for minutes but must have only been seconds. Then, gratefully, Commander Anderson cackled.

It was a good-natured laugh, not cruel or clever but relieved. The man was genuinely happy, and he wore it on his sleeve like a military honor.

"The workshop's clear," he declared. "Ditto with the vault, the ranges, and anything incriminating in HQ."

Carver paced in a circle, unsure what to say. A cleanup job like this would've taken hours at best, and that was with all hands on deck. He turned to Anderson for explanation.

The man hiked a shoulder and coyly said, "A good commander has contingencies."

Sam, Holt, Johnny, and Victor had followed them into the workshop. The others waited outside. The tension lingered, but the hostility was gone.

"What did I say about him?" Anderson asked his deputy, a proud glint in his eye. "You swore he was here to destroy us. I promised you otherwise, and here he is, breaking the law to do his part."

Samantha's hands moved to her hips.

The commander laughed again, this time more subdued. "Vince didn't need to come here today. It's a risk for any of us to be here right now. But he used that Homeland agent for information, and he's passing it on to us." Anderson shook his head as he walked outside, waving for them to follow. "You see this, boys?" he announced. "This is what a real operative looks like!"

Victor patted Carver's back. A few others offered words of appreciation. If he wasn't one of the guys before, he was now. Of course, Holt and his buddies were pissed their little show didn't go the way they'd expected. They stormed off. To her credit, Sam was back to work directing the troops to finish various tasks.

"I want those weapons locked up!" she called out while Holt was still in earshot.

The gathering dispersed. Carver took a long breath to calm his nerves. He had narrowly avoided disaster, gained the trust of the majority, and it had cost him next to nothing. The evidence had already been removed. Which still didn't remove the sick pit in his stomach for repeating Guerrero's information.

Carver's jaw worked as he studied the commander. Anderson ordered the cleanup because he had already received intel about the raid. There was a leak in Homeland Security or the associated chain of command. That proved the militia's sponsor had legitimate access. They were either a real red cell or a real threat.

Carver converged for a private conversation. Anderson greeted him with a smile that said he now trusted Carver implicitly. It was a useful position to be in.

"That applies to you too, Vince," said the commander. "I have to ask you to secure your weapon."

Carver glanced at his hip holster. "Sure." He frowned. "About the raid—"

Before he could form the question, Anderson's phone rang.

"Yeah," he answered. "It's in process?" A beat. "Okay, then. Do like we said." He hung up and rallied the troops. "This is the real deal, gentlemen! HSI is on the premises!"

Everyone shuffled to the front yard where a convoy of white SUVs, white vans, and a drab-green BearCat rumbled in. The large armored vehicle stopped in the rear, imposing even at a distance. Its four doors and back hatch opened at once and the HSI Special Response Team filed out in tan uniforms with black helmets and vests. The SWAT tactics weren't all show, either. SRTs regularly trained with Delta and DEVGRU.

Conventional HSI agents exited the SUVs in familiar blue windbreakers. Special Agent Bentley approached the commander, warrant in hand.

The SRT troops didn't wait for the documents to be reviewed. They were trained to serve high-risk warrants as efficiently as possible, which meant hustle. They split off into teams: one toward HQ, one into the yard, and another on crowd control.

That meant them.

"Hands where we can see them!" ordered one of the agents. They closed in on the group with weapons ready.

"Gun!" warned another, training his rifle directly on Carver.

"Hold it!" called Bentley. "He's mine."

Carver didn't give anyone a reason to be nervous. He kept still, hands visible, and bit down a grimace as the special agent from New Jersey took great pleasure in relieving him of his pistol. Bentley slipped the SIG into a plastic bag.

"Per the stated terms of the search, your firearm is now confiscated by the federal government."

Carver ignored the frat-boy snicker and focused on Special Agent Guerrero exiting the SUV. Their eyes met for the briefest of seconds before she turned to the scene. He wanted to say something, but she kept her distance.

"Clear," called the SRT team leader. The agents pressed on to secure the rest of the premises. Anderson was calm, well prepared for this. It was unlikely HSI would encounter any resistance.

Bentley pounded a finger into Carver's chest. "You just don't know when to quit, do you?"

Carver licked his lips. "I don't know what you mean, Special Agent."

"My ass you don't. Keep up the stupid act. See how stupid you feel in prison."

Without waiting for a retort, Bentley shuffled away and began assigning duties to available HSI agents. They had visited the site before and had apparently rehearsed a plan of action because they were quick and knew what to do.

An entire team focused on searching HQ, rather

ungently tearing the place apart. Members of the militia funneled into the front yard where they could position themselves to watch the search, but from a distance. Only Anderson and Sam were allowed to accompany the agents throughout the property. The commander objected to the necessity of all this, but he played the part of a law-abiding citizen to a tee.

Holt sneered defiantly as he rejoined the group. Carver thought it was a dumb move to antagonize HSI. Even if S2 was untouchable right now, making a powerful enemy had long-term consequences that would one day see a reckoning. Carver wondered if he needed to take his own advice when it came to Agent Bentley.

Homeland Security moved through the property with respectable precision, and it was only twenty minutes before their cockiness began to wear thin. Soon after, anger and frustration marred their faces. They gave it another hour and some before the operation slowed down. Teams regrouped in the front yard, heated orders were repeated, and various important phone calls were made.

But no evidence was uncovered. No substation maps. No SKS carbines. No Soviet ammunition. Every firearm onsite, of which there were plenty, was legally registered. A couple of hours into the momentous HSI raid on the militia compound, not a single arrest was executed.

It was an operational disaster.

As the search wound down, the congregation of footdraggers in the front yard grew. SRT collected and packed their gear into the BearCat. Carver paced in the hot sun. He caught site of Guerrero heading toward the SUV and split off to intercept her.

"How long is this going to continue?" snapped Sam, stomping after her too. Guerrero ignored while Sam made a show of following a few yards before stopping and calling out. "This is harassment!"

The deputy had been doing a fair amount of harassing herself. While Anderson played the helpful citizen, Sam Grafton took on the role of aggrieved innocent caught in the gears of government overreach. She was making HSI pay for every minute they were in her company.

Guerrero reached her vehicle and shuffled some papers into a folder on the back seat. She noticed Carver and blew air through her bangs. "Hell of a day," she muttered.

Carver stood beside the car, at a professional distance. There were many eyes on them, but at least their conversation was private. "Sorry for not taking your advice."

"You don't have to explain yourself." She turned to him. She was firm and detached, not openly hostile but with ice in her veins. "Nothing about this makes sense. Is there anything you're not telling me?"

Carver crossed his arms over his chest. "Look, Isla, I would have mentioned if I saw something illegal. The truth is, we're just out here shooting guns."

She studied him carefully, and something in her hazel eyes softened. Then their attention turned to a black SUV entering the property.

"Great," she huffed.

Guerrero slammed the door shut and trekked over.

Carver felt slimy. He wasn't sure how else to play things, but he was losing her. Guerrero's attitude toward him felt different. Like he was on the outside now.

A short, bald guy got out of the black SUV's passenger seat. He scanned the yard, located Guerrero, and converged on her with a series of demands. Judging from his demeanor, and from Bentley's hustle from across the yard to join them, it was clear he was their direct superior. Carver wandered within earshot of their raised voices.

"Do you realize how much money this little stunt cost us?" he seethed, facial pallor going a translucent shade of purple that resembled a jellyfish. "Do you know what kind of phone calls I'm getting? You swore to me you weren't chasing your tail!"

"It's a complication, sir," replied Guerrero evenly. "But we have an inventory of weapons we can schedule for analysis—"

"That's not going to fly again, Guerrero. I gave you a lot of leeway to manage the Secret Service's mandate, but this is a stride beyond."

"There's something here," she insisted.

"All anyone's gonna be talking about tomorrow is how my department infringed the constitutional rights of a law-abiding local militia. What happened to your probable cause?"

Her lips tightened. "There's a digital trail—"

"An *anonymous* digital trail which you've been unable to validate. Let's face it: you were hoping SRT would achieve what you couldn't. Only this isn't how we break cases,

Guerrero. DHS is not the place to bruise through investigations."

Carver was surprised by how publicly he chewed her out. Federal agencies didn't usually air their dirty laundry in sight of the victims. By now, most everyone in the yard was catching on. The deputy pulled beside Carver with the flattest smile he'd ever seen.

"I've heard enough out of you," snapped the boss. He fanned his open jacket to cool off. He was dressed for an office, and Carver was willing to bet he spent ninety-nine percent of his time in one. "What's your take on this, Bentley? And no bullshit protecting-your-partner. I know you had reservations from the start. Given what you've seen today, where do we stand?"

Guerrero's partner took a breath, glanced at her, and shook his head. "Honestly? This is a dead end. Our resources are better spent elsewhere."

Guerrero didn't look betrayed. She'd known what he was going to say. They'd probably argued the point countless times already.

"Good enough for me," said their superior. "I'm pulling the plug, effective immediately. I want everyone off this property in fifteen."

"Yes sir," responded Bentley.

The boss broke away and noticed Carver and Samantha watching them. "Who's in charge here?" he asked.

"That would be me," announced the dutiful citizen, joining them. "Commander Lester Anderson, veteran of the 1st Marines." He offered his hand, and the man accepted.

"I'm ASAC Covington, sir, out of the San Jose field office, and I cannot express my regret at this inconvenience strongly enough." Covington had silver eyebrows and a barren head that emphasized overlarge ears full of fuzzy hair.

"I consider myself a patriot and a supporter of the people's government," replied Anderson. "All this is really unnecessary, however."

"At this juncture, I couldn't agree more."

Anderson nodded. "You know, I can look past an honest mistake when someone admits it. As long as the mistake isn't perpetrated for longer than required."

"Say no more, sir," assured Covington. "We're not confiscating any property, and we'll be out of your hair in time for lunch. If that's agreeable."

Anderson eyed Sam and Carver with a cool smile. "That's quite agreeable, sir. Quite agreeable."

Covington turned to Sam and Carver. Head on, the ASAC has scraggly black hairs protruding from his nostrils too. The man had never met a manicure kit he liked. "Sorry for the trouble," he grumbled.

Amazingly, Sam held her tongue as he returned to his vehicle and left.

Covington had said fifteen, but he got ten. Once he was long gone, the rest of his department was eager to follow. Guerrero was dejected and avoided Carver's gaze. Bentley didn't have the same problem. With everyone else loaded up, he trudged over to the undercover operator.

"You know," he started, voice gruff but introspective, "I

don't get you. You have a commendable military record. A worthwhile career. You're not like the rest of these guys."

Sam and the others were listening, but Bentley didn't hide his contempt for them.

"HSI is here as a favor to the Secret Service, doing our best to make sure everything is smooth for the president's visit, yet you don't have a care in the world." The special agent leaned close, though he didn't have the heart or energy for intimidation. Instead he watched Carver with disappointment and asked, "Where's your sense of duty, soldier?"

Carver ground his teeth as Bentley jumped behind the wheel and joined the line of departing vehicles.

17

Carver was at his office the next morning, locked in, alone, and not sure what to do with himself. With the increased federal scrutiny, Anderson had ordered everyone out of the compound for "realignment," whatever that meant. Despite the vague nomenclature, staying away was a sensible security measure, even if Homeland Security had come away from the raid with nothing.

Well... next to nothing would be more precise. It turned out the only personal property HSI hadn't returned was Carver's SIG Sauer P320. Coming from Bentley, it was not so much an oversight as an overt slight.

As far as anything else still missing, the CIA ranked at the top. If Williams was curious about the raid, she hadn't made contact. For better or worse, she didn't want to put Carver in danger and was prioritizing caution. He had only himself to blame for letting Holt follow him a couple nights before.

Carver's many ruminations were interrupted by a call from Guerrero. He went into the front lobby hoping to see her arriving outside. They hadn't spoken the night before and skipped their rendezvous at the Signia. He was eager to talk in person, but she wasn't waiting at his window. Carver picked up.

"Isla." He stopped there. He hadn't actually worked out what to say.

"It's a mess, Vince."

"What's is?"

She sighed. "I know you don't like talking about work, but it's who I am. I've fought hard to get here."

"The raid is a setback," he conceded. "Nothing more."

"It's a lot worse than that."

He wanted to reassure her somehow. Play up the silver lining. "So what if you don't get them on illegal weapons charges? Something bigger will come along."

"This is as big as it gets, Vince. The dark web marketplace is a clearinghouse for military-grade equipment. The transactions are anonymized, but I've identified radar components with S2 fingerprints on them."

"Radar?"

Carver hadn't come upon anything like that. Radar wasn't the type of thing used for hitting unsecured substations, it was for attacking and fending off armies. Guerrero must be figuring S2 was a weapons-dealing operation, buying and selling on the dark web. It was a viable business model. There were a lot of Russians and Ukrainians who desperately needed anything they could get, not to mention plenty of growing unrest in Africa to profit from.

But S2 didn't seem a good fit for such an international operation.

Which perhaps explained the biggest unknown—the militia's sponsor. If he wasn't running a red cell, he had another long-term motivation for the substation attacks. Was it all just a front? Anderson a levelheaded businessman, making foreign deals abroad while courting radicalized civilians who like to take potshots at the power grid?

Carver didn't like it. The size and scale of things didn't line up. His silence extended long enough to jar Guerrero from her despair.

"God, I shouldn't have said so much," she muttered. "No wonder I'm being suspended."

Carver snapped back to reality himself. "You're what?"

"Are you surprised?"

"They can't do that. So what if the digital trail is unsubstantiated? You made one bad call."

"Bentley thinks I'm compromised."

Carver blinked. "You've worked together five years."

"Closer to four, but it's what he thinks. He won't say it outright, but I can read it on his face. He's been acting differently since this whole business with S2 started. He brushed off the digital angle, tried to steer me away from the raid. Now he's giving me the cold shoulder." She sniffed, and he realized she'd been crying. "I just... I don't know what he thinks I did."

The pangs of guilt hit Carver hard. Guerrero had warned him about the raid in advance, and he had attempted to use that information to warn them.

Luckily for his conscience, the militia had known about it without his intervention. But his indiscretion was still a tangible fact. It had happened, and he wondered if Guerrero suspected as much. Just as she'd read Bentley's face, he had read hers as she was leaving the compound.

"You didn't do anything..." he mumbled, but the encouragement trailed off as weakly as it started.

If Guerrero hadn't done anything, who had?

Someone was lying. And Carver couldn't tell her because word would find its way to S2.

He had to isolate the leak. If Bentley was in on the plot, getting Guerrero suspended would be a clever way to deflect suspicion from him. But then it could have been anyone, including the ASAC, or the ASAC's boss. There were a hundred other people in the chain of command from multiple agencies who could have tipped off Anderson. It was premature to conclude it was anyone. The only thing Carver was sure of was to be careful who he trusted.

The locked glass door rattled in its frame. It turned out Carver did have an office guest, it was just the wrong one. Anderson knocked before peering through the glass and spotting him.

"Um... Isla?"

She sniffled again. "Yes?"

Carver winced. "I'm really sorry. I have to go."

"Vince?"

"I'm sorry." He ended the call and unlocked the front door. "Lester, I wasn't expecting you."

The commander stepped inside. "You closed for business?"

"Given the state of things, I figured a little time off was

called for. You know, realignment."

"So Nick and Juliette?"

"Below the radar. You don't need to worry about them."

Anderson nodded as he leaned against the front counter, hands in pockets. "I don't mean to pry. I know you above anyone else will be on top of OPSEC. That's not why I'm here."

Carver glanced into the parking lot to confirm Anderson had come alone. He put his hands in his pockets to mirror the man's casual demeanor. "No problem, Lester. What's up?"

"I wanted to thank you again, one on one. The fact you were willing to come to me, well, that told me a lot about you. I wasn't kidding when I said I needed someone like you around. Someone to watch my back. Someone to look after Lorelai."

It was apparent the commander's casual posture was not reflective of the subject. "What are we talking about here?" Carver asked.

Anderson mulled over the question before saying, "Nothing." He stood straighter. "I'm here this morning as your commander, Vince. The compound's shut down. From this point forward, no personnel will meet or coordinate there. We're a go the day after tomorrow."

It took a second to sink in. "A go for what, Lester?"

"It's commander, Vince."

"You mean to go ahead with the substation attacks under this kind of heat?"

"It's been decided. There's no going back and there'll be

no objections. I'm your superior officer and I expect you to obey my orders to the fullest extent."

Carver watched him for a moment, and then sighed quietly. "Yes sir."

Anderson gave a curt nod. "Good. In two days, everyone will attack their target as planned. This will be a coordinated strike at 3:20 pm. Discrete teams will have no further inter-communication. We will not meet the day of or afterward. This is the real deal."

Except it suddenly seemed anything but real. S2, setting up shop on the dark web, running with activated cell structures. This was sophisticated domestic terrorism in the United States.

"Understood, sir," was all he said.

"Tomorrow is the staging day. You will make all necessary preparations with your team to ensure things run smoothly until you complete your objective. Holt will pick you up at 8 am sharp. I trust you can take it from there."

Carver witnessed the determination in Anderson's eyes, but he saw something else too. The inevitability of it, the nihilism. The commander couldn't have called this off even if he wanted to.

"You can count on me, sir," said Carver.

"I know I can," replied Anderson.

They shook hands.

* * *

Carver was, if anything, a consummate professional. As an asset, he was pivotally placed, and the stakes were growing in importance. He resolved to get through the next day without a hitch.

Shaw and Morgan locked up the office at two minutes till eight. Holt pulled up in an old white panel van they had never seen before. Everybody wore plainclothes. Left behind were any and all phones, smart devices, and trackers so there would be no GPS or network record of their locations. Even though Carver's team was op ready, Holt made a show of double-checking. He ran down the checklist until he was satisfied, and they all climbed into the back of the van.

"How about a little breakfast to set some ground rules?" suggested Holt.

"Already ate," said Carver.

"Coffee then."

Carver returned a shrug. "It's your show."

The team went to an unassuming little diner on the outskirts of Coyote, the type that most people see but don't think twice about. Being witnessed together in public was a risk, but people here seemed to mind their own business. There were no security cameras or surrounding storefronts to complicate matters. The seven of them took two tables along the back wall and settled in.

Johnny was tatted up with a spiked leather bracelet and belt, going for the rock star look but only getting as far as druggie. Steve was stocky like a wrestler, with thinning hair and a trimmed beard. Beau was the hardest to read because he was inward and quiet by nature. In stark contrast, Holt led them around with gung ho pride, smoothing his blond buzz cut and squeezing jokes through a ten-dollar smile.

It was a lot to bear, but Carver and his team got through it like good little soldiers. As breakfast wound down, Carver excused himself to the back hall where two single-room bathrooms were demarcated by an ancient pay phone. He strode to the door at the end and checked the exterior lot. The cracked asphalt was populated by a dumpster, a couple of parked trucks, and an overturned plastic crate orbited by a smattering of cigarette butts. On the way back inside, he peeked into the small kitchen to find line cooks tending the flattop. Carver returned to the table just as Holt was paying the bill.

"Big day tomorrow," the XO coolly announced. "Which means a lot of work today. Might as well get to it."

Carver couldn't agree more. They took the van one stop down the highway to a busy cross street. Past a gas station and some warehouses, Johnny turned into a public storage facility. They stopped at a check-in booth with a swing-down gate and an actual, live security attendant. After scanning a key card, the guard lifted the gate and waved them past.

So this was where S2 had stashed all their contraband in preparation of the raid. Carver had half a mind to report it to Guerrero to get her reinstated, but it was only a passing thought. The mission came first. He would deal with the collateral damage later.

They parked at the end of a string of road-facing storage

units with wide rolling service doors.

"Get the lock, would you?" said Holt.

Johnny said "yup" and pulled the keys from the ignition.

"Now, it's gonna be tight back here," explained Holt, opening both back doors of the van. "It's just for a minute until we get to the safe house. I want everybody carrying their share, got it?"

The team nodded and followed Holt just as Johnny bent down to put a key to a heavy-duty Master Lock.

"Not that one," snapped the XO, putting his boot against Johnny's backside and shoving him toward the next unit.

Johnny cursed under his breath and moved ten feet over while Holt kneeled down. Carver caught the lock clicking back into place. A jiggle of keys later and Johnny was rolling up the next unit's door. The team moved into the medium-sized room. It was maybe eight by twenty. Stacked against the wall were the same weapon crates Carver had seen at the compound and some empty duffel bags. Other equipment they didn't need was there too. The militia had rounded up anything and everything that had a whiff of impropriety.

"Keep watch, honey," Holt said to Morgan.

She sharpened an eyebrow but skipped the rejoinder and followed orders. The rest of them packed just enough SKS carbines and ammunition to complete the mission. Beau checked over two small cases that housed the components of a consumer quadcopter.

"These aren't all the guns," noted Carver, wondering if they had a problem.

Holt shook his head. "Victor and Davie beat us here. They got an early start because they have longer to travel."

"No breakfast for them," laughed Johnny.

That meant the individual cells were already armed and proceeding to their targets. The wheels were in motion.

Carver figured as much, but said, "I thought maybe the rest of the guns were in the other unit." Holt stared at him blankly and Carver pointed. "Next-door."

Holt snorted. "Nah, it's just the one. Johnny's an idiot."

Carver nodded like it was nothing, though he was sure he'd see that lock click back into place. S2 had a key for it, which meant it was their unit too. The secrecy only added to his curiosity.

The last item on their Christmas list was a single red cylinder modified for use as a drone payload. The M14 incendiary grenade is an anti-materiel munition meant to cause structural damage, with a thermate reaction that can burn through steel. Beau carefully secured it and they were on their way.

Carver was almost disappointed. At this point he had crossed off two of his case officer's three objectives. Date of the attack and the type of payload used. This was progress but only scratched the surface.

The next stop was a residence near the Metcalf substation. The short-term rental was booked anonymously over the internet for the whole week, with enough padding before and after the attack to keep nosy parties away. The ranch-style home had a driveway leading to a rear garage with high cinder-block walls lining the property. They had plenty of privacy to break the equipment down and make plans.

Carver went through the motions, handling what needed to be done while his mind was somewhere else. Like a Vegas bookie, he measured the odds of the militia being a legitimate red cell versus an arms-dealing outfit. Every rundown ended with more questions than answers. If S2's sponsor made money by selling military arms, why risk exposure with localized terror attacks?

The hypotheticals didn't add up. Yet this, right here, right now, was anything but hypothetical. These attacks were happening. And if Carver couldn't get in touch with the CIA in time, he was going to need to stop them himself.

Over the course of the day, Carver engaged in small talk to gather what information he could. Other times he kept his mouth shut and listened. He learned that Sam was lying low with Lorelai and some others, but not the commander. Anderson was left without a group, likely to coordinate the big picture, whether out of the compound or another undisclosed location. His part in this whole thing was a bit of a mystery. If anybody knew what he was up to, they weren't saying.

The afternoon consisted of a drive-by and walk-through of the target site. They knew the locations, but smoothing out the timing was important. When the day was finally done, Johnny dropped them off back at the office park, just as if they had all gone out for a movie.

Holt walked out with them. "Be ready at noon tomorrow," he said, slapping a hand on Carver's shoulder.

"Now, Vince, you and I have had our differences, but it's go time."

Carver nodded. "We have, and it is."

"Good. I know you excel at these situations, and I'm excited to finally work with you." Holt's grin was infuriating, even when he was giving a compliment. "I'm expecting your best out there."

18

Carver didn't wait for the morning. He did a little planning, a little prep, and, after evening hit, headed back to the public storage lot. He lacked access credentials to drive past the gate. Under other circumstances he might have rented a new unit to gain access, but the office was closed for the night.

Still, watching the storage unit from his pickup parked across the highway, Carver decided it didn't matter. The iron fence was high but lacked razor wire, and the adjacent lot provided ample privacy from which to breach. The main problem wasn't the perimeter itself, or the guard for that matter, but the few customers currently unloading items near his chosen entry point.

Waiting in the Ram, Carver listened as an NPR affiliate replayed a story about Ukrainian soldiers navigating the grueling conditions of trench warfare with modern drones. It was a sympathy piece. An information campaign designed to steady the American public for a long and slow war of attrition.

The truth was the American people didn't much care. That wasn't to say they were heartless. It was more that the conflict was so distant in both territory and consciousness that it was difficult to describe to the average worker why it was their business at all.

The United States military and its NATO partners had a very different take on the matter. This invasion had given them the bargain of a lifetime. For the expenditure of pocket change and zero American lives, they could expend generations of stockpiled munitions to destroy generations of Russian armor. All the ordnance of the Cold War was finally going hot, and the inferno of gunpowder and metal was continent shattering.

The radio piece inevitably veered into politics. That was the purpose of an information campaign. It touched on the strong bipartisan support for Ukraine, but highlighted the dangers of the West growing complacent. This wasn't bound to be an issue under President Diaz. When the leader of the free world finds dual-party support for their policies both foreign and domestic, it's hard to stop them.

Finally, Carver's patience was rewarded. The last customers on the storage lot hauled away a trailer with four Jet Skis. After a few minutes of inactivity, he shut off the truck, waited for a car to speed past, and hurried across the street holding a rolled-up rubber welcome mat. He made his way through the adjacent property to the darkened area equidistant between two light posts.

The vertical bars of the iron gate were designed to foil attempts at scaling, but Carver made quick work of them, even with the welcome mat over his shoulder. The top bar featured sheer spikes. Laying the rubber mat over them allowed him to easily roll over and drop to the bottom on the other side.

At the storage unit, Carver palmed a few lockpicking instruments he had looked up on YouTube. He'd identified the Magnum Master Lock earlier and now knew exactly what was needed to overcome it. He set the turning tool into the bottom of the keyway and applied pressure with his thumb. Then he went to work picking the single pins with a hook tool. The Lockpicking Lawyer was right about Master Locks. While it wasn't as easy as the video made it look, in a handful of minutes the latch clicked loose.

Carver rolled the door up halfway, ducked into the dark room, and clicked on a tac light to illuminate several covered objects. Sliding the drape off one exposed a pair of stacked crates. They were desert-colored, nearly six-feet long, and made of hardened plastic banded with military identifiers.

He snapped pictures with his phone before swinging the lid open to reveal a long tan cylinder and assembly. It resembled tube artillery, but Carver had a different idea. The packout was similar to the Switchblade launchers used by the Army, though this was larger and longer than the loitering munitions he'd seen in operation. He took pictures from opposite angles.

Before digging deeper, Carver peeked outside to confirm he was clear. Then, instead of checking the bottom crate, he undraped another stack. These boxes were black and contained a small radar dish, a laptop control unit, and what looked like an infrared camera on a gimbal. The pieces were modular and disassembled and difficult to identify, though they had signs of aftermarket alterations. Sanded paint, welded joints, and other work that could be accomplished with an angle grinder and other hand tools. Carver took more pictures, focusing on the markings.

This was it. This was everything Guerrero was looking for, and possibly what Trent had stumbled on. These systems were definitely not for civilian use. Yet they also hardly represented the makings of a weapons-dealing empire. If this was a smuggling operation, S2 was only in possession of a handful of components.

Carver worked his jaw and considered the red cell angle again. A single drone would make a good test. A proof of concept. It didn't make a robust business, but maybe the business would follow.

He absently checked outside again and turned back to the crates before doing a double take. Carver shut off the tac light and kneeled by the door. A black van had pulled up to the guard gate. It wasn't the same model Johnny drove, but it did share other notable similarities. Old, private, nondescript. The kind of thing that screamed eighties, with a weathered antenna at the base of the hood that cricked sideways at the top. Carver tensed when he zeroed in on the driver through the large windshield. It was Sam. The deputy was here for her military supplies, and she wasn't alone.

He drew his gun and the inched the door lower. Then he shut the crates, drew the drapes over them again, and hurried back to the entrance to check on their approach.

Carver had a split-second decision to make. The man in

the van's passenger seat spoke to someone in the back. If this team was anything like Holt's, it could be a full house in there. Carver bet there were four of them, at least.

But he possessed the element of surprise. Attacking unsuspecting targets was a decisive tactical advantage that he could put to maximum effect. His backup weapon, a Maxim 9 with an integrated suppressor, was the perfect choice for this kind of wetwork. Then again, once he went against Sam, the whole game was over. She might not reveal who S2 was working for. She might not even know. Or she could get killed in the firefight, which would altogether alleviate the usefulness of an interrogation.

"Shit."

If Carver rolled the door down and waited, they would notice it was unlocked. They would be ready for anything, maybe even weapons-free. The risk-reward calculation was plummeting.

The militia scanned in and the attendant waved them on. Carver bit down as he made up his mind. He rolled under the door and shut it from the outside. He hastily clicked the lock down and scurried away as headlights flared over the driveway. Planting his back against the far corner of the next building, he listened as his quarry went to work.

"That one too," ordered Sam.

After a twenty-count, Carver risked a peek. Both units were open. Six militia members, Lorelai among them. Going in hot wasn't an option.

But following them was. And seeing what the deputy's secret team was up to could lead to the answers he needed.

Carver eyed the rubber welcome mat on the fence.

It was in view of the militia, which meant inaccessible to him for the moment. But the spikes weren't that dangerous and getting out elsewhere was worth the pain. He crept along the building's edge to the next lane of storage units. A crew of workers loaded tools into their truck not fifteen feet away. Carver had to wait for them to leave or risk causing a scene and being exposed.

The deputy ran a tight ship, though. After only a few minutes, the militia rolled down the service doors and loaded back into the van. Sam idled forward, coming toward Carver instead of making a U-turn. The lot didn't have anything in the way of cover, so he pressed against the dark wall and ducked as the van drove right by him. It looped past the work crew and headed for the exit.

Carver bolted toward the welcome mat. He scaled over the fence and sprinted to the highway. Sam's van was already at the gate. He grimaced as one, two, three cars passed. Then he sped across the wide street to his truck.

Just as he opened the door, red and blue strobes lit him up. A police cruiser slowed to a stop beside him, middle of the lane, window rolled down.

"Sorry," hurried Carver.

"You can't park there," admonished the officer.

"I'm sorry," he said again. "I was just leaving."

"Hold on."

Carver glanced at Sam's van, blinker on, waiting to turn onto the highway headed away from him. "Officer, I only stopped a second. I can be out of here—"

"Sir," intoned the officer with authority, "I need you to cool your jets. Do you have a license and registration for that vehicle?"

"I do but—"

"Don't worry. If everything checks out, this will be quick. Wait right there."

The officer threw the cruiser into reverse and pulled behind his truck on the swale. The moment dragged as he punched the pickup's plate number into his computer. Sam's van turned onto the highway.

Carver considered evasive action, but escaping police in a state that liked to televise high-speed chases was the opposite of covert. Plus, he lived here. There was nothing to do but lean on his pickup with a wince and watch the best lead he had recede into a sea of tail lights.

True to his word, the police officer made it snappy. Seven minutes later he handed Carver his license back with a warning. Busy highways like this have a lot of wide trucks coming through. There was no stopping here for a reason. That kind of thing, with a have a nice night at the end.

Unfortunately, a nice night wasn't in the cards. Carver spent a chunk of it attempting to reacquire Sam's van, but it was impossible to know where they had gone. His best bet was due north, so he jumped on the freeway, hit the gas, and weaved through traffic at full speed, risking a ticket again in the off chance he would catch up to criminals dutifully obeying the speed limit.

Sometimes you get lucky. This wasn't one of those times. After thirty minutes of fruitless pursuit, Carver turned the truck around and headed home empty-handed.

Empty-handed but not empty-headed. He did come away with new intelligence, at least. And he still had friends in the military machine. A few phone calls, some open source internet research, and Carver should have a better idea of what the equipment now in Sam's vehicle was built to do.

19

It all came down to payload.

It was noon, Carver waited outside the office with his team, he was operating on limited sleep, and all he could think about was payload.

His search of the storage unit had been interrupted. He didn't get the time he would have liked to examine the components, but he did manage to identify the familiar tube overnight. It was a Switchblade, but an upgraded model developed just a few years ago, after his exit from the military.

The Switchblade 600 was a man-portable loitering munition. It packed a much heavier punch than its smaller cousin meant for soft targets. With the recent explosion of Ukraine aid and quick-ramping of Switchblade manufacturing, S2 had somehow found a way to smuggle them.

"Here they come," called Morgan, making her way back to the walkway.

The white panel van turned into the parking lot and coasted through the lanes to meet them. Carver glanced at the cell phone in his hand. So much for giving Williams until the literal last second to reach out.

Shaw trudged to his side. "We still on?" he asked under his breath.

"We're still on."

Carver's phone buzzed. He had reached out the night before, but the late hour proved imposing and he met with limited success. Now a Lieutenant Colonel in the Army was finally calling him back.

"Late as always, Howie," Carver answered.

Howie's real name was Dave, last name Howser. Being a hard-ass military instructor, Howser became Howitzer, which select friends granted the honor shortened to Howie.

"Where'd you get those pictures, Vince?" came the familiar gruffness.

"I told you. I'm helping out with inventory after that mess of a pullout in Afghanistan."

"Civilians aren't supposed to have access to that kind of materiel."

"First thing, the military is more and more relying on the services of the private sector. I provide a valuable service. You should look into it."

"What's the second thing?"

"The second is that I don't have access. There's nothing to worry about. I'm just going through pictures and making classifications to move the process along."

The panel van stopped at the curb and Holt exited the back doors.

"Buy me a few seconds," said Carver to Shaw.

The former SEAL nodded and moved to intercept Holt.

"Well, let's see," continued Howie. "Your initial assessments are partly correct, but partly wrong."

"How so?"

Holt watched expectantly over Shaw's shoulder. Carver put a single finger up before unlocking his pickup and perching inside for privacy. The sun was bearing down and the cabin was stuffy, but as Carver rested on his seat, Holt loitered in the rearview mirror. Carver shut the door and pushed the ignition twice to put the truck into run mode without the engine. He cranked the AC to max as Howie set him straight.

"You properly categorized some components as ECM," he said, referring to electronic countermeasures, "but you misidentified the camera. That's a directional infrared countermeasure unit. Its integrated processor aims a laser turret at incoming missiles, overwhelming the IR missile seeker."

"It's an anti-missile system for a drone?"

"That's the thing that stood out to me. DIRCM class systems are meant for protecting large military aircraft. They're not designed for drones."

"But they'll work."

"I suppose."

Between the loud AC fan and yesterday's NPR station playing, it was difficult to hear. Carver turned down the radio so he could focus on figuring this out.

"There's more," said Howie. "The other electronic warfare devices are fairly straightforward, but there's a subtlety to their classification. Electronic countermeasures are a form of electromagnetic attack, but they're often utilized in a defensive posture. Think signal jamming."

"Or a laser turret confusing a missile."

"Exactly. But some of your components have a subtle overlap. They're not electronic countermeasures, they're electronic counter-countermeasures. Not ECM but ECCM."

Carver cut through the military's love of acronyms and boiled it down. "Defense against electronic attacks."

"That's right. Electronic protection. But just like electronic attacks are used defensively, electronic protection is used offensively. It's confusing, but take that spread spectrum unit in your picture. Standard procedure to counter drones is to sever its command-and-control signal with an RF attack. That's your ECM. So you equip the drone with ECCM. The spread spectrum counter-jams the jammer, preserving your drone's C2 signal and allowing for the successful completion of its mission."

"Defense that preserves attack capability." Carver eyed the mirror again. Holt impatiently paced and occasionally berated Shaw, no doubt harping about Carver's nonprofessionalism.

"Okay, Howie, is that all you have for me?"

The lieutenant colonel laughed. "Is that all? No thanks? No offer to buy me drinks next time you're in town?"

"You always have both of those. You know that. I'm just a little preoccupied right now. Rain check?"

"Sure, sure," said Howie. He had a hard reputation but was agreeable with the soldiers he respected. "Hey, Vince, are you in a tight spot or something?"

The man was also shrewd. Which was why his insight was invaluable. He could take what looked like one thing and make it into the opposite. ECM into ECCM. Gruff into agreeable. Dave into Howie. But Carver had to do the same thing and make all of this seem like nothing.

"I'll tell you what, Howie. Next time I see you, I'll pick up the tab for the whole night and give you the gory details. Right now I got to get back to it."

"I can't complain about that. Until that time, Vince."

"Until that time."

Carver ended the call thinking about electronic warfare and electronic counter-countermeasures. The realization supported the idea that these weapons were being sold to the belligerent of a foreign conflict. Nobody had need of ECCM unless they were going after somebody with ECM. That meant military, and that meant soldiers.

Carver shut off the truck and sat idly, playing catch-up in his mind while the AC died down and the radio continued to play at the lowered volume. The system was mostly off but retained limited functionality because he hadn't opened his door yet. It was noon so NPR was covering the top news stories of the day. The market was down almost a whole percent, tech company employees were organizing a union vote, and President Diaz was primed and ready for his big Silicon Valley speech at three o'clock Pacific Daylight Time.

Blood flooded Carver's head as the story discussed the technology arm of the president's "Strength at Home" initiative. The closure of tax loopholes discouraged extradition of American technology to China. Tax incentives would fund domestic production and pipelines. STEM education, vocational training, jobs. Washington was investing heavily in domestic industry and Big Tech, and the administration was making a spectacle of it in the heart of San Francisco. "Technological security is national security" was the president's sound bite, but all Carver could think about was the timing.

3 pm. San Francisco. Today.

The schedule was set to kick off right before the planned substation attacks. Homeland Security was investigating possible threats to the White House visit, and their scrutiny of S2 had hit the mark dead on.

The power outages were a coordinated effort to douse excitement for the president's stimulus announcement. The event headlined the leader of the free world postulating on technological security in the epicenter of the tech industry, and it would be punctuated by a citywide blackout. Nothing could be more embarrassing. If that wasn't a shot across the bow, Carver didn't know what was.

Holt knocked loudly on his window and opened the door, cutting the battery power to the radio.

"What the hell are you doing in here?"

Carver placed his phone in the center console and exited the vehicle. "Just finishing up."

"Who were you talking to?"

"None of your business."

"I'm your XO. Everything's my business."

Carver patiently stared him in the eye. "Listen, it's personal, so it's not your business. If it had anything to do with the militia, or the op, or law enforcement, or *anything*, I'd let you know. But it doesn't. It's personal, and it's going to stay that way."

Holt's eye contact tripped up after only a few seconds. His gaze flitted to where Carver had dropped his phone. Perhaps in an attempt to save face, he said, "Fine, but I have to search you."

"Search me for what?"

"You don't have any extra phones or devices? No firearms? Nothing traceable?"

"I know the operational parameters," he said, but he allowed Holt to pat him down all the same.

"No firearms?"

"You asked that already."

"And you didn't answer."

Carver sighed. "No firearms."

The power trip itself wasn't out of place. It was that Holt was so much concerned than the day before. This from the guy who had snuck a pistol himself. Maybe it was projection. Or maybe it was payback for Carver sitting in the Ram and making them wait.

"So you're ready then?" asked Holt, stepping away.

Carver shut the door and clicked it locked. "Now I am."

"Great. Let's load up."

Carver noticed Holt waited for them to get in first. It felt odd, half like a game of chicken and half like they were prisoners, but they were all operating under the same parameters. Nobody had weapons that he saw. Carver headed to the van while flashing Morgan and Shaw a look of warning. It was just a vibe, but it communicated a whole lot in a passing second. That was the purpose of body language. Stone-age instant messaging. It got everybody on the same page, often without conscious realization it was happening. Body language wasn't about the details but the generalities. Awareness. Carver had news. Something was going down. Keep your guard up.

"About time," carped Johnny as they climbed into the back. His head craned around the driver's seat, watching them with a wicked set of clenched teeth, like he was strung out. Steve silently stared at Beau, who silently stared at his shoes. So much for a welcome.

Carver didn't like imagining what these boys got up to without Anderson's calming influence around. But again, he didn't spot any immediate threats. Everybody was a little on edge, probably because they had a job to do. Nerves were only soothed with experience, and the combined amount in this van, without Carver's team, was laughable.

Despite the impending objectives, their timeline was sufficiently relaxed. They had a few hours to gear up, drive ten minutes away, and get into already prepared positions. And maybe the schedule wasn't the only thing that needed to relax. Holt made a command-level decision to return to the same diner for breakfast part deux. It was one of his better ideas.

The full van bobbed on its loose suspension as quiet unease persisted among the passengers. The silence suited

Carver, because he was still thinking about Strength at Home.

A stimulus announcement was a decidedly odd choice of event to disrupt. Granted, Big Tech was an easy punching bag. For both parties. The Left takes issue with corporate overreach and abuse, and the Right opposes control by big-city elites. Bridging these differences was what made the Diaz-Bennett ticket so unstoppable in an otherwise contentious political climate.

Alex Diaz was a strong-willed young go-getter with a Hispanic father and an infectious smile. He always had a clever response locked and loaded, but rarely did he take aim at his political opponents. His debates were something else. Instead of getting into the mud with the pigs, he moved the pigpen to the grassy lawn. Instead of ranting, he affably rapped about the big picture, like a conversation at a hot dog cookout between friends passing beers. It felt personal, and genuine. And if he was perhaps too much of an idealist, he tempered that by surrounding himself with a staff that aggressively attacked downstream problems.

Exhibit A was Vice President Elizabeth Bennett. She came from a traditional northeastern family. Far from a soft and smiling personality, she was known as a viciously effective prosecutor. One who had eschewed politics her entire career, choosing to do the hard work instead of seeking out the glowing praise. Not nearly as charismatic as Diaz, but in a way that was her value. Her no-nonsense approach set the standard for the rest of the administration. It was a match made in Heaven, and, after years of escalating political cage matches in the national dialog, the American people were amazingly receptive.

So if this wasn't about politics, maybe it was about business.

But which business was that exactly? Because, from where Carver was sitting, he saw two profitable enterprises: arms dealing and government stimulus. Illegal weapons were endlessly in demand. The rub was the supply, as in where S2 was sourcing military components.

Stimulus was a different operation altogether, in that it was charitable and altruistic, at least on its face. Backroom deals would compromise ideal goals, as they always did. But S2 wasn't promoting the stimulus, they were shutting it down. Metaphorically. That wasn't about making money but suppressing it. Raining on the president's parade in San Francisco would have a damaging effect on business, depending on the actors involved. There was, of course, money to be made too. Every tragedy is an opportunity.

The trick was identifying the opportunity crossover of smuggling weapons and power grid blackouts. Those two lines formed an X, and at the center was his answer.

20

They took the same two tables as before, and the diner was just about as empty.

"Look at us," crowed Johnny, getting comfortable with his back against the wall. "A proper crew."

"Proper would include Chuck," grumbled Steve beside him.

"Amen to that," said Holt. "But let's not sell our new friends short. They've carried out their duties admirably. I'd buy a round of drinks but it's hydration and caffeination only this morning."

Steve's mouth cracked in dry amusement. "Maybe we'll have a party tonight. The new team with the old, sharing drinks over the pitfire."

"Maybe," said Holt noncommittally.

"OPSEC dictates we split up," noted Morgan.

"He doesn't mean tonight literally," said Holt. "Just after everything calms down."

A different waitress took their order today. She was young and unsure of the menu. It was waters and coffees all around, except for Shaw who had a cosmopolitan streak. He ordered tea with a spot of milk, how they did in Europe, and his expression dared anyone to call him less a man. The rest of the ordering slowed to a crawl. At least for the other side of the table.

Carver didn't eat much when he worked. It was a common trait among special operations forces. Digesting food expended energy and slowed you down. As long as you were well nourished and your action plan was in the time span of hours rather than days, it was better to go without a heavy meal. Morgan ordered toast with jam, and Carver and Shaw stuck to liquid.

"That's all you want?" pressed Johnny. "We're pre-celebrating."

"We'll celebrate when the job's done," said Shaw.

"Come on, live a little. Don't you want some eggs or bacon or something?"

"Leave it alone, Johnny," said Steve.

Johnny snorted in their direction, eyes dark, like they were spoiling his fun. "Hell of a last supper," he muttered.

Holt smacked him on the shoulder. "Would you stop being a dumbass for once?" The XO worked his jaw and added, "It's bad luck."

"I'm just saying is all."

"That's the problem," intoned Steve.

Johnny dutifully unrolled his silverware wrap and nobody said much of anything for a minute.

The table continued the weird vibes of the van. Here they were, the day of the attack, and this team was too adversarial with itself. The battle lines were drawn. There was Carver and his two versus Holt and his two, with Beau the lone drone operator caught somewhere in the middle, but likely leaning with the legacy S2 members just out of habit. Judging by his quiet discomfort it was even more likely he didn't want to be here at all.

This breakfast was meant to cool nerves, but Carver preferred to cool heads. The best way to accomplish that was by talking, finding common ground. And if the conversation also inadvertently bumped against actionable intelligence, Carver would be receptive to that too.

After the waitress dropped off their drinks and left he said, "This feels like the mess on the first day of basic," which only half caught their interest, so he drilled deeper. "You served, Holt, didn't you?"

"Still do in fact," answered the XO. "I was three years active in the National Guard, but it's an eight-year contract. I'm on reserve."

"Keeps you sharp?"

"If I'm honest, not as much as I'd like. I do most of my own training these days at the compound."

"I hear that. People think discipline is taught, but it isn't. What your parents and superior officers drill into you is order. Discipline is when you take ownership of that order to shape yourself."

Holt appraised Carver with a grunt, not overtly agreeing but at least seeming to view him in a different light. Carver had his attention, so he studied the others at the table. Johnny was next up and avoiding his gaze. That was because he had never enlisted in anything in his life. Steve watched without saying much. He was confident in his answer but wasn't the type to boast. The waitress returned to top off Beau, who over the last minute had given his full attention to his coffee, and after finishing it had been intently staring at the empty mug. Beau was nervous, no doubt about it.

"You must be thirsty or tired or both," joked the waitress. "Either way, this'll do you, honey."

Beau barely mustered a thanks before she returned to the kitchen.

"You've ever done work like this?" Carver asked him.

"Steve served," interrupted Holt. "In the Army, like you."

The stocky man dipped his head once. Steve was a man of few words, like Beau, but for entirely different reasons. Carver got the feeling he didn't like them much.

"You deploy?" Morgan asked.

"Kabul," he said.

Morgan's brows went up. "You probably have stories."

"Mostly about how much money the US taxpayer wasted propping up an army that only existed on paper."

"It would have only been surprising if it had worked," remarked Shaw. Then, in a rare moment of introspection from the southerner, he added, "It's good to get overseas, though. On a personal level. See the world from a different angle."

Steve didn't reply for or against. Tough crowd.

Shaw checked everyone's faces for agreement and didn't get what he was after. "What?" he prodded. "You don't think so?"

"I don't think about it at all."

Steve's expression was blank, but it wasn't empty. It was cold and detached. Dangerous. There they were, getting adversarial again.

"No worries," appeased Carver. "I didn't think about that shit when I was your age either. What are you, twenty-five?"

"Twenty-seven."

"The man speaks," said Shaw, which may have been counterproductive. But clipped answers were better than wordy dodges.

Carver nodded. "Fine, twenty-seven. And I don't mean offense. The truth is, Steve, I'm a lot like you. Talk when you have something important to say, keep an eye on things when you don't. It's a trait that has got me out of a lot of sticky situations."

"Yeah?"

"Yeah. I can tell you're a survivor. And I'm good at reading people."

He watched Carver like a mouse might a snake. Cautious, trapped. Only he wasn't about to run. Steve grunted and picked up his coffee mug. He might be observant and capable, but he was unsure of how to navigate a simple conversation.

Johnny laughed and smacked his friend on the shoulder. "Look at you, the survivor!" he teased.

And then there was Johnny. He wasn't worth psychoanalyzing. It was the usual wasted years, squandered potential, and real resentment about it. His usefulness amounted to him being an idiot who followed the crowd.

Morgan joined the effort to get the guys to open up. She scooted her chair on the end closer to Beau, so that their knees accidentally touched. His apology was the most he had said at the table, but it was a start. After that he had trouble avoiding her eye contact.

"How'd you get into quadcopters?" she asked.

Beau shrugged. "Just, just a hobby, I guess."

"They're not your specialty?"

"I mean, they're easy enough. I do a lot of computer stuff mostly. Network setup, security systems, video production."

"You're not making a movie of our little escapade," said Shaw, "are you?"

Beau chuckled nervously. "No way. We won't be recording. That would be stupid."

"Really stupid," agreed Holt, in case his leadership was in question.

Morgan sighed. "I don't see the point of the drone then."

Now Holt took offense. His face hardened. "Hold up. We are not going to discuss your objections again."

"It's not that," said Morgan. "It just seems like a waste of resources to me." She planted an elbow on the table to box Holt out of the conversation. "Did you at least get to help the deputy on the tech side of things? She should recognize your worth."

"No," Beau said unevenly. "She has her own thing going on."

"What's that?"

"Beau," warned Holt.

The drone operator's gaze flitted to his XO and back.

"You'd need to ask her."

"Am I seriously hearing this?" exclaimed Carver. "We're a team. With what we're about to undertake, we're not trusted with a few details?"

"It's called compartmentalization," said Holt.

"And what about coordination? Wouldn't it help us to know her side of the plan? In case something goes wrong."

"There is no plan. She's not part of this."

"Part of what?"

"Project Sundown," chuckled Johnny.

Steve and Holt stared at him and his stupid smile vanished.

"I don't get it," said Carver. "Everyone knows she's leading a drone team. Everyone knows we're utilizing them to take down the power grid. What's the big secret?"

They were getting sick of Carver's questions, and he was pushing extra hard, but they were running out of time. Their growing exasperation was a possible benefit, as the more they scrambled the more they might reveal. And what other option did they have? In an hour they'd be gearing up and moving out together. Holt was in charge of the operation. His job was keeping Carver's team happy. At least until they completed the mission.

Unfortunately, the empty kitchen moved faster than the conversation. Right when the buildup threatened to show results, the waitress set their plates on the table. Everyone stared quietly over runny eggs and breakfast sausages. The silence seemed to harden Holt's resolve, and Carver was worried they would need to start all over again.

"I'll take a fill-up, too," he said, sliding his mug over.

After making sure they all had setups, and coffee and tea and water, and butter and syrup, and extra packets of sugar for Johnny and artificial sweetener for Steve, the waitress left them to it. The tension at the table evaporated as they dug into their bounty.

It was obvious any discussion of the deputy was off-limits, so it was time to try a different tack. Holt had a piece of buttered toast in his mouth when Carver said, "Lorelai okay?"

The XO paused, cleared his throat, and chewed angrily.

"With Sam, I mean," explained Carver. "I don't want to overstep. I just want to make sure she's safe."

Holt finally swallowed and said, "Worrying over her isn't your job."

"Come on, Holt, it doesn't need to be like that."

"Like what, exactly?"

Carver sighed. "Look, we're guys. We have that neanderthal lobe built into our brains that we can't always turn off. We see each other as competition for resources. For mates. I get why you might feel threatened—"

"I'm not threatened," he scoffed.

"No, but you perceive the threat. And that's a compliment. That's the smart reaction. You should be cautious, and aware, and ready. That's just reality."

Though Holt dipped his head in agreement, this was very much a contest to him. "And what is it you think I need to be ready for?"

"Anything," said Carver. "That's my point. But I'll tell

you what you don't need to worry about, and that's me going after your girl. That would be disrespectful to you and her. And you know what, in all honesty?"

Holt blinked. "What?"

"I think you're good for Lorelai. She needs someone strong. A born leader. That's fair."

Holt swallowed again, even though there was no food in his mouth this time. Saying the opposite of what these guys expected put them on their heels.

"What's not fair is telling me I can't worry about her. Not after her crying the other day. Not after what she's been through."

Holt wasn't sure if he should go hard or go soft, but he wasn't the silent type, like Steve. He was a leader. He had to say something. "She just overreacts sometimes."

"Wouldn't you?" directed Carver. "Look, I don't give two shits about your occasional spats. Who am I to judge? But she's the victim of trauma."

"Victim," snorted Johnny. "She's ain't the one who died."

This time, no one needed to tell Johnny to shut up. He got the hint quick. Holt worked his jaw a moment, eggs going cold on his plate, and he decided to talk.

"She was the victim," he agreed. "And if I could get my hands on that piece of shit who beat the hell out of her, he'd be in pieces."

Carver set a clenched fist on the table. "Hell, I'd bring the machetes."

Holt studied him a beat and nodded slowly. "You know

what, Vince, I believe you would. But Lore's stronger than people think. She took matters into her own hands. Even when the useless police wouldn't help her because her husband was a fed. And he let her know it, too. Always waving his badge in her face like he was untouchable."

"Holt," Steve warned.

"No, no, it's okay. I can say this." He focused back on Carver. He wanted to talk now. He wanted Carver to know. "So Lorelai did it smart, being small as she is. She waited till he got home. Cooked him a nice dinner. You ever had shrimp and grits from the low country? It's her specialty. She made a feast of it. Had a healthy portion of whiskey to with it, too. And she got him real drunk, even though it increased the chances of him getting violent. And she waited till he got nice and sloppy, and even a little mean, and she took it because she was used to taking it. She kept waiting till he got comfortable. Took off his shoes, his pants, his gun. And when he was half passed out on the sofa she blew his brains out and shoved that Secret Service badge down his sleazy throat."

Steve ground his teeth, Beau was wide-eyed, and Johnny chuckled, a fan of the story. Carver was quiet a second. There was a lot to process in there. Lorelai was a victim, no doubt, but that sequence of events sounded awfully premeditated.

Lorelai tried a normal life. It didn't work out.

"That couldn't have gone down easy with the feds," he said.

"Hell no. She was a badass, but she couldn't stop them

arresting her for it."

"She do time?"

"It was a close thing," admitted Holt. "But they decided not to press charges. The history of police calls, the interviews with neighbors, they all backed her story. It was a righteous kill. And I'm proud of her."

"The police hassle her after that?"

Holt inconsequentially hiked a shoulder. "Sure they did. But Lore packed up, left Oklahoma, and landed with her dad at the compound."

"And that's where she met you."

"That's it. We had just moved down from Washington ourselves, met the commander, and started building something special."

"Like fate," said Morgan.

"More like it just happened. You can't control who you meet and when."

Carver wasn't sure if that was a philosophy or an excuse. "But that was the end of her troubles?" he pressed. "Feds aren't local police. You can't just move four states over and leave their radar."

"It's not a problem," insisted Holt.

"Maybe she could tell me her secret then, because Special Agent Bentley's still holding a grudge. He hasn't returned my pistol yet."

Steve and Johnny snickered, and Carver couldn't help laughing with them.

"He the one with the stick up his ass?" asked Holt.

"A description like that would pick him out of a lineup."

The laughs came louder the second time. Their plates were half finished now, the heavy eating was out of the way, and everybody was filling up and relaxing and easing off the throttle. Carver knew how fleeting the moment could be but, for now, it was smiles all around.

"Well, good for Lorelai," announced Carver, lifting his coffee mug in a toast. "She's not as fragile as I thought."

"No she is not," said Holt, holding his in the air as well.

Shaw's mug was empty but he lifted it all the same. "And to hell with the feds."

"Yeah!" agreed the others, saluting their drinks.

"With any luck," added Carver, "this operation of ours will finally put the feds in their place."

"At least one of 'em," cracked Johnny.

The smacks to the back of his head happened without delay, Steve on one side and Holt on the other. "I said shut the fuck up!" seethed the XO.

Johnny sorely rubbed his hair. "Come on! Like you said, we can talk now."

"One more word," cautioned Holt, eyes flaring, "and you'll be talking through a broken jaw."

Carver traded a glance with Shaw. He had expected the table's mirth to run dry, but not that suddenly. Holt dead serious again, Steve quietly pissed, as if nobody ever listened to him and that was his lot in life. Beau picked up staring at the bottom of his mug again. All for what, a sideways reference about sticking it to the man? The reaction didn't reflect the offense.

Unless Carver and the CIA had been looking at this

whole thing wrong from go. *At least one of 'em*. This was about a specific federal employee, not the power grid.

Which meant Project Sundown was a reference to something else, something Carver and his team hadn't foreseen. Just another in a string of inconsistencies that had started as soon as Carver uncovered the Switchblade. Then identified the ECCM. Then learned of the link to Lorelai's dead husband.

And there it was. He had found it. The intersection of the two lines that made the X.

Switchblade 600s and ECCM were overkill for attacking the power grid. But this limited stock wasn't for sale. Sam and Lorelai made up a fourth covert team with a separate objective, one Holt and his friends knew about, one that taking down the grid was ancillary to.

Project Sundown all came down to payload. That was still the missing piece, but the picture was clear enough without it.

Sun wasn't a reference to the power grid but the leader of the free world. Everything revolved around Alex Diaz.

Project Sundown was a kill mission, and the target was the president of the United States.

21

Carver went numb as he realized the full scope of the militia's operation, smiling when Holt spoke, nodding along with the others, but he could barely process anything except the doomsday scenario in his mind.

Taking down the Silicon Valley power grid was the side mission. Cover for assassinating the president. A sudden blackout would cause panic and compromise the Secret Service's security cordon.

When the president travels, the FAA issues a Notice to Airmen with a Temporary Flight Restriction. The airspace in the control area is completely locked down.

The Secret Service employs a variety of C-UAS tools to counter unmanned aircraft systems. Carver should know. With a career in security, he had used and directed the use of such tools. Any capable security detail would utilize a combination of radio-frequency detection, radar imagery, and electro-optical and infrared cameras to intercept threats.

DroneShield uses RF attacks to sever an operator's command and control link. SkyWall fires a physical net and parachute to force land a drone. Radars detect, track, classify, and respond to all skyborne objects. Most of these handheld countermeasures are tailored for consumer quadcopters whose negligent operators are hoping for eyes in the sky at the Superbowl. They aren't formidable enough to defeat military-grade fixed-wing aircraft.

The more capable systems are plugged in, often in military vehicles, but also on rooftops and perimeters. They provide intelligence of the local skies with RF sensors, thermal imaging, and drone C2 detection. A blackout would disrupt these active protection measures or at least hinder their effectiveness.

Carver rested back in his chair, laughing at stupid jokes, hours away from the presidential visit, grid attack, and drone strike. He waited till one woman, elderly and overweight, waddled to the restroom with a full belly. Carver made a show of killing his coffee mug. He sighed, set it down, and announced, "Duty calls."

On his way to the bathroom, he tried the occupied one in plain view. The door jiggled against the deadbolt. He called out "Sorry" and headed down the hall, out of sight of Holt and his crew. Instead of going for the second door, he picked up the pay phone and got a dial tone. Thank the inertia of old infrastructure.

Without a direct line to his handler, he called the state department on a number he had long ago memorized. It wasn't a public-facing line, but it wasn't a privileged one either. Just a way for insiders in the know to cut through the noise.

"How many I direct your call?" asked the woman

without an introduction.

Under his breath, "Case Officer Lanelle Williams, CIA."

A pause. "Excuse me?"

"You heard right."

"Who is this?"

"Vince Carver, former special forces in Detachment-Delta."

The woman clacked some keys in the background while her neutral voice continued. "Sir, there must be a misunderstanding. The state department doesn't handle that kind of business."

"Just check it out. I told you who I am."

"It doesn't matter who you are."

"I know this isn't the best method of reaching out, but I'm an asset and this is an emergency."

She waited a minute. He figured she was looking something up. He set the phone down for a quick second to stroll into Holt's view, looking bored and waiting for the restroom. He tried the door again and paced back to the phone.

"Can you get Williams?" he asked.

"I don't know what you're talking about," she said evenly.

"The hell you don't," Carver growled. "Just reach out and see what she says."

"Sir..."

"Transfer me to their office."

"Sir, I can't do that."

"You have to."

She sighed curtly. "Mr. Carver, Officer Williams and the CIA have no working relationship with you."

He paused a second. "So you do know who I am."

"From a bulletin."

"Then you know I'm serious."

"I know you are a private citizen with no legitimate business with the federal government. Don't contact us again."

Carver grimaced as the line went dead. A shadow shifted in the hallway. He returned the phone to its base and spun nonchalantly. A young boy wandered back and waited behind him in line. Carver waved him toward the second bathroom and he disappeared inside. He breathed slowly, rubbed his head, and paced in and out of view again.

The attack team was minutes away from finishing up. Carver didn't have time to go through a complicated vetting process, and there weren't a lot of useful numbers he knew by heart.

But there was one he used several times recently. He put another quarter in the pay phone and dialed Guerrero.

Just his luck, she didn't pick up. She was probably pissed, ghosting him after the news of her suspension and the cold way he had left her. Maybe she figured him for the leak. Her voicemail greeting didn't sound like her. It was professional, without feeling. He almost second-guessed leaving her a message at all. It wasn't like she could call him back when he didn't have a phone. He decided to simply say, "You were right. About S2. They're going after the president with a drone."

He hung up and turned just as Holt almost bumped into him walking into the hallway.

"What are you doing?" he asked.

"I'm done," said Carver, ignoring the suspicion cast his way. "I'd wait on this door," he said, pointing to where the kid went, "because this lady's taking forever."

Holt glanced at the bathroom, and the back door, and the pay phone, and his eyes narrowed. The kid suddenly kicked open the door next to them and strolled past.

"Called it," said Carver, brushing by the XO on the way to his seat.

* * *

The team huddled in the back of the van on the way to the short-term rental.

"Everyone know their exit plan?" asked Holt.

Johnny snickered from behind the wheel. "I know what needs doing."

"Wasn't asking you," bristled Holt. He shook his head and said, "Johnny's with me. We're heading up to Oakland."

"I'm taking Beau to Santa Cruz for a few days," said Steve.

"Right," said Holt. "Vince, I don't even want to know. The three of you can probably return to your office and act like it's any other day."

Carver wasn't sure why Holt felt the need to review the plan. Maybe it was just something to talk about. "Will you be contacting the commander in the next few days?"

"Zero contact," stressed the XO.

"What about with your mom?"

Holt bit down. "Don't worry about it. Don't worry about anything except executing this op."

Carver nodded absently. Unfortunately for Holt and the boys, Carver was determined to worry about it. He was measuring all the angles, figuring the best way to foil this attack and keep the power grid running smoothly.

The van bobbed as it turned onto the driveway. Johnny drove past the house and turned onto the patio so he could reverse into the detached garage.

"Steve, get the door," said Holt.

The big man squeezed between the front seats and exited through the passenger door. The engine idled and the team waited silently in the dark cabin. There were no windows in the back, but Carver leaned forward to catch the right angle with Johnny's left mirror. He watched Steve lift the manual door, walk to the side, and wave them in.

Johnny didn't back in completely. The garage was mostly full of storage for the mission. By backing the van in a couple of feet, they had all the privacy they needed in the off chance a neighbor peeked over a wall.

Holt tapped the ceiling twice. "Let's load up."

They went to work. A duffel bag for the SKS carbines, another for the ammunition. They had scoping equipment, bean bags for the rifle rests, and Beau's drone components.

"Where are the side arms?" asked Carver.

Holt double-checked the load so far. "I'll distribute those

inside."

"Distribute? Why not put them in a bag in the back?"

"Why not shut up and listen to your commanding officer?" scolded Johnny.

Beau's hand slipped and the grenade canister bounced on the concrete floor. Everybody flinched.

"Sorry!" he said, scooping it up and wiping a scratch in the metal.

Carver looked around. He hadn't seen Steve in a minute. Holt headed toward the house, calling back. "When you're done loading, meet us inside."

"Hear that, Beau?" crowed Johnny. "That means you too."

The drone operator focused on his task with stark precision. He had reservations about the mission.

Shaw and Morgan keyed off on Carver's tension. While Johnny prodded along the drone setup, Carver nodded for them to follow him around the van. They took a knee beside the front wheel.

"We're going to stop this attack before it happens," he whispered. "Understood?"

"Lima Charlie," replied Shaw, giving the radio code for loud and clear.

They spun as Johnny converged on them. "What's this powwow about?" he asked snidely.

Carver knocked the tire with a knuckle. "The sidewall has a rip in it. It wasn't here yesterday. You must have scraped a curb somewhere."

Johnny peered at the gash in the rubber. It was large but

shallow, just barely exposing the steel cord underneath. He gave it two sturdy kicks and grunted. "It'll hold for what we need." He pivoted to the back. "You done yet, Beau?"

The drone operator hurried over. "I'm here."

"Good. Let's get on with it, then." Johnny shoved him ahead. "Hurry up."

The group strolled to the house as Johnny double-checked the van. That gave them a second alone. Carver and Shaw flanked Beau on both ends.

"We know what's going on," Carver muttered.

The drone operator stiffened. "Wh— What?"

"Don't play dumb," growled Shaw. "You have exactly one minute to come clean with us."

Beau shook his head. "I just do what they tell me to."

"And what's that?" pressed Carver. He checked over his shoulder. Johnny was still futzing in the back of the van.

"I'm sorry," whispered Beau.

Shaw leaned on his shoulder. "Sorry for what?"

The poor guy was trembling.

"Screw this," muttered Morgan. She wrapped an arm around Beau from behind and pressed her knife against his stomach. "What's going on?"

He stopped in his tracks, shaking like a nervous wreck. "They're... they're going to kill you."

Morgan blinked back surprise. "After the job?"

Carver turned back to Johnny, shutting the van door with a loaded SKS in his grip. "No," he growled. "This is going down right now."

22

It was too late to surprise Johnny with a direct charge. He held the carbine low and at his side, unthreatening on his approach, so Carver rolled with it. He strode toward Johnny, guileless but with urgency in his step.

"We have a complication," he said.

Johnny scrunched his face, leaning his head to the side to see what Morgan was doing with Beau. "What complication?"

Steady strides. "The op is blown."

Johnny put an arm out. "Now hold on right there."

Carver pointed his right hand to the sky over Johnny's shoulder. "You see that?"

Johnny couldn't resist an instinctive glance. But the sky was clear today. There was nothing to see up there. Johnny's suspicion overrode his confusion. He spun to see Carver's left hand slip around his knife's grip. Johnny swung the SKS up as Carver's blade knocked the barrel askew.

The Colonel was shaped like a pistol, blade forward, grip lateral, right down to the trigger guard for the index finger. That meant when Carver had a chance to grab the SKS, he took it. The knife pushed flat against the barrel but couldn't be dropped as long as it was hooked around his finger.

With the rifle in control, Carver slammed his right fist into Johnny's nose, crushing the soft bone. The militia member staggered backward, yanking on the trigger. The gun went off close to Carver's ear.

He yanked the gun high to spread Johnny's body and sent a heavy kick to his groin. When he doubled over, Carver delivered a hammer fist to the neck that put him on the ground.

The house's back door creaked open and Steve pointed a pistol. Morgan spun Beau as the gun barked. Carver's team wore minimal ballistic protection, unassuming low-form-factor vests beneath their shirts, but Beau turned out to be the bigger shield. Bullets cut into flesh as Morgan kicked him into Steve, with Holt bumping up behind.

Carver swiveled the SKS, having no choice but to fire high over the heads of his team. The rounds impacted the stucco above the door frame, but that was close enough to get the message across. Their attackers tripped over each other to scramble back inside, Steve firing wildly and leaving Beau to collapse and bleed out on the stoop. Morgan bolted past Carver to get a rifle from the back of the van.

"Come on," said Carver, waving Shaw to follow suit as he covered the back door.

The Navy SEAL instead pressed against the wall of the house just beside the door. He shook his head once and drew a Cold Steel Recon Tanto knife. Someone stirred inside.

Johnny jumped and grabbed Carver's gun while he was

distracted. They twisted together, struggling. For a druggie he was surprisingly tenacious, not like a bear or rhino but more like a cockroach.

Carver's knee connected with Johnny's stomach. He was light and loose this time so the blow didn't do a lot of damage. With both of Johnny's hands pulling the SKS, Carver was forced to follow suit or lose the weapon. While not posing any immediate danger to the larger Delta operative, Johnny was proving to be a pest.

Instead of using the back door, the kitchen window popped open and out came Steve's gun. This time, at least, he didn't immediately fire. Maybe he liked Johnny more than Beau, or maybe he figured he'd be outnumbered if he kept killing his own guys. Either way Carver was dangerously exposed.

What Steve didn't figure on was Shaw planted at the wall directly below him. He grabbed Steve's wrist and jerked him forward, pulling the top half of his body outside. Then Shaw plunged the seven-inch combat blade upward into the big man's chest. The damage was sudden and catastrophic. The large knife ripped Steve's heart open, and he immediately slumped into the windowsill with a muffled choke.

"So much for being a survivor," muttered the SEAL.

Carver swung Johnny around in a wide circle, released the SKS they were fighting over and giving it completely to his opponent, and kicked him three yards into the garage.

"About time," said Morgan, loaded carbine against her shoulder. A single shot at point blank exploded Johnny's head. He hit the floor with wet thump.

"Fuck!" yelled Holt. He fired wildly out the window over Steve's twitching corpse.

Morgan returned suppressive fire while Shaw grabbed Steve's dropped pistol. He fired backwards, sprinting into the garage and joining them behind the van.

"Damn it, these bastards are cold," he snarled. "They could've at least waited until we completed the op to turn on us."

Carver grabbed a new rifle and used a clip to load it. "Smart play on Holt's part. Even if we were suspicious about being betrayed, we wouldn't expect it beforehand. We almost walked right into a prepared kill zone."

Morgan took up position over the hood on the far side of the van. "I hate to break it to you," she called, "but that prepared kill zone still exists." A single shot dinged off the garage, and she fired back to keep Holt honest.

Shaw checked the magazine of Steve's Glock and opted to stick with it. "The windows give him a choice of firing points. Even if we breach from multiple entries at once, the danger is high. He might get the drop on one of us."

Carver bit down. Holt would have worked out the firing positions and angles in advance. He was fortified and ready for them. And worse, despite the young man's misplaced bravado and confidence, he was an okay shot who had nothing to lose.

Well, almost nothing.

"You're not getting out of here!" Carver shouted from behind the van.

"You killed them all!" cried Holt.

"Was that not the plan?" he replied. "You wanted a shootout, you got a shootout."

"That was a dirty trick with Steve."

Shaw scoffed. "Shooting us in the back any less dirty?"

"Screw you! I'm not coming out of this window. I'm not exposing myself. So if you want me, come get me!"

Shaw locked eyes with Carver. "I'm about to," muttered the annoyed SEAL.

"No," said Carver. "Holt's the one in a strongpoint, but we're the ones holding the cards." He crouched and peeked out from the van's bumper. "Covering fire, three times."

Morgan popped the window three times over three seconds, giving him enough time to duck into the exposed section of garage, grab Johnny's boot, and drag him back into cover.

"Safe," said Carver.

"Reloading," she called.

Carver handed Shaw his loaded carbine and he took her position. Meanwhile, digging through Johnny's pockets produced the keys to the van. Carver held them up with a jingle.

"We have what Holt wants. We don't need him anymore."

"We're going to run?" she asked. "He could cause trouble for us if we leave him behind."

"Oh, we're not leaving him behind," grated Carver. "He just needs to *think* we're leaving him behind."

They grouped behind the van as Carver explained. The drive past the house exposed the vehicle to fire from the windows, but chances were Holt would be on the defensive until he realized what was going on. Then it would be too late. Morgan crawled through the back of the van, into the driver's seat, and started the engine. Shaw handed the carbine back to Carver and loaded in, shutting the rear doors.

The van lurched out of park but then moved down the driveway at a steady roll. Carver walked on the side of the vehicle opposite the house, using it for cover until they were flush with the building. Then he crouched low and glued himself to the wall. Morgan hit the gas. Boots stomped across the interior and paused suddenly as Holt watched the supplies necessary for his operation drive away.

"Shit!" he screamed.

Carver waited silently, but it wasn't long. Holt wasn't the patient sort. He burst onto the front porch muttering to himself. Carver crept along the sidewall, but Holt was panicking and unpredictable. He suddenly stormed back inside. Carver listened as the XO did a lap of the house. The back door shoved open and his boots hit concrete, pausing to take in the sight of Steve bleeding down the wall.

"Yeesh."

The son of the deputy crossed the backyard and stopped at the entrance of the garage, crestfallen at the sight of his friend.

"Stupid idiot," he said wistfully. "You—"

Holt stiffened as he sensed something. A scuff against concrete. A waft of gunpowder. He paused longer than he should have, really. Maybe because he knew he was done.

"Drop the gun," ordered Carver, rifle beaded on his back from ten feet.

Holt's head bobbed side to side in deliberation. "Or what?" His grip tightened around the pistol.

"What's your mother doing, Holt?"

"The deputy? You think you can stop her?"

"I can and I will."

He snickered, still facing away, afraid to make a move because it would be his last. "You're too far and don't have enough time."

"Distance doesn't matter. She's not getting her power outage."

"*One*. She's not getting *one* power outage. There are two others. The plan has redundancy. Besides, we don't need it to stick. It only needs to happen. One. Single. Blink."

Carver crept forward. "Why? Why doesn't it need to stick?"

The XO took a long, resigned breath. "You putting your money where your mouth is, Vince? Are you in a squared-off shooting stance, or bladed to reduce the size of the target?"

"I am wearing a vest. You tell me."

"Of course you are," he chuckled bitterly. He hadn't even noticed.

"Holt, why doesn't the grid outage—"

The XO ducked and spun at the same time. It was probably something he saw in a movie. Carver's weapon barked and the body shot punched into Holt's shoulder. The kid managed to get the gun up and fire before being pelted again. Holt's legs twisted under him and he hit the concrete. He coughed up blood, and gently eased onto his back.

Carver held his aim steady until Holt's fingers on the pistol went slack. He stripped the XO of the gun, dragged him into the garage, and put a bullet into his head. Carver casually strolled through the yard, past the house, and into the street, where Morgan spotted him from a distance and pulled the van up so he could climb in the back.

"I'd hate to see that Airbnb review," remarked Shaw.

"Actually," countered Morgan, "it's the cleaning fee that'll hurt."

They drove away.

"We have a problem," said Carver, and he wasn't talking about the distant police sirens responding to the gunfire. He scooted behind his team in the front and told them about S2's plan to assassinate the president.

"This bunch of idiots?" exclaimed Shaw in disbelief.

"Some of them, like Johnny, I can't account for," admitted Carver, "but maybe that's the point. They're societal outsiders. They want to take down the power grid and destroy the federal government. They're the perfect patsies."

Morgan frowned and met his eyes in the mirror. "Patsies... Are they meant to fail?"

"They're meant to die. To be the lone gunmen who had crazy ideas and killed the president. If they die the buck stops with them."

"And the militia's sponsor stays in the wind."

"Exactly. This is his op and the militia are his sacrificial pawns. That's why Holt wanted to take us out before the attack. The grid is child's play. They don't need us. Not balanced against the risk of keeping us around. Holt couldn't take the chance that we'd disappear after the job, that we'd realize the true mission objective after news of the assassination got out, and that we would turn them in."

Shaw worked his jaw and let them continue the talking. Morgan said, "Okay, that tracks. But Anderson's the one working directly with the militia's sponsor. If we were a loose end, why would he go out of his way to hire us in the first place?"

Carver shook his head. "It's the part I can't quite work out. But I've been getting the feeling that Sam Grafton's the one in charge of the real play. Smoke and mirrors with the substation attacks while she's the one handling the Switchblade. The other XOs don't know any better either. Only Holt because he's her son."

"Plus she needed us dead."

"That too. So I was thinking. Been doing a lot of that today. At the diner, Holt mentioned he and Sam moving down from the Pacific Northwest shortly after Lorelai moved back. He made a weird comment, something about not being able to control who you meet."

Morgan nodded. "Like his love for Lorelai was tragic."

"Which it would be, if the commander was the target of their operation."

"The Montagues and the Capulets."

"You're not far off."

Shaw finally jumped in. "Your theory is that, not only is Sam working with the sponsor without the commander's knowledge, but that they infiltrated the militia, just like we did, except with the purpose of setting them up to take the fall for killing the president."

"Shakespeare left that part out."

"Which puts a cork in all that red cell business. That was just a pretext to get Anderson to play along."

"If I'm right about him at least," said Carver. "He doesn't strike me as having a big grievance against the government."

Morgan huffed. "So Agent Guerrero was wrong about S2 setting up shop, which is why she had trouble proving it. The militia isn't selling the drone, they're using it for a single strategic blow. And the coordinated timing of the substation attacks will prove the militia's involvement."

"Along with tactical objectives," added Shaw. "I'd guess a power loss would soften the security perimeter and drone defenses."

"That's another thing I'm running into a wall on," muttered Carver. "Holt said keeping the grid down wasn't important. They just needed it to happen. He called it a blink."

Shaw shrugged. "Any outage will create an attack window."

"I didn't get that impression. I'm thinking, if there's an active threat at a preplanned event, something like gunfire or a drone in the sky, then the president would be smothered, whisked away, and taken to a bunker or other secure location. But what if that bunker was compromised? What if the entire city was struck by a power loss and a large coordinated attack? I'm thinking the president would be shoved into the Beast and his convoy would make a beeline to Air Force One. Or at least to a remote fallback position. Away from the bulk of the Secret Service's prepared countermeasures."

Morgan said, "A mobile retreat would be susceptible to a drone strike."

Carver nodded. "Any threat to the grid would trigger escape maneuvers."

"Which are the kill parameters," finished Shaw.

"With the two other substations being hit at the same exact time, it wouldn't matter that we prevented our attack. The power will blip. There'll be flashy explosions from the drone strikes. The president's team will identify the threat and scatter."

And it wouldn't matter if they put him in a tank," said Shaw. "The Switchblade 600 uses a Javelin warhead."

He didn't need to state that it was an anti-tank guided missile. It all came down to payload.

They mulled the problem over as the sirens receded in the distance. Instead of being comforted by the quiet, it reinforced how isolated they were. "Can we call anyone?" asked Morgan.

"Maybe. I tried. I'm not sure we can reach anybody in time who'll help. But I have another idea. What if instead of stopping the attack on our power station, we go ahead with it?"

Morgan spun around in the driver's seat. "What?"

"Follow me, here. The substation attack is the shock to the system that warns the president's security team. Taking the grid down, even partially, puts them on alert to get them out of Dodge."

"That's the precise problem," countered Shaw. "They get in that convoy and the Switchblade's gonna zero them."

"Not if we take the power down before the 600's ready." Carver checked his watch. "We have two hours till go time. But if we don't wait, if we take down that substation right now, the president and his team will have hours of advance warning. We can get them out of harm's way before the Switchblade ever goes airborne."

They looked at him like he was crazy.

"It's a solid attack plan," Carver insisted. "We've worked it over for days."

Morgan chuckled, and Shaw laughed.

"And Williams knows about the attacks, she just doesn't know the timing. I have no way of contacting her, but if we hit our target first, I bet she immediately routes authorities to the other locations, before they're in progress, ensuring no further grid interruptions."

"You're forgetting," said Morgan. "The CIA's quick response will send police our way too."

Carver hiked a shoulder. It wasn't perfect. They just had to be in a different zip code by the time the authorities arrived.

"Vince," chuckled Shaw, "either you're getting smarter or I'm getting dumber, because I think I'm actually on board with this."

Morgan allowed a sideways smile. "Don't discount it being both."

Carver was relieved they didn't need a lot of convincing, because every second wasted was a second President Diaz didn't have.

Morgan cocked her head and stepped on the gas. "Boys, let's go take down the power grid."

23

The midday sun beat down on the ridgeline. Carver and Shaw lay prone in the dirt, carbines resting on bags as they finalized their shoot prep. The Monterey Highway had only occasional traffic at this time of day, and the security guards were predictably lax. The pair in the substation were far from the road, and the one in the nearside energy center had just disappeared on his lunch break.

"Change in the target," instructed Carver. "Instead of transformers, we're going to hit the radiators now. They're filled with oil. We put a bunch of holes in them, they'll drain and overheat. It'll shut them down and cut the power without catastrophic damage, and they'll be cheaper and easier to replace than the actual transformers."

"Ever the good Samaritan," muttered Shaw. The Russian Simonovs didn't have modern sighting tools, so he analyzed their new targets through a separate scope. "Four hundred fifty meters to the target. Wind, two miles per hour, no value."

Instead of a classic sniper-spotter relationship, they both manned their own weapons. It wasn't like they were dealing with a hard target here. Carver made the distance adjustment on the elevation slider of the rear sight. They wouldn't be adjusting for windage in the field with these rifles, but the environmental dynamics were good to know so they could make the necessary tweaks in their head.

The radio crackled. "Security line is cut. Road is clear. I'm heading back to the van."

"Copy," returned Carver.

The internal magazines were loaded with ten 7.62x39mm cartridges. With each fire at just under two seconds, they would do significant damage before anyone realized they were under attack. Carver locked his target into the hooded front sight of the rifle, and the M43 cartridge exploded from the muzzle at nearly twenty-five hundred feet per second.

The carbines barked evenly, inducing some muzzle rise but low kick due to the twenty-inch barrels. Realigning the large targets with each shot was an easy matter, and holes popped into the distant machinery at a steady pace.

After ten cartridges went through the ejection port, Carver took the first of three loaded stripper clips lined up before him. He slotted it on top of the receiver and slid the ammunition down, then set the disposable clip aside and released the bolt back into position. He sighted the carbine with his next target and made some holes all over again.

The first round of shots had the guards idly looking around, musing at the distant pops that echoed overhead. The second clip's worth had them scanning the horizon, trying to figure out who was shooting what, where. It was only after Carver was well into his third magazine that the guards finally realized that, just maybe, somebody might be shooting at them.

Oil drained from the damaged radiators, still unnoticed by the guards. The SKS carbines moved from target to target as the tanks swiftly emptied, sensors detecting low fluid levels, futile attempts at sending emergency notifications to the energy center disrupted by the severed lines of communication.

Carver loaded the last clip into the rifle and examined the damage. They had to ensure every single transformer grouping was compromised, and it appeared like the job was already done.

Shaw was faster on his trigger. He finished the last of his ammunition and said, "Easier than shooting varmints." He backed out of his perch and started collecting spent shell casings, counting each one.

Carver expended his last magazine on whatever targets best guaranteed a successful operation. He also recovered his ejected shells. They packed up forty to a man, as well as the leftover stripper clips, and the rest bags, and any other traces of their presence. They scuffed the dirt where they had rested and backed away from the ridge as the security guards yelled into radios and finally found each other, only just beginning the process of figuring out what the hell had just happened.

Carver and Shaw sprinted to the van, where Morgan waited behind the wheel. They unassumingly rolled out of the terrain and onto the highway. Clean, pro, and easy, past the ailing substation. Electricity arced across one of the radiators. A sudden explosion boomed, followed by a shutdown, and the three operators melted into the haze of the horizon.

24

Carver followed Shaw out the passenger door, boots hitting the asphalt of the Kinetic National Security shopping plaza. He shut the door and spoke through the rolled-down window.

"You clear on the breakdown?"

"This ain't my first rodeo," drawled Morgan.

He nodded, pounded twice on the van's body, and stepped away as she drove off alone, back onto the street. The weapons and vehicle had to be dumped. Luckily, they only needed to go unnoticed for as long as it took Lanelle Williams to clean it up for them. That meant stashing it somewhere discreet, out of the way but unsuspicious. It also assumed they would ever hear back from the case officer.

Shaw was already striding to his parked G Wagon. The Mercedes was a gleaming silver monstrosity that was somewhat out of step with his unassuming friend, but then everybody was entitled a foible or two.

"Is your phone in there?" asked Carver.

"In the center console."

"Make sure not to walk it over to the pickup."

"Got it, boss."

Shaw wouldn't follow Morgan too closely, nor park within a block of the van. Both his phone and SUV could be tracked, so he would pick up food, head to the recreation area, and jog over to give Morgan an assist. Then they would enjoy lunch in the great outdoors and return to the office together.

Carver was already mission clear. He unlocked his pickup and retrieved his phone. As expected, local cell service was unavailable.

The three of them had done their job well and this stretch of San Jose was without power. Cell towers and switching equipment require electricity to operate. Most sites are mandated to have backup generators, but the FCC is toothless as an entity. Whether or not backup power is actually installed on critical systems relies on the telecom's cost-benefit analysis. If the current outage was extended, the problems would be worked out, but it'd be some time before service was fully restored.

Carver entered the KNS office. Except for the bell jingling above his head, everything was quiet. No drone from the air purifier. No buzzing of the lights or electronics. The UPS units had long-ago put the computers to sleep to preserve battery power. It was a graveyard in here.

He clicked on a tac light in his personal office and opened the safe, equipping a Maxim 9 in a shoulder holster under a windbreaker. He also slid out a rifle bag and dug some clamshell packages from his desk. The sharpened blade of the Colonel made short work of the plastic, and Carver moved to the lobby as he checked the batteries.

Guerrero waited in tactical gear, pistol pointed. "Where are you off to in such a hurry?"

Carver eyed her, and then the slightly ajar door. She had opened and closed it in a way as to not ring the bell. Good for her.

He gritted his teeth, placed the two phones for his team on the welcome counter, and slipped his into his pocket. "I was hoping not to run into you just yet."

Her nose twisted. "I would ask why, but I'm guessing it has something to do with dead militia members in a short-term rental in Coyote."

Carver raised his eyebrows. He was starting to be impressed. "I thought you were suspended."

"I am, but my partner's on the scene. Bentley caught the alert Santa Clara put out."

"Quick work."

"What are you into?" she hissed. "You can't just leave a message like that without explaining yourself."

Carver's rifle bag was locked and in the back office. He made no move for the pistol in his jacket. "I was offering you a warning of the militia's intentions. Or a faction within the militia."

"You were the leak. You warned S2 about my raid."

"They already knew, Isla. There's someone on the inside. It could be anybody. Hell, it could be you."

"You really believe that?"

"It's hard not to with that gun pointed at me."

Her eyes quivered. What did she want. How involved was he. Guerrero swallowed and lowered her gun. "You think HomeSec is compromised?"

"It's someone. What about Bentley?"

She forcefully shook her head. "I don't believe it."

"The guy was sinking your investigation all along."

"He pushed back on my lack of evidence."

"The guy's an asshole."

"Maybe, but he's my asshole. I can't accept that the man I've put in four years with is a traitor."

He took a long, introspective breath.

"So what now?" she prodded.

"Crisis averted, hopefully. Did you report my warning?"

"I sent a threat notice up the pipe. High priority. It could be my ass if nothing comes of it, again, but I figure they've already got me in a sling. And I want to trust you."

"You can."

She sucked her bottom lip. "Some corroboration would go a long way."

"Fair enough. Let's go get it."

He went back and retrieved his rifle bag. By the time he returned Guerrero had holstered her weapon.

"Where are we going?" she asked.

Carver cracked a smile. "To see Commander Anderson. He's not the type to save his own skin, but he *is* the type to do anything for his daughter."

25

She rode with him to the compound. They hit a bit of traffic due to disconnected traffic lights, but the San Jose outskirts were easier going. On the way he checked both his regular cell phone and the burner. No signal. Recovery of the network and grid were underway but slow going. Meanwhile another side effect of the outage was made manifest. Jammed communications.

The gate at the militia compound was open and unmanned. Carver rolled forward slowly.

"Maybe he left in a hurry?" suggested Guerrero.

Carver hoped not. If Anderson wasn't home, he wasn't sure how soon he could reach him.

"No," he concluded, pointing at the heavy chain hanging on the fence. "Somebody used bolt cutters on it."

They found a white SUV in the yard, unmarked but a match to the other Homeland Security vehicles.

"This isn't good."

Carver shifted to park and exited the truck with his weapon drawn, not bothering to shut the door. Guerrero followed suit. A generator rumbled somewhere in the background. HQ had lights on inside. Which made perfect sense. What good was an apocalypse compound without a power generator, especially when you were the only one expecting a blackout?

They rushed the building, its front door still open. Carver cleared the opening and moved inside. Anderson was on the floor of the war room, propped against one of the filing cabinets. There was a pistol on the hardwood beside him, but both hands attended to his bleeding belly.

Carver swept the room as he advanced. Splayed on the floor opposite was ASAC Covington out of the San Jose field office. His face was frozen, eyes wide, nostrils flared. Maybe the mortician would finally give him that nose hair trimming.

"They got me, Vince," coughed Anderson. "The bastard turned on me. I knew he would."

Carver holstered his weapon. Guerrero didn't. She wasn't up to speed and had no reason to trust the commander. On the other hand, Carver felt like he knew him well.

He also knew what had happened. The ASAC was the leak. He had ordered the raid of the S2 compound, but not before making sure it would fail. He was part of the frame.

In all likelihood, Holt was supposed to take out Anderson just as he had attempted with Carver's team. Loose ends neutralized and patsies set up. Only Homeland Security learned of a shootout that killed the conspirators. Then the power went down early. The ASAC knew the plot had imploded and came straightaway to erase the only evidence that pointed to him.

"It was Covington sponsoring the militia?" asked Carver.

Anderson winced. He was in a bad way and was worried about the gun still pointed at him. "Special Agent Guerrero, right? You a part of all this?"

She advanced and kicked his pistol away. "You killed a federal agent."

He sighed painfully. "He was the leader of the red cell. The one who planned the substation attacks. Vince, why did the power cut early?"

Guerrero swiveled her crazy eyes to him. "That was *you?*"

Carver hiked a shoulder. "Holt and his team turned on us. They tried to take us out too."

"Holt?" Anderson's eyes closed. He knew all-too-well what had happened next. "I had no idea, Vince."

Carver canted his head. "Yeah, well, given that you're bleeding out on the floor, I'm inclined to believe you."

Carver checked his phone. He got a weak signal and tried 911. Even in times of high traffic, emergency calls have a higher priority. He tried to get through, but the combination of weak signal and downed power thwarted his efforts.

The commander shook his head. "It's a shame to see a good kid like Holt go out like that."

"You did hear the part where he tried to kill me."

"You know how the world works, Vince. He was pressured into it. Everybody always is."

Carver knelt by his side and checked the wound. It looked bad.

Anderson pressed his hands back over and said, "I knew this thing was trouble."

Carver wondered if the commander realized Sam and Holt had purposely infiltrated his organization from the start.

"Juliette?" he asked weakly. "Nick?"

"They're okay. Lester, I need you to tell me where the deputy is."

Guerrero checked the rest of the small house, even though Carver sensed it was clear.

"Sam's job is just to get video evidence of the fallout. Eyes in the San Francisco sky. The tech capital of the world brought to its knees by a few boxes of old ammunition."

"That's not her real mission, Lester."

"Of course it is. I set it up specifically so Lorelai wouldn't be involved in the substation attacks."

So the commander didn't realize the scope of the infiltration. "I'm not talking about the power grid," said Carver. "I'm talking about the plot to assassinate the president."

Anderson's eyes went wide, but he didn't jump straight into the expected denials. Instead, acknowledgment crept over his face. The red cell attacks, the secrecy, the double dealing—all the concerns and fears that had accumulated over the last weeks and months finally clicked into place. The larger plot explained it all.

They had played him.

Pained tears broke free. Anderson was defeated, dying, and realizing that everything was so much worse than he had possibly imagined. Carver let him sob a moment.

Guerrero returned to the room and gave him the all clear. She checked the landline and hung up, shaking her head to communicate the lack of dial tone. It used to be the old copper lines would deliver their own power even in a blackout. Now they were all digital, if not at the house then at the switching stations. With Guerrero off duty and without a government vehicle, they had no immediate methods to call for help.

"I knew something was off," said a teary Anderson, mustering whatever strength he had left. "Covington wasn't trustworthy. That's why I needed you around, Vince. If this red cell business was on the up and up, why threaten Lorelai over my compliance?"

"The ASAC made you do it? What threat?"

The commander sighed. "My daughter's had some... unfortunate incidents in her past."

"She killed her husband. He was a fed, right? But he's dead."

He squinted at Carver. "You know about that?"

"Lester, I need you to focus. Right now your daughter is collaborating with Sam and the others to kill the president of the United States."

He blinked several times like he was losing steam. "Covington said I needed to lead the red cell or he would make sure she was in federal prison the rest of her natural life."

Carver nodded. "Let me guess. He knew Lorelai's ex and this was payback for killing him?"

"What? No, he didn't know Ray. He just found out about it somehow. He wanted S2 to work for him so he ran deep background and discovered a way to put the screws to me."

The explanation was plausible, if unsatisfying. The dead husband and Covington were both employed by separate divisions of the same department. It may not have been a close-knit family, but it was incestuous enough to trade in gossip.

"I'm sorry I used you, Vince. But I needed help, one soldier to another. I didn't know what was going on, but I knew it was something. I was out of my depth."

"Don't worry about all that. What's Lorelai's part in this?"

Anderson shook his head. "Nothing. Same as Sam. I mean—they were supposed to put together a video of the power loss. That's it."

Carver bit down. "Lester, I'm gonna need more than that."

The man looked around the room, barely registering Guerrero now. He was fading fast. But then his eyes lit up. "Lorelai called this morning from the hotel." A smile crossed his features. "She wasn't supposed to, but she did. Nerves, you know?"

"Where is she staying?"

"Sam was in charge of logistics. Compartmentalization and all that. But the number's on my cell phone." He looked down and patted his pockets. Carver helped him dig it out and located the number. He handed the phone to Guerrero.

"Lorelai..." mumbled Anderson, adrift.

Guerrero copied the number to her phone. Carver tried 911 again, with both phones, but nothing was going through.

"I want to thank you, Vince," said the ailing commander. "Working with you felt like being in the military again."

It was a nice sentiment, but Carver was ridden with guilt. He didn't know how to respond, or what Anderson was expecting.

"I can't feel anything anymore..." The commander stared into far focus. "They were some of the proudest moments of my life, you know. Back when I didn't have a care in the world, when I could put everything on the line. Back when I didn't have a soft spot." He released a jerky sigh. "Now I have a daughter... I did my best to protect her... but my best wasn't enough."

Carver dropped his head and said, "Lester, I'm sorry things didn't work out," but Anderson's eyes had already glazed over. He was dead.

In a strange way, Carver sympathized. The man had been a loner, like Carver. A patriot. A warfighter. No attachments to hold him back. Then one day he had a daughter to protect, and with Lorelai moving back home, so came the wolves to his door. The commander's mandate would have been clear: play along or see Lorelai punished.

That plot was why Sam had been so opposed to Carver joining the militia in the first place. He and his team were outsiders. Loose ends. But the commander intentionally made the effort to welcome them. Anderson realized how precarious the whole thing was. He was being extorted, but hoped he could get out the other end. He watched the militia slipping into the hands of the deputy. He was losing all power and agency to control his own destiny. Until one day at the gun range he met a special operator, a special opportunity, and he set his own plan into motion.

Without the capability to resolve his problem, Lester Anderson had found someone who could.

Except he never conceived the true plot until the end. He had never suspected the severity of the infiltration. Carver was never a guarantee, just a fallback plan, a contingency to have in his back pocket in case everything went south.

Rather than be angry at the man, Carver decided that Lester was a patriot and father till the end.

He went outside, walking the property in search of a better signal. Guerrero went with him, weapon holstered, eyeing him curiously. He stopped when his phone spiked to two bars.

"Should I ask who you're working for?" checked Guerrero, hands on hips.

"You really shouldn't."

A string of missed calls flooded in. Guerrero had tried him multiple times after his warning, which also explained the incoming voicemail notifications. Still nothing from Williams.

"Damn," he said.

Guerrero crossed her arms. "You're worried."

"That man's daughter is out there somewhere, with a

Switchblade 600. The whole system takes ten minutes to set up. If they don't use it today, they could use it tomorrow. We need to find Sam before she goes to ground. And save Lorelai if possible."

"The girl conspired to kill the president, Vince."

"Can you locate that hotel?"

She watched him evenly, aware that he had ignored her point. Then, "Assuming no hitches in communication, we can have that location in a matter of minutes."

Carver bounced the plot around in his head. "And your threat notice. About the attempt on the president. Who did you send it to?"

Her active eyes went dead. "ASAC Covington."

"Shit."

He sprinted to the pickup and she hurried to follow. As he waited on her to climb in, his phone buzzed. He had a message from Shaw.

"Bentley outside office with SRT." Another message quickly followed. "They'll be onto you next, especially if you're where I think you are. Gotta go."

Carver slammed the dashboard. The sudden emotion startled Guerrero, but he didn't explain. Tires kicked up gravel and they sped down the country road before another Special Response Team arrived.

He no longer had a team, but the operation wasn't over. He needed to move ahead without them.

The good news was, if Morgan and Shaw were back at the office, they had successfully dumped the weapons and the van. Bentley couldn't hold anything over them.

Guerrero watched as he swerved his way through the roads and onto the freeway. He was worried she was going to pull rank on him, order him to stop, but for some indecipherable reason she didn't.

They were going ninety when he said, "How much do you trust Bentley?"

The special agent swallowed. "I'd bet my life on him."

"Good enough for me. Call him and catch him up. I don't want him to shoot my people."

She lifted her phone to tease out the best possible reception. The power was still out in the city. "Where should I tell him I am?"

"We're going to San Francisco to finish this thing for good."

26

There was no power outage in San Francisco. Once they left the southern Bay Area, everything was completely normal. Too normal, even. Nobody shared Carver's urgency as he weaved through freeway lanes, making every minute count. For her part, Guerrero was on multiple calls to ensure the president's team was aware of the situation.

The 101 routed through the president's security cordon in the Financial District. It would needlessly slow them down. Instead they took the 280 and the CA-1, cutting through the west end of San Francisco on the way to the north-side Marina District, replete with a beautiful view of the Golden Gate Bridge.

"It's no good," complained Guerrero after ending a tense conversation with the Special Agent in Charge. "The local offices are scrambling to make sense of ASAC Covington's death. The red cell explanation is farfetched."

"That's because it was made up. Don't they get it? Covington doesn't matter. What are they doing about the president?"

"We've warned his security team. I've had confirmation from multiple sources..."

He didn't like how she trailed off. "But... ?"

She huffed. "The White House administration is moving ahead with the speech."

"How could they possibly come to that decision? Do they not believe us?"

"We're taking this seriously too, Vince. We have a shootout, a grid attack, and a dead ASAC in the mix. DHS is taking every precaution. But this call comes from the president's team. All we can do is assist."

Carver cursed as he exited the freeway and began to navigate the city streets. His plan to warn the president had worked too well, if such a thing was possible. The San Jose power outage was noticed all right, but on its own it wasn't deemed a coordinated action. Threat assessment wasn't overly concerned with an incident an hour away. With his reputation on the line, President Diaz was urging his team to proceed as planned.

On the flipside, the early warning should have signaled Williams to take down the other attack teams. Being busy with that effort would be the best explanation for why she hadn't contacted him yet.

That meant the secondary and tertiary grid attacks should never take place. It was something, but it was cold comfort if the speech was moving forward. With the Switchblade still in play, the president was susceptible. Carver could only hope the CIA would catch on in time and do what Homeland Security couldn't.

They cruised past the Super 8 motel on Lombard. Carver didn't bother stopping. Here and now, the location didn't do them much good. Sam's team had spent the night here, but they wouldn't be hanging around. Assuming there were no delays, they only had ten minutes before the president's speech was scheduled to start. Thirty minutes till the planned strike.

Carver looped the pickup down the various side streets, looking for anything amiss.

"We're in the wrong part of the city," said Guerrero.

"The hotel will be close to their staging ground. Five minutes away, like the Airbnb in Coyote. It's how they operate."

"The president's in the Financial District."

"Exactly. The deputy is positioned outside the Secret Service's security cordon, with a fire control system that has the capability to fly, track, and engage a target without external ISR. The Switchblade 600 has a cruising speed of seventy miles per hour. At three miles away, that's... two and a half minutes from launch to touchdown. They only need to be close enough to manage the operation and any local assets. It's what I would do."

A mix of awe and suspicion crept into her eyes. He supposed that was how most people would react if they discovered his inner workings. He kept busy scanning the local alleys and substructures. San Francisco was a densely populated city. The odds of running into Sam's team were low. But, assuming a small radius to the hotel, he was hoping to spot something out of place within the next half hour.

He was on the money, and it was only one block over on

Greenwich. A modern cement structure under construction between traditional three-story wood-paneled homes caught his eye. The new building was a shell, no windows or doors, and fronted with scaffolding. Sitting in the empty and doorless garage, backed in, was a nondescript black van with an old, cricked antenna.

Carver continued down the street without slowing. He didn't see anyone but it would make sense if they posted a lookout. Five houses down, he double parked in front of a broken-looking garage door and hoped it didn't see much use.

He got out of the truck and crossed the street to get a better angle of the operation. The house was mid construction, with a portable toilet booth on the curb beside a sign advertising the developer. No active work was underway. No crew, no inspectors, no owners. Except for the van, it wouldn't have appeared occupied at all.

The next-door houses were built in the San Francisco style, very close to the property line and without side windows. Combined with the construction tarps hanging on the second and third floors, anyone inside would have plenty of privacy.

What stood out to him most was one of the tarps on the third floor. It was drawn aside, offering a limited window within. While Carver couldn't make out the interior from the ground, he noted that the opening was wide enough to allow the egress of a tube-launched drone.

Carver marched to the Ram, turned off the engine, and unzipped his rifle bag.

27

"Stay behind me," said Carver after they geared up.

"I'm a trained shooter, Vince."

"Been in a firefight before? Right in the middle of one?"

Guerrero bit down, frustrated that she didn't have a good answer.

"I'm sure you can handle yourself, but this is my operation. Stay behind me, watch my back, and don't shoot when I'm in your firing lane."

"Fine."

"One more thing. We're going in quiet. Hopefully we surprise them, but we have to assume they'll spot our entry. That means continual forward motion. We fly in quick and act without hesitation." He held her eye so she would pick up on his gravity. "This isn't a Homeland bust, Isla. You got that?"

Her jaw clenched again, but this time with resolve. "Got it."

"Let's go."

He pointed the rifle down and hustled along the sidewalk in broad daylight, cutting into the construction yard at the edge of the property line. The building husk had no front door, just a doorway leading to an entry with concrete stairs on the left and the unattended garage on the right. It would have been nice to check the van, but surprise was the priority. He marched up the stairs. It was only once there that he realized the exterior stairwell could potentially serve multiple units, each floor fronted by a concrete wall and an open doorway.

The bullpup rifle breached the floor line flush with Carver's head. There was a small landing, with the next set of stairs continuing after. The platform had no railing or wall blocking the open stairwell, but that just meant he had an unobstructed view of the exterior wall.

He suspected Sam's team would be entirely on the third floor in a makeshift nerve center, but he had to perform basic precautions. Running into a stray militia member unprepared could be disastrous. He advanced on the door to find his instincts were good. Brushing aside the small tarp, he could see the main portion of the second floor was clear. Carver pivoted to the next flight of stairs, this time slowing his stride.

The third-floor landing was at the rear of the building, which didn't give him a central sight line from the stairs. Once Guerrero was in place behind him, he advanced to the doorway. The tarp had been disturbed, partially folded down to allow entry. Without touching it, he shifted his view along the opening to take in the full scene. A pair of folding tables were set up with computer equipment. A mazework of cables snaked across the raw floor, probably to a transmitter of some sort somewhere. Two militia members attended the computers. Sam occupied the far corner, near the front of the house but out of sight of the windowless opening. None of them suspected a thing, and their weapons were holstered.

The same couldn't be said for the other two guys on the team. They weren't familiar to Carver, but the rifles they held ready were. FN 15s from the militia stocks. The men stood apart from each other, not offering a single easy target. They weren't especially vigilant—they should've been more interested in watching the yard and stairs instead of the monitors—but they were still dangerous, ready to respond to a threat. Carver gave it two seconds before they were on their triggers. Maybe another four or five for the others, depending on their focus.

It bugged him that he didn't see the sixth member of Sam's team. Lorelai had to be close at hand.

Without disturbing the tarp, he swept what he could see of the space a second time. A couple of partial walls led to bathrooms and bedrooms, but the husk of space was otherwise empty. Very little was carpentry. The building's main frame was steel, and the walls and central column were thick reinforced concrete that would stop all the bullets they had.

That resolved his avenue of attack. They were outnumbered. The element of surprise would give them the initiative. Past that, splitting their firing positions would give them optimal coverage of enemy targets, as well as divide their enemy's attention. Those vital seconds lost to confusion were the difference between victory and defeat.

Carver signaled Guerrero to take position at the doorway and stay there. Then he breathed in and out slowly as he had been taught. Box breathing, to calm his nerves, slow his heart rate, and improve his precision and decision-making. He watched the two guards with rifles, and he waited until they both had their backs to him.

Carver fired the X95, riddling the first gunman with bullets. He marched past the tarp and swiveled to the second man. He was fast, spinning with his rifle up. Carver hurried his trigger as he sprinted sideways, spraying the table and wall with rounds. But the sight of Lorelai in the other far corner halted his attack. He hadn't been able to see her from outside the doorway, but he sure saw her now.

The gunman opened fire and Carver dove behind the thick central pillar. Chunks of concrete chipped off, but the core of the structure held.

He cursed as he hid from the bullets. He had fumbled the entry. Seeing Lorelai there, in the line of fire, had caused him to hesitate. Now his precious seconds ticked. The militia infiltrators ducked for cover and drew their weapons. Carver was losing the initiative.

Luckily the whole crew zeroed in on him. Guerrero entered the fray, only armed with a pistol but a surprisingly confident shot. Planted in the doorway for cover, her rounds cut down one of the computer guys advancing with a pistol.

Sam retreated behind the small corner wall on the far side of the room. "Launch!" she ordered. "Launch!"

With the crew on their heels. Carver listened until the FN 15 went dry and the owner pulled the mag. He swiveled out of cover to take down the vulnerable gunman, but the other computer guy had a bead on him. His pistol barked and a divot of concrete shattered a foot from Carver's head. He ducked back behind the pillar, stone chips blanketing the area like snow.

The Switchblade tube was past the computer tables and cables, close to Sam and Lorelai. It was positioned at an angle, facing the open wall. Carver managed a peek from the other side of his column, but the reloaded FN 15 opened up on him again.

Lorelai was in her corner operating the drone with a tablet-based fire control unit.

Guerrero opened fire with a fresh mag, and the gunman with the FN 15 made the mistake of spraying the doorway in return. Carver swung out from his original side and filled the gunman with steel-tip penetrators.

Instead of ducking back into cover, Carver marched into the fray, squaring his body with his targets and firing a quick barrage of suppressive fire. The remaining computer operator retreated backward firing wildly, tripping over a thick clump of cables on the floor. Carver released his empty mag while pulling a new one from the attached mag coupler. It was in reverse position to allow a quick reload. The Switchblade tube thumped and a projectile blasted into the sky with a loud release of air, tarp flapping in the wind. The wings of the drone spun into place with a loud click as it disappeared above them. Scowling, Carver put down the fumbling computer guy with three rounds.

Seeing Lorelai wasn't armed, he pointed to the wall the

deputy peeked out from. They simultaneously fired at each other, but her pistol was no match for his civilian Tavor. She was forced back into cover, and the room went quiet.

"Guerrero," he called, "cover that wall."

Keeping on top of the deputy's position, he sight-checked the four downed militia members. They were all dead.

"It's too late," called Sam from behind the wall. "The Switchblade's in the air."

Carver gritted his teeth. One of the computers had live network coverage of the Silicon Valley announcement. No closeup of President Diaz yet, but there was movement onstage by his staff. Applause from the outdoor crowd. The speech was getting started. That gave him a floor of two and a half minutes until the drone acquired its target.

Carver's rifle mag was mostly full. Keeping his aim on Sam's wall, he marched toward the fire control unit. He had to stop halfway there. Going any further would open the angle to the deputy's cover, exposing him to her fire.

"Lorelai," he said, "call it back."

"Can't be done," said Sam. "The FCU is locked."

"I can destroy the antenna," Carver countered.

"Wouldn't make a difference. The drone's in autonomous mode. It's set-and-forget, Vince. Any interruption in communication will only take out our eyes. We won't see what happens, but that won't change what happens. Get it?"

Carver ground his teeth. The president would be speaking in a fixed location. With the San Jose blackout occurring early, it was possible the plan had changed to taking the target out at the earliest possible opportunity, collateral damage be damned. Absent live control from an operator, a GPS fix on the presidential podium was good enough to get the job done.

Sam wasn't trying anything stupid, either. Tucked into her hidey-hole, she was perfectly positioned to cover Lorelai and the FCU. Carver's options weren't great, the best being advancing to the wall and blind firing around the corner. Not bad odds for him hitting something, but if the deputy was ready for that, it was a good way to get disarmed or shot himself.

He kicked himself for not holding onto Beau's incendiary grenade.

Carver weighed attacking the deputy with attacking the drone. Taking out the comms would be counter-productive, because he bet it was still possible to send a kill signal, no matter what Sam said. But systems like this had strong encryption. Lorelai was no longer touching the interface, just nervously shifting her eyes from the X95 to the screen with the bird's-eye-view of a low-flying UAV passing over San Francisco highrises. It was going too fast.

"Lorelai," he said evenly, "unlock the fire control unit."

Uncertain eyes met his.

"I told you, she can't do that," argued Sam.

"Of course she can."

The deputy was silent.

Carver knew Switchblades had wave-off capability. All he had to do was get access to the FCU. "Unlock it, Lorelai," he repeated.

"Now why would she do that?" gloated Sam.

"You're being used," he asserted. "I don't know if you think this is real or a war game or what, but there is no red cell. If you don't unlock that console, you'll be responsible for murdering the president."

Lorelai's gaze spun to the deputy. She had a clear view from her position, and something like love and hurt flashed across her face.

Why hadn't Carver seen it? The motherly attention, the bringing the girl into the family. With a father who wasn't always the best at showing his emotion, it was all too easy for Lorelai to get sucked in by Sam's support.

"Think of your father," urged Carver. "He wouldn't want this for you."

A scoff came from behind the wall. "Don't listen to him, Lore. Your father's your commander. These are his orders."

"Your father was killed a little over an hour ago by the man who planned this mission."

Lorelai tensed, eyes locked with his in a silent plea of disbelief.

"Sam doesn't love you," he said. "They were always going to blame this on him from the start."

"Girl," called Samantha, "are you gonna believe this Johnny-come-lately, or are you gonna believe your family?"

Lorelai watched Sam for several seconds. Then her eyes flitted to Carver's. Emotions crisscrossed her face, struggling for dominance. Decision. And she saw a decisive man. A man she perhaps had a crush on. A man she perhaps trusted, even though their time together had been fleeting.

Lorelai, for once, saw the truth.

"I can't do this," she cried. She tapped the touchscreen, unlocked the interface, and activated the wave-off.

Shots rang out, and too late Carver realized the depths of Sam's dedication. He propelled forward, opening fire on Sam's position, rounds chewing into the wall but closing on her angle. A bullet popped Lorelai's arm. She recoiled, eyes panicked and full of tears and shock and absolution. Carver barreled into her and the table, gunfire tearing up the room in two directions. The table upended and everything crashed down hard.

Carver popped up on all fours as bullets whizzed by. One impacted his side, contacting the vest and sending a jolt of pain through his ribs.

On the tablet, the view from the Switchblade veered skyward as it transitioned to a standby altitude.

Carver dragged his rifle close but it caught when Sam stepped on it. Her pistol clicked empty, but her boot didn't need a mag. The steel-toe knocked his forehead, and his attempt to rise ended on his back, without his rifle, just as Sam slid another magazine into her Glock.

* * *

Carver breathed heavy, hands spread above his waist, showing that he was disarmed and no longer a threat. The deputy was standing out in the open, not shying behind cover. Which didn't make sense to him. Guerrero should have been covering the room.

The knock to his head had filled it with haze. He squinted toward the doorway, trying to make sense of it. The special agent wasn't there. She'd been MIA since the rifleman sprayed her position. She'd been hit.

And she wasn't the only one.

Lorelai was also on her back, body heaving. The blood on her arm had nothing on the pools welling on her chest. Despite the irregular jerks of her torso, her head was motionless, against the floor. She blinked weakly, watching him. Her arm reached to him and sagged. Her breath stuttered, then stopped, and the militia's nerve center went eerily quiet.

"Oh dear," sighed the deputy with a modicum of actual feeling. "Holt is going to be upset."

She raised the gun to him.

"I don't think he'll mind," rushed Carver, fight or flight ramming interfering signals through his brain. But the fog was clearing. "Trust me," he said to stress his point.

Instead of her trigger finger twitching, Sam's eyes narrowed. "What makes you say that?"

The deputy had a tactical head. She stood two yards from him. Far enough that he couldn't reach her with a kick, but too close to miss if he tried anything. For now, he was at her mercy.

Carver cocked his head. "You must know. He hasn't contacted you. Or maybe you've been black and you haven't heard."

She was annoyed now. "Heard what? If you're here, that means you didn't go with him to the substation. You must have ratted him out. He executed the attack early after you didn't show."

"You mean after he didn't kill me?"

She blinked, like how did he know about that. The annoyance fled her face.

"I know the whole thing, Sam. Your sponsor in Homeland Security, your infiltration of S2, your plan to set them up for the president's assassination, but only after they were dead."

Her mind was scrambling. She half shook her head and said, "Where's my son?"

Carver took a patient breath. "Ask yourself how I know?"

"Tell me where he is."

"Ask yourself, why. If someone tried to kill me, why would I still be around?"

She stepped close and brandished the Glock. "I asked you a question and I'm not going to do it again."

Carver didn't make any sudden movements. Slow is smooth and smooth is fast. "Ask yourself," he said in a grinding tone, "if I'm here right now, what happened to Holt?"

It was Sam with the sudden paroxysm. She got in his face, shook the gun wildly, and screamed, "WHAT DID YOU DO TO MY BABY?"

Carver gripped the Glock's slide and forced the weapon sideways. It went off once as he swept his legs into hers. Sam tumbled on top of him, intercepting his reach for his sidearm.

The deputy screamed bloody murder, shaking, face violet. She grasped Carver's neck with her free hand and squeezed. But she was much smaller than him. He bucked, and she thrashed, and he bucked again. She hung on for dear life, unable to concentrate on anything but squeezing the breath out of him.

"I HATE YOU!" she yelled. "I HATE YOU! I HATE YOU!"

When the gunshots rang out, he hardly heard them. The clacks of metal on metal sent a pair of 147-grain hollow points from Carver's Maxim 9 into her chest. The deputy's grip went lax and she collapsed onto an elbow.

Carver slid her Glock aside and backed away on the floor, sitting, allowing his lungs time to fill. Past Lorelai's body, the fire control unit showed the view from the drone doing laps high above its target. It had been successfully waved off, but it was still active. Still waiting.

"You did it," Carver whispered to the dead girl.

He spun his weapon to the sound of the tarp brushing aside.

Guerrero leaned weakly on the doorway, blood streaming from her head. She held her pistol up halfway and with great effort. Taking in the room, her arm relaxed. She hopped toward him, leaning on the wall and favoring one foot.

For a brief moment, Carver wasn't sure who or what to trust. But here was Guerrero, struggling with each tortured step, and still backing him up. The HomeSec special agent checked the bodies of the dead militia members before stopping at his side. Sam was alive, but unmoving, much as they had found her commander less than two hours prior.

"You hit?" asked Carver.

"I took a rifle round in the vest. Maybe two. I fell down the open stairwell trying to get out of the way. Broke my fucking ankle."

His eyes widened. "You okay?"

"I'm alive."

"Your head's bleeding."

She nodded slowly. "I'm a little woozy."

"Join the club."

At the mention he noticed his own hair matted with a spot of blood. It was just a cool tickle, a shiver of annoyance, but it was enough to set him on edge. The slight euphoria from the deprivation and acquisition of oxygen fled his system. He had to deal with the Switchblade once and for all.

Knowing Sam was covered for good this time, he crawled to the FCU on the floor beside the upended table. Carver switched to manual mode steered the loitering munition away from the crowd, past the skyscrapers, past the docks, and directly into the choppy waters of San Francisco Bay. The screen went black. It was over.

Sam grunted as she watched the screen, bleeding, losing some fire in her eyes but wearing a defiant scowl all the same. Her hatred was the only thing pumping her heart.

"I have to call this in," said Guerrero.

Carver nodded. "Sit down. Tie that up. Use one of their

boots if it's big enough."

The special agent sighed. She was putting the mission over her own well being. There was a time for that, Carver knew, but there were also precious few moments when you needed to take care of yourself. Guerrero lowered to the floor beside the same guy who shot her and began unlacing one of his stiff combat boots. If she could get her foot into it, wrapping it extra tight would give the joint added support.

"You think you've won," growled Sam.

Carver hiked a shoulder. "We didn't lose. You going to tell me why you targeted your president, or would you rather wait till you're spirited to a black site on an unnamed Pacific island? Either way works."

"You don't get it. If they want the president dead, he's dead."

His eyes narrowed. "Who?"

"The peons! The true believers! We were just using them, but you think they give a shit? They enjoy being used. They enjoy being useful." She stopped to hack up blood, then continued with the same fiery determination. "People like you don't stand for anything, Vince. The true believers are on my side. They might be pathetic, but every one of them is willing to die for the cause."

Her conviction was something awful.

Before he formed a response, his phone buzzed. A new text message read, "Need car insurance NOW?" and ended with a number. Only then did he notice previous message sitting in his spam folder. It was a longer-winded car insurance ad with the same contact info.

He snorted. This wasn't unsolicited advertising, it was a covert communication request.

"That important?" asked Guerrero.

"Depends on your opinion of the CIA," he said.

He could've kicked himself. Williams *had* reached out, at least an hour ago. Whatever automated system she had used to make sure the message was lost in the mix had sent it to his spam box. Too authentic by half. But now, with a mysterious Unidentified Airborne Phenomenon buzzing over the president's speech, Williams had broken protocol and sent him a more direct message.

Direct for the case officer, anyway.

"Sky Strike down," said the deputy. "Commence Ground Strike."

Carver looked up to see Sam speaking urgently into a small radio.

"I repeat, proceed with Ground—"

Carver punched the radio out of her hand. Sam lunged and went for a knife strapped to her leg, but she was too slow. Carver twisted her wrist until it popped. She screamed and kicked, so Carver tied up her legs with his boot. Still she didn't give up. Sam was feral now, like something out of a zombie flick. She leaned in baring her teeth.

He met her power with his, butting his head right into the bridge of her nose. The blow flattened her face and stunned her a second. Before she recovered, Carver hit her with a body shot center mass. The deputy careened across the floor and hit the tarp. It tore from the wall and engulfed her as she fell two stories and hit the patio.

Guerrero sighed, wincing from the effort of jumping to her feet. "Any chance she's still alive?" she asked.

Carver looked down and said, "No."

"That was too good for her." Guerrero's face tinged with pain as she tightened the boot around her ankle. Carver went over and took the laces from her hands.

"This is going to hurt."

She nodded and closed her eyes.

He pulled the laces taut and wrapped them around the backs of the boot, then up and again. When it was over, Guerrero took two calm breaths before picking up her phone. Carver figured he should do the same. He dialed the number. It quickly connected to a silent line.

"I, uh, heard I could get a good deal on my car insurance," he said.

"I thought you might be dead," replied Officer Williams. "Then I saw pictures of Holt Grafton's team in Coyote. Looked like your handiwork. Same with the clean strike on the substation. Are you off the rails, Vince?"

"It was the only way I could warn you. They were plotting to kill the president."

"I figured the timing was suspicious. I dispatched teams to the three targets. We didn't find a trace of evidence in Coyote, but the other two XOs and their crews are wrapped up. They're in custody and being interviewed as we speak."

"They don't know anything."

"That's what they say. Where are you now?"

"Marina District in San Francisco. I just sent an armed

Switchblade 600 into the bay. Sam's dead. Anderson, Lorelai. They're all dead."

"We need some of them alive, Vince."

"Extenuating circumstances. There was a dirty ASAC who got to Anderson. He was keeping HSI off S2's scent, which is why Guerrero had such a hard time of it."

He eyed the special agent, on the phone with her partner or her boss or whatever other relevant authorities needed to be in the loop. This kind of thing was all hands on deck.

"This ASAC Covington," pondered Williams, "he was the militia's sponsor?"

"I don't know. There's no motive besides being bent. But listen, Project Sundown is still live. Just before Sam died she radioed a distress signal. Another team. There's going to be some kind of ground strike against the president."

"We've been attempting to contact his team, but they've been radio silent."

Carver's brow creased. He walked over to the monitor of the live feed. It was a picturesque day in the city, sunny, clouds breezing across an azure sky. President Diaz made pronouncements from his podium, and his onlookers cheered. None of them had any idea how close to tragedy they had been.

"This isn't right," muttered Carver. "No speech is worth this security risk. An anonymous tip is one thing. The president probably gets threats every time he makes a public appearance. But word from the CIA should be the gold standard. The Secret Service should be moving him out."

He checked Guerrero. HSI was also having trouble

convincing the president's team to abort the event. The whole thing smelled. Sam's words haunted him.

"I can't raise them," said Williams over the line. "The Secret Service isn't responding."

"There's one explanation for all this," he said. "The president's security team is part of the plot."

"What are you talking about?"

"The Secret Service has been in the background of this thing from the start. They offloaded their due diligence to another department, HSI, who were themselves hamstrung by a corrupt ASAC. They aren't warning the president of the threat to his life."

"We don't know that."

"Lorelai's ex-husband was Secret Service, and she killed him. That's the leverage they used against the commander. It's tied together."

A keyboard clicked over the line. "Yes, I have that right here. She goes by Lorelai Anderson but her legal name is Hanna, from her marriage to Ray Hanna."

"That's the link."

There was more typing, and Williams sighed. "I don't see how. Ray was part of an anti-counterfeiting unit. He didn't have— Wait."

Carver paced the room and scooped up the deputy's radio while Williams did her thing. He wondered why he hadn't heard any return calls after Sam's order and checked the volume. He wondered if anybody had copied and, if so, if the seconds were ticking again.

"This is bad," muttered Williams. "Ray's older brother,

Alex Hanna, also works for the Secret Service, except he's in personal protection. He's in San Francisco right now, leading the president's mobile team."

"That's it. He must have had it in for Lorelai ever since she killed his little brother. He's how the ASAC learned of the leverage. He knew the militia connection and sent Sam and Holt to infiltrate."

"That's a grievance against Lorelai, not the president of the United States."

He shook his head. "He's the guy. I'm not saying I have all the answers, but he's the guy. We can ask him why he did it when he's safely in cuffs."

Lanelle Williams only took a moment to process it all. The fact that she took that much spoke to the gravity of the situation. "If what you're saying is true, the president's about to be attacked and the Secret Service won't do anything to stop it."

"I'm sure of it, Laney. It was something Sam said. Every true believer would willingly die for this. They'd be put down to serve the cause. The only way for Sam Grafton and Alex Hanna to escape scot-free was for her faction of true believers to be killed and blamed for the assassination. And they were confident of it because Hanna is leading the team that will make sure it happens."

This time the line was silent.

"I need to hit the streets," decided Carver. "This isn't over by a long shot."

"This is... I'm not sure I can sanction this, Vince. You're talking about storming the president's position and potentially engaging in a firefight with Secret Service agents."

"Then talk me out of it. Get the president to stand down. Get word to someone you trust. Get proof that I'm wrong."

"... And if I can't?"

"Then you can catch the fallout on the evening news."

28

Guerrero stayed behind to secure the scene. Not only did her ankle take her out of commission, but authorities were on the way and she had to be the official face to meet them. She had done enough. The last leg of this operation was Carver's. It was better that way because he wasn't sure if he'd be walking away from this one.

He swapped out spare mags in the truck and peeled out toward the Financial District. The speech was at an outdoor plaza near Market and Montgomery, which was as close as you could find to Wall Street on the West Coast. It wasn't more than ten minutes away under good conditions, but this was a city that rarely had those. Carver sped eastward as the buildings changed, wood to glass, three stories to ten, then twenty, then stretching to the sky.

He made good headway down side streets, and when that was no longer possible due to traffic and closed roads, he skipped the Ram onto a sidewalk and ditched it. He also left behind the X95. Weighing the odds, he didn't think a man scurrying through the crowd holding a bullpup rifle would get very far. As a special operator, his job was to blend in until he didn't.

Carver jogged three blocks. Not with the urgency of a man trying to save the president, more like a guy who had slept in and wanted to catch the end of the speech. Once he spotted the police vehicles, he slowed to a brisk walk. No need to stand out. It was what everybody else was doing.

The outer perimeter wasn't a real perimeter. There was no access control. It was about visibility. The cops were saying *here we are. Everything is under control.*

But it wasn't, and only Carver knew that. It was just him against a sizable conspiracy.

The sound of spectators intermingling with the president's voice made everything suddenly real. It was all at once strange and familiar. Carver was used to operating in non-permissive territory. This was functionally the same except for being a city street in the United States. The special operations checklist would have him recruit local assets. A badge or two on his side would drastically increase the odds of success. But the idea had problems.

Any one of these officers could be dirty. He figured that was only a small chance. You tell enough people a secret and it becomes gossip. XO Victor and the other militia members weren't aware of the true scope of their plot—it was doubtful a random cop did.

So, assuming the guys with guns were good guys, recruiting them to his cause was appealing. But Carver had no credentials. They would have no automatic assumption of duty toward him. Short on time, he was never going to convince a police officer to take whatever drastic measures were necessary to prevent an impending assassination.

Trying to do so would only call attention to himself, so recruiting local assets was out.

Carver pushed into the thick of people. For now, the herd was his weapon. Standing half a foot taller than the average man, he adjusted his aviator sunglasses and took in the faces, postures, and actions of everyone he passed.

It was like using his hands to catch water from a faucet. They got wet, sure, but it was impossible to contain it all. Faces slipped between his fingers. The sheer magnitude of the crowd he was trying to take in, on ground level and without optics, was staggering.

Finally he entered the wide intersection at the center of the event. The further he closed toward the president, the more dense the obstacles. A barricaded subway entrance on a brick sidewalk. A row of trees and bollards. President Diaz's words were everywhere. His optimistic voice reverberated over a network of loudspeakers. But it would be difficult to get to the man.

President Diaz was the gregarious type. Handsome enough to disarm with a smile and a wink, self-deprecating enough to recruit opponents to laugh alongside him. Only a decade older than Carver, he possessed the youth and vitality to serve the American people. More importantly, he had the right mix of idealism and savviness to convince them that exceptionalism was possible.

The plaza itself was small. Not an ideal space for mass gatherings, but it probably looked great on TV. On the street among the people. Bank towers in the background. Spectators filling three wide crisscrossing corridors, each closed several blocks down.

But the claustrophobic affair didn't translate to easy access to the VIP. His podium was on a custom-built elevated stage. A barrier at ground level wrapped the front of the platform, with a moat of security personnel in between.

Crowds like this do something to your adrenaline. With so many people packed tightly together, something primal creeps into the brain. Not open aggression, but an underlying level of hostility that spreads across the throng like a virus. It's a defensive precaution. A realization that, if something goes horribly wrong, nobody is fully in control. Everybody is at the mercy of the collective mob.

Under other conditions, Carver would do what he had in San Jose when he took down the grid. He would make a scene. He would step into the center of the crowd and repeatedly fire his pistol into the air. What would happen to him next would be a crapshoot, but it would all but guarantee the president be whisked to safety.

But, in this scenario, the president's team was compromised. Leaving him to the mercy of the Secret Service was no longer an option.

In fact, that had been the original plan.

Carver rotated three hundred and sixty degrees. There were more windows around than he could count. He could only hope whoever was in charge of vetting those vantages was loyal and had done their job well. Otherwise things could end badly.

Sky Strike down. There was no more drone to worry

about. *Commence Ground Strike.* Whatever was coming was coming on foot.

The crowd applauded the president's mention of revitalizing the tech sector. Carver's eyes shifted to the people on the ground. The wave of cheers was useful to him. These events were just grandstanding. Anybody present and listening would be showing their support every thirty to sixty seconds. Separating those interested in the politics from those with other purposes was beneficial.

Carver didn't have the capacity for small details. This was about large coordinated movements. A group closing in. Conspirators in a huddle. Oversized duffel bags. But barring the bad guys wearing matching black cowboy hats while twirling thin mustaches, he wasn't going to get anywhere. The throng was too massive.

Carver couldn't know who Sam had radioed before she died. Any full-fledged militia members wouldn't be cleared for Secret Service detail. He supposed one could be a sympathetic cop, but even that kind of access was overkill. This was a teeming mass of spectators. If Carver could openly walk in with a gun, so could everybody else. The threat could be anywhere.

He next surveyed the Secret Service detail. Also easier said than done. For every visible agent there might be three or more unseen. A couple at the base of the stage, a pair at the steps in the rear, ten manning the barrier, and several others at strategic choke points.

There'd be others at the perimeter, in the buildings, on the roofs. Specialists too. First responders, bomb squad, snipers positioned at multiple vantages. Killing the president wasn't the type of thing someone walked away from. Not on the ground. Unfortunately, it was impossible to distinguish the Secret Service agents diligently doing their jobs from the bad actors. Carver was in the middle of a haystack with at least one well-placed needle somewhere.

He texted Williams. "Need photo of AH."

The head of the president's security detail should have a prominent position. Alex Hanna would be visible, but not necessarily front and center. If it were Carver's team, he'd place his best agents close to the president while staying further back himself. Somewhere still in the action but with the space and awareness to take in the larger security picture.

His gaze traveled from the stage's rear access to the adjoining street. This corridor was clear, barricaded by motorcycle cops so the crowd couldn't get behind the president. Black Chevy Tahoes with tinted windows lined up where Montgomery bent into New Montgomery. Secret Service agents clustered and spoke into radios and checked sight lines.

President Diaz continued his speech at a casual pace. He wasn't anywhere near winding down, yet his security detail was active. They were prepping an extraction.

Which had a few possible explanations. One was that this was exactly what it looked like: the Secret Service preparing the president's scheduled exit, better early than late. It could also be that word of the threat finally reached somebody who was doing something about it. They were going to cut this short and get him out of here before anything happened.

The final possibility was more concerning.

Carver backed out of the dense crowd and circled around the more maneuverable outskirts. He had to approach this from the perspective of an inside man. One who had the power to move and funnel his target wherever he liked. That was the key. Carver didn't need to get to the president, he needed to set things up so the president would come to him.

He crossed a wide street to reposition at the edge of the spectacle, stepping over steel cable car tracks. Using a slick new bus stop installation as cover, he approached the corner of the building at the mouth of the barricaded street. Carver was as close as he could get without raising eyebrows. His prime view was no longer of the president but his custom-built Cadillac sedan.

Nicknamed the Beast, the monster of a vehicle featured eight inches of armored walls, five inches of ballistic glass, kevlar-reinforced run-flats, and was hermetically sealed against chemical attacks. No wonder S2 had gone through the trouble of acquiring a warhead designed to take out a tank. Once the president was inside the Beast, barring the use of military munitions, he was safe.

Williams texted back with Alex Hanna's federal identification photo. He had short black hair and a straight mouth that passed for a smile. He didn't look like a bad guy. Maybe the face of an entertaining storyteller at a bar. The broad shoulders of a high school quarterback who couldn't make it far into college.

Carver studied the security detail. It was hard to make out their faces. Many had their backs to him. A few had similar builds, but the ID photo wasn't current. Spotting Alex Hanna might have worked in a lineup. Here, in the streets, the best he could do was rule out the agents that definitely weren't him.

Carver pulled Sam's radio from his pocket. It was a civilian walkie-talkie, but military grade. He clicked the transmitter twice and waited. When no one responded, he clicked several times in rapid succession.

A Secret Service agent put his finger to his earpiece. He stood on the side of the motorcade opposite the president's approach, practically right under Carver's nose. Only the back of his head was visible but the hair could be a match.

Small-arms fire broke out across the street. Carver peeked from behind the bus stop to locate the source. The horde of people reacted like a tidal wave, rolling outward in a large swell, screams roaring ahead of movement and spreading like napalm.

The security response was swift. Close protection smothered President Diaz. A wall of Secret Service agents jumped onstage to block their VIP as he was discreetly swept offstage. Police at the barricades stepped forward to manage the crowd. The agent by the motorcade ordered other nearby personnel to advance toward the threat.

As spectators fled from gunfire, ground zero was quickly exposed at the rear of the intersection. Two, three men in the cheap seats, brazenly discharging pistols.

Police officers at the perimeter swarmed first. They had the challenge of dealing with fleeing civilians blocking their firing lines. Even worse was the collateral damage behind the gunmen. Hollow points were designed to break up inside soft targets instead of punching through and hitting unintended victims, but they couldn't account for the police missing in the first place.

The air filled with competing screams of surrender and bringing down the system and dropping weapons. Jolted spectators washed out those commands with hectic shrieks. But none of those outbursts pierced the intersection quite like the methodical report of firearms.

One of the officers took a hit. Two others joined together to cut down the guilty militant. Onlookers scrambled. A gunman grabbed a woman for a hostage. Another ducked behind the tiled wall of the barricaded subway stairs.

The cover didn't do him any good against the elevated snipers. When the militant peeked out to fire, his chest burst open in time to a loud crack echoing off surrounding buildings.

Throughout the clamor and chaos, all Carver could think about were Sam's words. True believers willing to die for the cause.

They were dying all right, but what was their cause? The president's men hustled across the plaza toward Carver and the waiting convoy. None of the Secret Service agents onstage or in this direction were taking fire. They might as well have been a mile away.

In fact, aside from shooting back at the police officers, the gunmen had been firing into the air, just as Carver had considered doing. This was the militia making a scene.

They weren't a threat. They were just the distraction.

After sending reinforcements away, the Secret Service agent on the nearside of the convoy was alone now. He turned to check the corner, almost staring right at Carver, and it was unmistakable. A little weathering around the eyes, a few more pounds at the waist maybe, but it was definitely Alex Hanna.

The conspirator turned back to oversee the president's men closing on thirty feet from the Beast. He placed his hand on his holstered pistol. Could the plan be this brazen?

Carver jostled forward as a man in a suit shouldered past him from behind. Carver spun at the ready but there was no one else. Just this new man in a dark suit and sunglasses striding past the security barricade and toward the president's car. His hand, low against his pants, clenched a machine pistol with an extended mag.

Carver had never seen this man before, and Alex Hanna was looking the wrong way.

Being caught off guard was one thing, but the gun and the timing had only one explanation. The assassin strolled right by Alex Hanna, his suit blending in with the rest of the security team's. As he stepped around the hood of the Beast, Hanna pulled his pistol and pointed it at the mystery man.

Only he didn't pull the trigger.

This was the play. The assassin was a patsy, or a militia fall guy, or a true believer—it didn't matter. He was going to kill the president, and then he was going to die, with no one the wiser that Hanna had enabled the plot.

From his cover at the bus stop, Carver pulled his Maxim 9 and took aim.

The mass of Secret Service agents escorting President Diaz converged on the Beast and went for the door, only at the last second noticing the gun on them. The machine pistol exploded with a series of pops. The agents, drawing weapons and covering the president and taking automatic fire, commenced a chaotic dance. Then a well-placed nine-millimeter hollow point punched into the back of the assassin's skull and scrambled his brains.

Everybody collapsed together. The anonymous assassin pitched over like a felled redwood. The jumble of agents fell on top of President Diaz. It was unclear who was hit and who wasn't. Only Carver and one other Secret Service agent stood tall.

Hanna spun. Carver's weapon had an integrated suppressor. No one had noticed it above the racket of the machine pistol, but Hanna had watched the killer's head explode from a few yards away. He swept his readied pistol up and fired three shots into Carver's chest.

Twisting away, he tumbled behind the bus stop and bounced his head on the concrete. Carver winced as he rolled behind cover.

"Sundown," called Hanna over the radio. "I repeat, Sundown."

As the pile of agents recovered their footing, Hanna swept his legs onto the hood of the Beast. Seeing his men lift an unharmed President Diaz to a crouch, he stood on the hood of the black Cadillac and stepped closer.

Carver sprang to his feet with a pained grunt. Hanna lifted his gun and fired. One of his agent's saw the threat and jumped in front of the president, taking the next bullet.

Carver charged the motorcade, Maxim braced in both hands, and opened fire.

Bullets peppered Hanna's back. Like Carver, he wore a vest. The small rounds couldn't get through. But Carver spent the entire mag, adjusting his aim down, striking Hanna's posterior and legs. The agent stumbled against the windshield, momentarily losing his fix on the exposed president.

By the time he raised his gun again, his window was closed. Two agents dove into the back seat on top of Diaz, and the other three had their own weapons ready. A barrage of gunfire cut into Special Agent Alex Hanna from head to toe, and he listed backward and crashed down onto the asphalt.

Carver backtracked across the street again. A ray of light shone into the Beast's open door and caught the features of a savvy idealist behind the tinted black window.

Then the Secret Service turned their guns on Carver.

Amid the gunshots, he threw down the Maxim 9, surrendered his hands, and retreated behind the bus stop. Holes popped into the metal construction, and Carver ducked down, grabbing his side just under the vest where Hanna's bullet had penetrated.

"Don't shoot!" he yelled. "Don't shoot!"

Strangely, through the haze of adrenaline, over the barking of gunfire, Carver heard his own words echoed back at him. "Don't shoot," they said. "Don't shoot *him!*"

The gunfire slowed and Carver heard it again. Unmistakable this time, in the same voice that had blared over the intersection's loudspeakers moments before.

"Don't shoot him!" ordered President Diaz.

The agents stopped firing. Carver lay low on the sidewalk, head propped up by the concrete footing of the bus stop. He bit down in pain. Rubber screamed as President Diaz's motorcade peeled away. Carver's back was wet.

Between shouts for medical personnel and cries from whichever citizens remained in the vicinity, three Secret Service agents rushed around the wall of the bus stop with their pistols drawn.

Carver slowly raised his palms, one of them painted deep-red with blood. "I'm one of the good guys," he said, right before he passed out.

29

The next time Carver woke he was in a hospital bed somewhere, post-op, with bandaged stitches on entry and exit wounds closely spaced on his right waist. The bullet had grazed the edge of his vest and cut through his side, puncturing fat and muscle but missing all blood vessels and organs. His energy levels were in the gutter, and he wasn't sure if that was due to his injury or the meds. It was only painful if he moved. After the attending nurse apprised him of his condition, he decided he'd had enough for the day and went back to sleep.

That evening, he was up again. A police officer was posted outside his door and he noticed, for the first time, that his left wrist was handcuffed to the bed frame. Since he was officially under watch, he didn't bother waiting for any visits. He did manage to stretch for the remote and watch a bit of TV.

The news was all S2, all the time. For most of the general public, learning of the radical militia who wanted to bring down the government must have been shocking, and the media coverage was squeezing the hell out of that orange. The running theme was the small, ragtag band of malcontents, Commander Anderson at their head, their political leanings, and their grievances with American values.

Investigations uncovered the militia's ties to white nationalism and, of course, Nazis. S2 was a play on the notorious SS. Several member manifestos referred to the United States as a bankrupt corporation enslaving its people. The militia had championed several petitions to secede or divide a number of southern and western states. They shared plans to bring down the power grid and supplant the corrupt police infrastructure and otherwise accelerate the fall of the Deep State. Strangely, mention of the actual grid attack in San Jose was omitted.

The narrative wasn't exactly a lone gunman on a grassy knoll, but it was the best they could do given the ties to a subversive militia. Call it the lone gun club.

Of course, President Diaz was alive and well and in fact had never been exposed to any real danger. The Secret Service had some wounded personnel but had otherwise displayed excellent courage and containment of the situation. And on and on and on.

As the words blurred together, Carver decided what he cared about most at the moment was getting more shut-eye.

* * *

"You're alive," said Williams.

Carver peeked an eye open. It was daylight, presumably

the next morning but how could one know these things, and the case officer waited at the foot of the bed with her arms crossed like she was losing her patience.

"Sorry to inconvenience you," he rasped.

It was harder to speak than it should have been. Maybe it was from disuse, or perhaps he'd been intubated during surgery. Whatever it was, it was going to interfere with their verbal sparring.

"The president's people never got the security alerts, and the ones who did reported it to Agent Hanna and that was that."

Carver ran his gaze across the room, easing the light into his eyes. The door was shut, and they were alone.

"Who let you in?" he said.

"Nobody, officially. The Bureau is still watching you so I've arranged a bit of misdirection to get a few minutes alone."

"Of course you have."

"Don't worry, you'll be taken care of."

"Nick? Jules?"

"They're fine."

"Isla?"

"She'll come out of this okay."

He swallowed a few times to massage his throat.

Lanelle Williams walked around the bed and spoke in a lower tone. "After your unofficial assignment, I'm here to unofficially debrief you. There's a sizable but contained number of officials who have most of the pieces of what happened here. Our job is to prevent that number from growing. In the public eye, Alex Hanna and Eddie Covington are heroes. There was no traitor in the Secret Service. There was no corrupt Homeland Security ASAC. And there definitely wasn't the illegal smuggling from the military of a Switchblade 600 loitering munition." The CIA officer sighed. "As much as the narrative might pain, the public can't know how close this thing was."

"You mean the government can't disclose the corruption within their own security apparatus."

"Your words. You know the drill. There are no bad actors in DHS." She nodded to the bedside table, where a folded newspaper lay under the remote control. "You can read all about it in the paper. It's yesterday's, but I figured you would appreciate it."

"Who were they?" Carver grumbled.

Her lips tightened. "There are no satisfying answers or master plans yet. Some of them are anarchists. Some of them disgruntled veterans. The dead gunmen in San Francisco have very clear radical histories. They're members of another S2 chapter from Washington, and may have orchestrated last year's attacks on the power grid. We're still tracking Samantha Grafton's ties to the organization, but she lived in the area and would have had plenty of opportunities to mix it up with them."

Carver frowned. "Militia members outside of Anderson's command."

"A separate chapter. That's the part we missed because we never saw these guys. But it explains how Sam and Holt were able to so easily move in on the operation and assume positions of leadership in San Jose."

He shook his head. "The militia eating its own. Does that sound right to you?"

"You know how these things work. The people on the ground floor, the ones pledged to the cause, they're the expendable ones."

The deputy's caustic words echoed through Carver's mind.

"Samantha Grafton and Alex Hanna were at the top of the food chain," relayed Williams. "They had no definitive ties to the militia, at least not until Sam infiltrated."

"You're not trying to tell me the conspiracy really was just about some crazies with an ax to grind."

"Isn't it always, though? No matter the motivation, it takes a radical to carry something like this out."

"But why did they do it?"

Williams took a breath, checked the time on her phone, and said, "The downed drone and communications equipment have been recovered. We know the attack was being recorded. This was meant to be a public statement, which means there's money or politics in it somewhere. Our best guess, at this time, is that Alex Hanna and Samantha Grafton were making some kind of power play. Graduating to the next level. Maybe Special Agent Guerrero was right about the storefront. Maybe they were looking for some cred to obtain state sponsorship somewhere."

Carver returned a discontented grunt. "You mean this was an audition."

"Once people strike out on their own, once they

consciously decide that society doesn't matter to them and they're in it for themselves, anything is possible."

Carver worked his jaw. Of all the half-assed reasons he could imagine for homegrown terrorism, the most frightening of them all was it being just business.

"My time's up," she said. "You take as much as you need. The security detail's just a precaution. You'll be extensively interviewed, but you're not under arrest. Get rest and get better."

As she walked to the door, he said, "Hey Williams." She turned and he took a moment, and then he simply said, "Thanks."

"No, Vince, thank *you*. The country owes you a debt."

She left the door open on her way out. It was a dry exit but heartfelt in her own way. Within a few minutes there was a huddle outside his room, some discussion, and a police officer returned to his post by the door. He was probably in charge of guarding Carver's Jell-O.

A tired sigh escaped his lips and he regarded the newspaper. The front page covered all the highlights bulleted by Williams and the nightly news. Something didn't sit right about painting Hanna as a hero who died protecting his president, or Covington being on the verge of discovering the plot and getting killed for it. Even worse was framing Lester Anderson as the bad guy. He was at the center of the plot, no doubt, but he was no mastermind, just one of the little guys who couldn't take on the world by himself. There was no context of extortion. No relatable element of human suffering. The commander would forever be a caricature of a villain.

The real tragedy was that this was exactly what the populous craved. They were only interested in single-picture memes and ideas that could be conveyed in two hundred and eighty characters. Context was king, but the king was dead. If you didn't have a zinger, you didn't have a point. It was the death of rational thought.

Carver perused various side stories digging into details related to the plot. A deep dive into S2's origins and goals. A wounded police officer's heroic point of view. A breakdown of the militia compound.

He shut the paper in disgust. None of it was relevant anymore. He had done his job. The remainder of the operation was informational now, relegated to the decision-makers who even Lanelle Williams answered to. It was out of his hands.

As he folded the paper to return it to the table, he noticed a dog-ear on the back page. Carver looked closer and found one more story that took just a small corner at the end of the main section, titled, "Mystery in Metcalf."

The report was an offhand mention of an already forgotten incident outshined by the momentous day. A number of unknown assailants fired upon and damaged an electrical substation in a well-coordinated attack before vanishing without a trace.

The brunt of the article focused on the fallout. San Jose had gone without power for two hours. The FCC was looking into why backup systems failed. Security was being overhauled across California. Wired alarms were moving to satellite. Fences would turn to walls. Vanguard Security would transition operations to Eclipsis. That sort of thing.

The story ended with a note of good fortune. The attack had luckily only damaged the substation's cooling systems, and full repairs were scheduled to be complete within the week.

Carver set down the paper and smiled. At least Williams had a sense of humor about the whole thing.

* * *

Carver stirred from sleep. People shuffled in and out of his hospital room with determined precision. They weren't doctors, but they were important. Carver's eyes opened and closed, each time capturing a slightly different picture, as if time was skipping.

As movement receded out the doorway, a singular figure stood at the foot of his bed and fixed into focus.

"How are you?" asked President Diaz. "Can you speak?"

Carver wiped his eyes, realizing then he was no longer handcuffed. He cleared his throat, and said, "I'm not sure how well, sir, but I can bull's-eye a target at a hundred yards if you need me to."

The president grinned. "I wouldn't doubt it. I've had time to read up on you."

Carver almost cracked a joke, but something about this man in this room held him back. The commander in chief demanded a level of respect from anyone who had ever worn the uniform, even from a special operator, even lying on his ass in the hospital.

Alex Diaz was a prototypical man of the people, but seeing him up close, he was more. Accessible but vaunted, ideal yet wise, sated yet hungry. There wasn't any more apt way to describe him than presidential, and Carver wondered if that had been the case his entire life.

"You're officially one of three citizens caught in the militia's crossfire," Diaz stated diplomatically. "I'm on a goodwill visit, kissing babies and shaking hands of the brave Americans affected by this violence."

Carver nodded. "It also doesn't hurt to show you're not afraid to come back to this city."

"That too," said Diaz with a grin. He turned to an administrator waiting outside that Carver was too tired to identify. Then he lowered his voice. "You and I, as well as a few select others, know the true magnitude of what happened that day. I witnessed you risk the wrath of my security team to get your man and save my life. You're the CIA man of the hour."

Carver shifted uncomfortably in the bed. "I'm, uh, not sure that's accurate, sir."

"Oh? Still preserving your cover?" President Diaz laughed and thrust a hand up. "Don't worry. I've spoken intensely with Case Officer Lanelle Williams. I've been apprised of your service overseas, your contribution to our domestic semiconductor pipeline, your assistance in Eastern Europe until you went rogue and may or may not have committed acts it would be unwise for me to avow, suffice it to say that you may have knocked down the first domino contributing to a notable Russian PMC's total collapse."

The president held Carver's eye with a measure of respect. "I know you did some private work, including your participation in a very public shootout in Mexico that upended Tijuana's leading narco cartel. And now, this operation, or whatever we'll call it, has left you out in the cold."

There weren't a whole lot of ways to answer that except for, "Yes sir."

Diaz nodded to acknowledge their understanding. "Not even the director of the CIA was aware of your going undercover in S2. Do you realize you were an illegal asset?"

"That was my understanding of the situation, more or less, sir."

"And how does that make you feel?"

"I'm sorry, sir?"

"What are you sorry for?"

Carver studied the earnest eyes of the president and said, "I don't understand your question."

Diaz took a step closer. "I'm asking if you're bitter, Vince. If you feel used. Antagonized."

Carver cleared his throat again and said, "Sir, I feel that this is pretty much what I signed up for."

President Diaz nodded in satisfaction. He appraised Carver an additional moment before hanging his hands in his pockets. "I suppose you'll be wanting a medal of some sort."

"No sir."

His eyebrows went up. "No? And why not?"

"I already have a few. I keep them in a shoebox in my closet."

The president returned a humorous snort. "I suppose that works out, because all I can offer you is my thanks for going above and beyond. And even that much is unofficial. You understand?"

"It was assumed."

The two men bit down. Their understanding was explicit. Matters of national security needed to be. But there was something that went unsaid between them as well. A measure of fight. The camaraderie of being in the battle together. No matter the votes or the campaigns or the politics, their concerns rose above the noise and formed true devotion to a way of life that neither of them had built, but both of them worked every day to sustain.

Carver chuckled idly.

President Diaz eyed his bemused expression, out of place in the formerly sober atmosphere. "Something funny, Vince?"

"I was just thinking, Mr. President, about the cyclical nature of unlikely events that brought us here. If you hadn't spearheaded funding for vital tech resources a few years ago as a congressman, I wouldn't have found myself in a Range Rover in the Arizona desert protecting a semiconductor company that was the target of a foreign plot."

* * *

It was another two days after the president's visit, and for once Carver was ready. He had taken to walking around the room for exercise, he wore loose-fitting pants under his robe, and it didn't hurt to swallow or move anymore. He figured no special operator worth his salt would be snuck up on by another politician, whether that was the director of the FBI, the Federal Communications Commission, or whoever else wanted a piece of him. Carver was awake, he was prepared, and he had slept enough.

So he wasn't caught with his pants down, metaphorically or literally, when Special Agent Isla Guerrero strolled to his empty doorway.

"You really all alone in here?"

She wore a tight-fitting tank top and baggy jeans, simultaneously less dressed but more put together than her professional wardrobe.

Sitting up in bed, Carver shrugged. "I guess the police are no longer concerned with Jell-O related crime."

"What?" She scrunched her dimpled nose and cheeks. "I was talking about your friends. If you have those."

"My guys have gone to ground. I communicated with them through a go-between. They know the drill."

"I guess I didn't get the memo." She leaned on the doorway, demurely kicking the floor before raising her gaze to meet his. Her lips upturned in a smile.

"I'm glad for it," he said, grinning himself. "You're a sight for sore eyes."

"You saying you missed me?"

He hiked a shoulder again. "The guard at the door

wasn't really doing it for me. But there is this one nurse who you might be in competition with."

She snorted. "You know how to make a girl feel special." She approached the bed finally and found a spot to sit. "Seriously, Vince, you have a way with people. You have a way with how you do things, too. I've been fully reinstated. In fact, I've gotten a promotion."

He took her hand in his. "You did all that yourself, Isla. You were given a temporary assignment you were never supposed to achieve, under the oversight of a crooked boss you were never going to convince to help, and you still cracked the case. You're a good agent."

She beamed at him. But then reality broke into their moment. "The promotion requires my reassignment to DC. It's a dream job. What I've always been working for."

He squeezed her hand firmly. "You'll do great."

They stared at each other. He could get lost in her expansive hazel eyes. Maybe he already was.

Guerrero licked plump lips, then smacked them together and said, "I'm flying out tomorrow afternoon. All my affairs are wrapped up and I'd just been waiting on you to... well... I figured I'd check up on you again."

"Again?"

"You didn't think I'd abandoned you here, did you?"

He didn't say anything.

"We worked good together," she said. "When we were actually working together."

"We did some other things good together too."

She smiled another moment, but it gave way to

dejection. "It's just... The job, you not being discharged yet... Our timing's off, isn't it?"

"Actually," he said, swiveling his legs over the side of the bed, "I think your timing's perfect."

"What are you doing?"

"I'm going to spend the rest of today and tomorrow morning with you. I figure we could start with a real steak, something with a lot of butter on it, and maybe find some nicer accommodations afterward. This place isn't the Hilton, you know." He stood, ripped the IV out of his arm, and reached for his shirt. "This is the first good reason I've had to get out of bed the whole week, and I got a visit from the president, so that's saying something."

She got up overly quick, like she was tense. "You're cleared to go?"

"Operational discretion," he said.

"Are you sure?"

"Don't ask questions. It's top secret. You're just going to have to trust me."

He walked around the bed and she met him halfway, slinging an arm under his shoulder for support. She leaned in for a kiss and said, "I can do that."

Carver walked out of the hospital without asking about insurance.

Afterword

The eagle has officially landed!

This next volume in the series is meant to hit closer to home —and closer to comfort—than we might like. For once Carver is staying put and tackling a domestic threat, and the stakes are taken to the extreme.

Project Sundown is a fictional portrayal of a lot of modern problems amped up to eleven. National security on a homegrown stage. The idea that our weaknesses, left unchecked, can fester and rot our country from the inside out.

The premise begins with the planning of attacks on our critical infrastructure. The twist is this part isn't fiction. The very electrical substation in Coyote, California that is targeted by S2 was actually hit in 2013 in what is known as the most sophisticated attack on grid infrastructure in US history, the Metcalf Sniper Attack.

A team of gunmen, at relatively close range, opened fire with rifles on the transmission substation after cutting its fiber-optic cables. Over the course of the next twenty minutes, they destroyed seventeen electrical transformers, costing $15 million and weeks to replace.

In the aftermath, Pacific Gas & Electric announced a huge spending package to upgrade security across its locations. The police found nothing but spent shells devoid of fingerprints. The attackers would not be caught. (Whether or not it was Carver's team saving the president's life is classified.)

Next up are America's very own extremist groups. It would be unjust to paint all militias with this brush, but S2 is specifically based on the Atomwaffen Division, a now-international neo-Nazi network formed the same year Metcalf was hit. (Coincidence, I ask you?)

The Atomwaffen Division makes no secret of their goal to overthrow the US government. They promote accelerationism in order to achieve societal collapse. They burn the constitution and the flag. Members have been arrested and charged with murder and terrorism. One planned to blow up a coronavirus treatment hospital with a car bomb and was killed in a shootout with the FBI.

This next part may sound familiar. As part of a presidential protest, a group of militants training on a private ranch planned to "wreak havoc across the nation" by striking the power grid in an operation they called "Light's Out."

S2 is a nod to the SS, a wink to the Secret Service, and also a possible future for former Atomwaffen members in their second endeavor.

Finally, the drone plot at the end isn't a threat specific to the United States, but the widening availability of FPV drones aren't just causing problems for Russia and Ukraine. Remote assassination is now a thing.

In 2018, Venezuelan president Nicolás Maduro was speaking in Caracas when a pair of drones may have triggered explosions overhead in quick succession. In Baghdad, the Iraqi prime minister's home was struck by a drone after two others were shot down. These assassination attempts ultimately failed but resulted in several injured soldiers and bodyguards.

A whole industry is sprouting to tackle the challenges posed by these sorts of attacks. This book highlights some of that, with the deputy going the extra distance of acquiring a military-grade drone to avoid such countermeasures. The one thing we can be sure of is that we will see more of these attempts in the future, and it's only a matter of time before one of them succeeds.

That just about does it for me. Thanks for fighting alongside Carver, Shaw, and Morgan. If you enjoyed the read and have anything at all to say, including setting me straight about an error, feel free to email at matt@matt-sloane.com. Input is always welcome.

-Matt

A Favor

It's not always easy to ask for a favor, even a small one, but I'm going to do it.

As an author, it's impossible to understate how much my career relies on you, the reader. Every purchase supports me. Every kind word helps my work flourish.

For that all I can say is thank you, from the bottom of my heart.

I know you're ready to dive into the next book, the next adventure, whether by me or another author, but it would be an incredible kindness if you could spend another single minute in the world of Vince Carver to leave me a review wherever you bought the book.

I guarantee that your words will make a difference. Not just to me, but to a random stranger stuck deciding what to read next and wondering if an author they've never heard of is worth their valuable time.

For that one guy, your input means everything in the world.

Also by Matt Sloane

VINCE CARVER THRILLERS
National Security
Ghost Soldiers
The Service of Wolves
Project Sundown

The latest books and information will always be on
Matt-Sloane.com

* 9 7 8 1 9 4 6 0 0 8 5 4 1 *